"*Promise of Deer Run* offers an authentic and engaging journey back to the challenges of rural, post-Revolution America, reminding the reader of the beauty of married love, the treasure of family, and the blessings that come with forgiveness and second chances."

— DENISE WEIMER, author of *The Georgia Gold Series* and *The Restoration Trilogy*

"Elaine Marie Cooper has crafted a beautiful tribute to those who have protected our country's freedom — no matter the century or war. Ms. Cooper doesn't dodge the trials of life, yet approaches them with the recognition and appreciation of finding God's grace in our worst circumstances."

— SANDRA ARDOIN, author of *A Reluctant Melody*

"Cooper's research runs true as mothers apply herbal treatments, infants die of illnesses that are curable with today's medicine, saffron creates the perfect yellow linen and women deliver babies with the help of a midwife. A farmer pays for his medical bills by chopping wood and married couples escape to a wigwam for an intimate retreat. Elaine Marie Cooper writes authentically, matching the rhythm of her words to the speech of that time period. The story flows so naturally, the reader escapes into a simpler yet challenging era."

— RJ THESMAN, author of the Life at Cove Creek series

OTHER CROSSRIVER BOOKS BY ELAINE MARIE COOPER

HISTORICAL FICTION

Road to Deer Run
Promise of Deer Run
Legacy of Deer Run (coming Fall 2016)

NONFICTION

Bethany's Calendar

Promise of
Deer Run

ELAINE MARIE COOPER

CROSSRIVER

BREWSTER, KANSAS USA

This book is dedicated to
Jack, Chloe, and Luke — GiGi's Triplet Treasures

This book is also dedicated to all the veterans
who suffer from post-traumatic stress disorder.
May the Lord bless and heal you.

Acknowledgments

*O*nce again, I am incredibly indebted to my husband, *Steve*, for the many hours of editing, support, and encouragement. And for your warmth and love, I am eternally indebted.

Thanks to my wonderful editor, *Debra L. Butterfield*, and my publisher, *CrossRiver Media*.

My sincerest gratitude to veteran and former Army Chaplain *Den Slattery* as well as *Pam Hays*, founder of The Arms Forces, which supports veterans with traumatic brain injury and post-traumatic stress disorder (PTSD). Your input from veterans suffering from PTSD was invaluable in adding depth to this novel's characters. Thank you from the bottom of my heart.

Two very special contributors to this novel are historians in Massachusetts: *Dennis Picard* from the Storrowton Village Museum in West Springfield and *Ralmon Black* from Williamsburg. Your knowledge of late eighteenth-century Massachusetts has been so helpful to the historical details of this book. Thank you, gentlemen!

I also thank so many *friends, family, supporters* and *readers* who have eagerly anticipated this sequel to *Road to Deer Run*. Many of you I have never met in person, but your encouraging words about my first novel have been such a blessing to me. I am indebted to you for your enthusiasm, and I pray that this book meets your expectations. It puts a huge smile on my face when someone gets joy from my writing.

And, as always, thanks to my Lord and Savior *Jesus Christ*, from whom all blessings flow.

Prelude

"Huzzah! It's over! The treaty's been signed! Huzzah!"

The news the troops had been awaiting for months was now a reality: the Americans had won the war against England. The United States of America was free and independent that spring of 1783. Eight long years of battle had proven victorious for the colonists.

Nineteen-year-old Nathaniel Stearns emerged from the small wooden barracks at West Point, New York. He had slept fitfully all night, finally falling into a deep slumber just before dawn. He awoke with a start when the cheers reached his ears. Rubbing his eyes, he squinted at the early morning sun.

"It's really over?" He shaded his eyes as he spoke to a jubilant private.

"Over and done, once for all! Johnny Bull is going back where he belongs! Come. Let's share a gill of the good creature to celebrate."

"You go on. I'll be there in a bit."

Nathaniel stood by himself as the others ran toward the hogshead of rum that the officers brought out for celebration.

The elation of this moment was blighted for young Corporal Stearns. The last three years of war had brought more than their share of personal losses, overshadowing the joy of victory. Nathaniel bore memories of his best friend's death, as well as the betrayal of his childhood sweetheart. He would never be the same after seeing his best friend's face blown away by enemy fire. That memory visited Nathaniel's sleep on a regular basis, like an unwelcome visitor you wish you had never met.

As he turned back toward the barracks, Nathaniel caught a glimpse of his father approaching. Sergeant Benjamin Stearns had been away from home for the duration of the war, with an occasional furlough to visit his family in Deer Run. The years away from home deepened the lines around his father's eyes and mouth. The jovial man of Nathaniel's youthful memories was replaced by a somber gentleman with a stoop about his shoulders.

Nathaniel immediately noticed the change the news of victory brought to his father's countenance. He was smiling.

"Father." Nathaniel stood at attention.

"At ease." His father grinned from ear to ear. "Nathaniel, I'm certain you want to celebrate with the lads." His face grew serious. "But I'm asking you to consider heading back home as soon as you can. Here are your discharge papers. I asked the captain to prepare yours first. I want you to go home and stay at the farm. Check on your mother and brother and sisters." His voice caught in his throat. "My heart weighs heavy with worry. Please—"

"I'll pack immediately, sir," Nathaniel interrupted him. "You can count on me." He saluted his father.

"I've always been able to count on you, son. You've made me proud."

His father held his gaze and tears began to well in Nathaniel's eyes.

"Well then." His father cleared his throat and set his shoulders at attention. "Be on your way, lad."

"Yes, sir." Nathaniel sniffed sharply and wiped off his face. "Father, when will you return home? What shall I tell Mother?"

"Tell her... I'll be home forthwith. Tell her to look through her golden curtains and watch me arrive with the sun." He smiled. "I know how much your mother delights in seeing the sunrise through her only window."

Nathaniel couldn't help but smile at the thought. The two men embraced and his father turned away to join the celebration.

Returning to the barracks, Nathaniel gathered his few belongings. When he stepped out the door to begin the long walk to Deer Run, he searched the crowd of joyous troops for a glimpse of his father, but he couldn't see him anywhere. Nathaniel approached the group, grabbed the half cup of rum allotted to each soldier, and downed the drink in two quick gulps. He threw his satchel over his shoulder and started the journey home.

It took nearly a week to walk from the encampment in New York to the outskirts of Deer Run. Nearing the family farm, he hoped his mother or brother or sisters — someone — would burst out the front door to greet him. It had been three years since Nathaniel was home and until this moment he did not realize just how homesick he was.

Approaching the log cabin, he only heard the wind as a hollow, haunting sound stirring the trees in the woods. Chilled air swept against his neck and he pulled his collar up higher. The smell of rain infused his nostrils.

"Mother?" His voice filled with apprehension.

He opened the heavy wooden door, crafted years ago by his father. "Ethan? Sadie? Hello?"

His heart almost stopped as he saw the cabin was deserted. He surveyed the room. There were no linens, no dishes, no food cooking in the hearth. Even the yellow curtains his mother was so fond of were gone.

What has happened? Where is everyone?

He noticed a letter nailed to the wall above the chest of drawers. He walked across the room with unsteady legs and removed the old parchment.

His hands trembled as he read the note, dated September 30, 1780:

Dearest Benjamin and Nathaniel,

　　It is with great sadness that I have been forced to leave our home. Ethan took ill some months after Nathaniel left. Despite our greatest efforts to treat his terrible fever, dearest Ethan went home to heaven. My heart is still breaking.

　　As I am unable to keep up the farm, my sister Abigail in Boston has kindly offered to take in the three girls and me. I am in despair that I may never see either of you again.

　　Please send word of your safekeeping and come to Boston as soon as you are able. I await word of my brave men.

With loving regard,
Your Wife and Mother

The paper dropped to the floor without Nathaniel taking notice. He stood without speaking for a moment before racing out the door to the burial ground up near the woods.

Tears stung at his eyes. Strands of his long blond hair whipped his face, clinging to the moisture on his cheeks. Frantic, he almost tripped more than once on the mass of weeds growing in the old cornfield.

"This cannot be!" he cried, but his voice was lost in the howling wind.

Arriving at the gravesite, the cold letters on the tombstone told the tragic truth: *Ethan Stearns, born January 19, 1766, died September 2, 1780.*

Nathaniel's fingers etched the chiseled letters. He outlined them repeatedly with trembling hands encrusted with mud.

Ethan was indeed dead.

Nathaniel fell to his knees and shook his head back and forth.

"No. No. No!"

Sobs wracked his body with rhythmic waves. He would have raised a fist toward heaven… if he only had the strength.

1

Nathaniel

Seven years later

The nightmare was back, plaguing Nathaniel Stearns' sleep. It was always the same.

He was eighteen once again and glancing over at his friend Isaiah. The two had been inseparable since signing on to fight the Redcoats. Now, covered in too many layers of dirt to count, they were poised like cougars, ready to leap at their lieutenant's order.

An unusually bright display of two planets in the otherwise pitch-black night sky seemed to shine a blessing on the battle. The anticipation was palpable in this company of Continental troops as they sensed impending victory in these trenches outside Yorktown.

"Be ready, men," Lieutenant Laurens yelled above the din of the French troops already attacking one British redoubt. The wooden fortification of the enemy was many yards up the hill, yet one could clearly hear the intense struggle between the English and French. The moans of the wounded and dying only increased Nathaniel's frenzied heartbeat.

He and Isaiah gripped their muskets with trembling fingers. Every muscle in their bodies tensed as the young soldiers readied to surge forward at the command.

"Up! Up!" The long-awaited order was finally given. As the Americans poured out of the dirt trenches, enemy fire lit up the sky, making the sweat glisten on the Colonial troops' determined faces.

Isaiah was closest to the edge of the fortification. Charging out of the trench, he glanced back at Nathaniel with a victorious smile. But the face of Nathaniel's comrade was suddenly wiped away. In an instant, it was replaced by red nothingness.

Nathaniel stared silently at his faceless friend lying in a pool of blood. At first, his mind could not comprehend the horrific sight. A moment later he dropped his musket and screamed a gut-wrenching cry.

"Isaiah!"

Nathaniel woke with a start, his linen shirt clinging to his body with sweat. His heart raced, his breathing shallow and rapid.

Was I screaming out loud?

Staring around the empty log cabin, there was not another soul who could answer him. He had pondered that question for the last eight years since that battle occurred. But every time he awoke from that recurring nightmare, he had no one to ask.

A cool breeze blew through the open window, carrying the scent of a burning hearth nearby. He smelled simmering gruel from a neighbor's home.

Nathaniel's heart and stomach ached. Not just from the nightmare about Yorktown but from the thought of awakening years ago to his mother's cooking. The memory continued to bring him sadness as he looked at the cold, empty fireplace.

He tried to sit up, but his throbbing head begged him to lie back down. As he plopped his head onto the pillow, the bristly edges of his beard caught on the old linen fibers. The smell of the moldy material made his stomach turn.

He forced himself to sit up despite the pain in his head. Then he remembered the night before, at Deer Run Tavern. The dry, wretched feeling in his mouth brought that memory back clearly.

How many gills of rum did I down with Dr. Burk? I should never have gone with him to the tavern.

But Nathaniel had nothing better to do on a Saturday evening when Dr. Burk came knocking on the door at dusk. "Come let us share our tales of war," Dr. Burk had said enthusiastically as he threw his arm around Nathaniel's shoulder. He had thought it odd that the physician did not wish to spend his evening at home with his wife. Robert Burk seemed to spend a great many evenings at the tavern instead of in front of the fire with Matilda. Nathaniel was lonely, however, and did not question the doctor's personal affairs. He was grateful for some company.

With head throbbing and vile tastes filling his mouth, Nathaniel wished he had declined the offer.

Pushing himself off the straw-filled mattress, he drew a deep lungful of the fresh September air. He walked to the front door, opened it, and in his sleepiness nearly tripped over a basket on his front step. A small smile pulled at the corners of his mouth.

I wish I knew who was sending me victuals.

Stopping to open the linen napkin covering the basket, he looked inside to find fresh bread from someone's oven. Nathaniel glanced around the front yard and down the road for any sign of the generous donor. But as always, there was no one in sight and no one ever came forward to claim credit for the gift. He felt embarrassed by this charity, but grateful. He knew no one wanted to make the ex-soldier feel beholden.

Groggily, he walked toward his mother's old garden. Searching for some parsley, he found a small plant tucked beneath a few weeds. He tore off the green stalks and crunched the leaves between his teeth. The bitter herb was preferable to the rank taste that assaulted his tongue.

Nathaniel hobbled on unsteady legs back to the house. He picked up the basket and brought it inside. Setting it on the tableboard, he looked with sadness at the long piece of wood that had once seen his parents, brother, and sisters enjoying a meal together. He could still see his brother Ethan, two years his junior, trying to keep up with Nathaniel's larger appetite.

I should never have left Ethan to take over the farm.

Tears stung at Nathaniel's eyes as he remembered how anxious he had been to fight in the Revolution, to free America from the ties that bound her to England. It was not two days after his sixteenth birthday in 1780 that he had bid his mother and siblings farewell.

"I shall find Father and we will fight for freedom together!" Nathaniel had said with youthful confidence.

He thought about his mother and sisters at his aunt and uncle's home in Boston. The childless relatives had a home as large as their hearts and provided well for Nathaniel's family. After he found the letter, he visited his mother and sisters in Boston, but he stayed only a week. His generous uncle offered him a job at the newspaper he owned, but Nathaniel's heart ached to return to Deer Run. He implored his mother and uncle to allow him to go back to the family homestead.

"If no one is there to greet him, Father may despair of ever seeing his family again." His mother and uncle could not convince him otherwise, and they consented. Nathaniel understood their reservations about his decision, but they did not understand the pain of returning to an empty house and an unexpected gravestone.

And so Nathaniel took on the daunting task of reviving the long-neglected farm. He owed this to his father. After all, had Nathaniel stayed behind in the first place, the farm would have been well managed, and perhaps Ethan would still be alive. So each day as he labored to bring the land back to its former productivity, he awaited his parent's return.

Seven years had now passed since bidding his father farewell at West Point, and there was still no sign of him. The many letters Nathaniel sent to the army went unanswered. With so many veterans anxious to return home, the inefficient communications systems were soon overwhelmed. Why was Benjamin Stearns not home?

Nathaniel rubbed his swollen eyes as he pondered this. He walked over to the basin of water by the open window and splashed the cool liquid on his face. Looking up at the bare window, he wished his mother had left the yellow curtains behind. They had given this rustic cabin a feeling of warmth. Now the window frame's bare wood stood out as a stark reminder of the emptiness in his home — as well as the emptiness in his heart. This was one of those moments when he wished he had not even returned from the war alive.

Dear God, why did you not spare my friend? Why was I not killed at Yorktown instead?

His prayers always flew silently heavenward. They seemed lost in the clouds of despair.

Only one purpose kept him going. One thought obsessed him as he trudged through each laborious day on the farmstead — he was determined to wait for his father's return. He would not abandon his parent who had promised to come home. It was Nathaniel's reason for survival, even if most of the townspeople of Deer Run thought he was quite strange for doing so. Everyone just assumed Benjamin Stearns was dead.

As Nathaniel splashed more cold water onto his bleary eyes, he heard a familiar sound, the bell at the meetinghouse. He had forgotten it was Sabbath.

Despite his weariness, he grabbed his razor from the wall hook and began shaving away the stubble that covered his leathery face.

No sense in looking like a drunkard.

He tried not to lament about his behavior of the night before — what he could remember of it. And as he walked out the door to go to the meetinghouse, he tried not to despair at the thought that God may have forgotten him completely.

2

Sarah

The bell at the meetinghouse rang so loudly Sarah cringed. She wanted to cover her ears, but she knew her mother would not approve.

The nineteen-year-old imagined her mother's stern voice resonating from so many previous admonitions. "'Tis *not* proper for a lady to react in such a manner."

Sarah Thomsen frequently caused her mother, Ruth Eaton, much consternation. It was not that she was trying to annoy her parent. It just seemed to happen that way. Sarah knew she could never be as polite and civil as her older sister, Mary. Her sibling was the good daughter.

Sarah always seemed to have a penchant for blurting out what was on her mind or reacting to circumstances without thinking first. Her stepfather, Myles Eaton, said she had a natural spirit for truth and adventure. Her mother said Sarah was self-willed and obstinate. Sarah just knew she was a sinner, barely saved by God's grace.

So as she and her parents approached the meetinghouse and the bell announced Sabbath services, Sarah merely bowed her head and prayed God would give her the strength to bear with the insufferable toll, however badly her ears might throb.

"Good morning, Mr. Eaton. Missus Eaton." Mehitabel Beal nodded her head slightly at the approaching family. "Sarah," she added in greeting, almost as an afterthought.

Did her lips draw into a fine, tense line at the speaking of my name?

Sarah ignored the thought. "Good morning, Missus Beal." She curtsied politely.

Richard Beal approached the Eaton family. The young boy with the puffy red hair had grown into a handsome, smartly dressed twenty-two-year-old. He winked at Sarah before turning to address her parents.

"And a fine good day to you, Mr. Eaton. Missus Eaton." He was all charm and perfect manners as he tipped his hat to her parents. Sarah rolled her eyes upward and then caught herself.

I must not be rude, especially not on Sabbath Day.

But Richard Beal definitely taxed her patience with his frequent rude remarks about others. And the fact that he was trying to make such an impression on her parents was most annoying. His charm did not deceive her.

With dramatic flourish, he turned to Sarah. "And a good day to you, Miss Sarah. Is not the weather perfect on this September morning?" He winked at her again.

"Good day, Richard." She attempted to give him a genuine smile but the effort felt labored. "Yes, the weather is lovely."

She glanced at her smiling mother, who was quite pleased at the thought of Richard Beal being a suitor for her youngest child.

"Sarah, Richard would make a perfect consort," her mother had said to her recently. "He is a successful dairyman with a prosperous business. Why, his family is quite well off since the war. You would do well to consider his intentions toward you."

Sarah attempted to change the subject, but her mother continued to press the issue. "That young man is the proper age to court such a young lady as yourself. You could not find a better husband in all of Deer Run. And you know that he has set his eyes on you."

"Yes, Mother, I know," was Sarah's only reply. Her mother had stared at her in exasperation and thrown her hands into the air. As Missus Eaton walked away, Mr. Eaton had given Sarah a sympathetic grin. He winked at his stepdaughter, cajoling a smile from her.

At least Father Eaton understands.

Sarah was now grateful it was time to go into the meetinghouse with her family. She gave a courteous nod to Richard and curtsied before walking away. She could practically feel Mehitabel Beal's glare upon her. Richard's mother thought her son could do better in finding a wife than the likes of Sarah Thomsen.

As Sarah and her parents walked into the old wooden meeting-house, she noticed her sister, Mary, and her brother-in-law, Daniel Lowe, already sitting in their family seat with their six children. Mary looked up and the two sisters smiled at each other.

James Thomsen, Sarah's older brother, who arrived with his wife, Hannah, directed his four children into their family pew. By the ap-pearance of both Mary and Hannah, it appeared there would be new babies added to the family before long.

Sighing, Sarah's spirits sagged. She turned her attention toward the pulpit, but her thoughts were not on the minister's words. She smoothed a wayward lock of blonde hair back and tucked it under her linen cap before looking back at her folded hands.

I shall never marry, I am sure of it. I will be the lonely old aunt who gets shuffled back and forth around the homes of her numerous nieces and nephews. "Poor old Aunt Sarah," they will say. "She was too obsti-nate to fit in as any decent man's wife. We shall just have to care for our pathetic Aunt Sarah."

She sighed again, so loudly her mother looked at her with disapproval.

See. I knew it. No one will bear with my disagreeable character. Not even Richard, once he realizes my ill manners and once his mother con-vinces him of how unsuitable I am for her perfect son. Perhaps my niece Lydia will have pity on me...

As she looked up with a hopeful glance at two-year-old Lydia on Hannah's lap, Sarah caught someone else's gaze. It was the sad but handsome blue eyes of Nathaniel Stearns.

As soon as Sarah turned his way, he shifted his eyes downward.

Sarah's cheeks grew hot.

Nathaniel Stearns? Looking at me? This makes no sense. He never pays me any mind.

She tried not to appear to be staring, but her occasional glances back at the man made her heart beat faster. Sarah had always admired his handsome face and thick blond hair pulled back in a ribbon. But it was a memory from long ago that came to mind and warmed her heart…

Sarah was a lonely eight-year-old and desperate to go to school. In those days, there was no schooling for the girls, except the lessons taught them at home by their mothers. But the headstrong youngest child of Widow Thomsen decided things should be otherwise.

So Sarah made her plan. When her mother was off delivering a baby one day, Sarah decided to go to school — the boys-only school. She was quickly escorted back home and her mother informed of the outrageous infraction.

The incident was not well received by the town leaders, who voiced their concerns in a town meeting, suggesting that Widow Thomsen was not a fit parent if she could not control her child's behavior. Widow Thomsen was humiliated. Mr. Eaton stood up at that town meeting and declared that the widow was a fit parent. She just needed a husband to ensure the child's adherence to rules. He gallantly stated to the town that he would gladly volunteer for the role of husband to Widow Thomsen and father to young Sarah.

As the story was later told to Sarah, one of the selectman hollered out at the meeting, "Well it's about time, Myles."

And as Myles Eaton made his way through the crowd to Widow Thomsen to ask for her hand in marriage, Ruth Thomsen wept while all the townspeople at the meeting cheered their approval of the engagement.

But as was customary penance for disobedient children, Sarah had to pay her dues by spending several hours in the stocks. The roughly hewn wooden apparatus that locked securely around the ankles of naughty children caused much discomfort. Even worse, the child was unable to eat or use the chamber pot for many hours.

So on the next chilly Sabbath day, the townspeople, with stares of disapproval, marched past a weeping Sarah, trapped in the stocks. Her clothing barely protected her from the cold and damp ground she had to sit upon. A few who were sympathetic to the child's plight — including Mary and Daniel — were outraged at this practice and refused to attend services that day, but most of the town agreed this was the proper means of dealing with disobedience.

During the lunch hour in between church services, the townspeople ate their food near Sarah, who was still locked in the stocks. She tried to ignore her growling stomach as she caught wind of the smells of fresh bread and cheeses. But it was no use. She was hungry.

She fought back tears as the townspeople marched back into the building for their afternoon service. Such humiliation!

As she heard the reverend preaching through the open windows, Sarah closed her eyes in despair. She knew her reputation was now cast as the town troublemaker. Suddenly, she heard quickened footsteps coming toward her on the dirt pathway. When she opened her eyes, she saw fifteen-year-old Nathaniel Stearns.

He spoke in a whisper.

"Here — take this quickly." It was a large piece of bread from his own lunch that he had hidden inside his shirt. "I told my mother I had to relieve myself. Do not tell anyone that I gave this to you."

With that he was gone. Sarah had not even had time to thank him.

Now as she glanced at the grown-up veteran sitting across from her in the meetinghouse, she was filled with gratitude for the kindness and mercy he had shown to a pathetic eight-year-old. And it relieved her that she had thought to bring him some freshly made bread before dawn this morning.

3

Arrival

"Daniel, wake up!"

Mary shook him with gripping hands. He snapped his eyes open at the sound of panic in her voice.

"What?" Daniel struggled out of a deep sleep, exhausted from a hard day's labor harvesting corn. He did not know the hour, but he knew by the aching in his bones that it was long before dawn. Forcing his mind and body to rouse, he realized the likely reason for panic in Mary's voice. "Is it time? I'll send the boys for your mother."

"It's too late for that, Daniel!" Mary paused a moment then made a deep groaning sound that could mean only one thing. This baby would not wait for the midwife.

Daniel broke into a sweat. "What do you mean too late?" Completely alert now and more than a little distressed, he threw off the quilt and ran for the door to the main room. He flung it open, nearly hitting himself in the head.

"Danny! James! Hasten to your grandmother's!" The boys awoke with a start and sleepily threw on their breeches. They did not say a word but headed for the main doorway to fetch the midwife.

The soon-to-be father of seven had to remind himself to breathe. Although this was not a new scenario for him, he did not recall Mary ever saying it was too late. Daniel was quite certain he would have recalled that phrase.

He hurried back to his wife, who writhed on the bed in discomfort.

"Daniel, help me!"

"Good heavens, what do I do? I know naught of this." His hands shook as he smoothed his hair back from his face. He sat on the edge of their bed, and held her hand. Sweat began to trickle down his neck as he watched his wife labor so intensely. "What can I do?" He stared helplessly, as she began to groan more loudly.

"Daniel, he's coming!" Mary threw the quilts off, bent her knees upward, and bore down with all her might. Before he could say another word, Daniel saw his child begin to emerge. Without thinking, he cupped the baby's moist head in his hands as the rest of the child quickly slipped out onto the bed. Daniel tenderly picked up the youngest Lowe child. "It's a boy."

Mary breathed hard and her brow was covered in sweat, but she smiled at the words. "Finally, another son!" Reaching down to take the squirming child from her husband, she cradled the whimpering boy next to her and put him to her breast. "Meet your son, Daniel. This is Ephraim."

Daniel wiped the sweat from his brow with bloodied hands. Sitting down on the bed next to Mary, he still tried to fathom what had just taken place. Reaching over to his wife, he gently smoothed the hair back from her face. He was just about to speak to her when there was a gentle knock on the door. Daniel stood up and went to answer. Opening the wooden door, he saw four sets of wide eyes staring at him, illuminated only by the dim light from the hearth. Nine-year-old Polly spoke for the group of girls.

"Papa," Polly said. "We heard the cry of a little one. Can we not see the new babe?" The other three girls nodded enthusiastically.

Daniel prepared to tell the girls to go back to bed when Mary spoke up. "Let them in, Daniel. Let them meet their brother."

Exhausted, Daniel stood back to allow the girls passage into their parents' room. First Polly came in and then seven-year-old Priscilla, five-year-old Sally, and two-year-old Alice. Polly hushed the girls and made them stand quietly in a row. They stared with awe at the sight of their nursing brother.

Young Sally could not contain her excitement. "Was he all wet and squirmy like Grandsire Eaton's little piggies, Papa?" Her green eyes sparkled as she spoke.

Mary grinned at Daniel, who did not know how to answer his daughter. It was all he could do to recover from the sudden arrival of his child. He realized he was still shaking.

"Well," Daniel stammered. "I would not say that your brother was like a piggie… but he was a little wet and squirmy…" He looked over at his wife for assistance.

Mary came to his rescue. "Girls, 'tis time to return to bed. You will see Ephraim in the morning." The four scurried back to bed, giggling excitedly about Baby Ephraim.

No sooner had the girls left their parents' bedroom than Missus Eaton came bursting through the doorway accompanied by her daughter, nineteen-year-old Sarah. When the midwife saw the child had already been birthed, she threw her hands into the air and sighed.

"Daniel, could you not have made Mary wait for me?"

"Wait for you? I would have liked nothing better, Mother Eaton. This child was on his way into the world before I could possibly have stopped him."

"Mother, do you think that Daniel wished to deliver your grandson without you? He had no choice."

"Grandson?" Ruth Eaton's lips broke into a smile. "Ah, and a fine boy he looks to be! Let me examine you both, Mary."

Widow Eaton clapped her hands together, all professional demeanor put aside as she cooed over the new child. She appeared to have forgotten any disappointment in missing the birth. Daniel went over to his wife and kissed her on her forehead.

"He is a fine lad, Mary. Thank you for another child — another son."

"Thank you for helping me, Daniel. I know you were terrified." She touched his cheek.

"You did all the work. I merely caught the boy." Kissing her tenderly, he then kissed the boy nursing on his mother. "I shall let Mother Eaton take care of you now." He smiled at his wife as he exited the doorway.

Wearily, Daniel limped over to the chair by the fire. His war injury was even more pronounced after several days of harvesting in the fields. Settling himself onto his chair, he smoothed his hands across the wooden arms and thought about the creator of this piece of furniture — Mary's father. Daniel had never met his father-in-law, who died in a drowning accident when Mary was only twelve. She still spoke of him often. Daniel stared at his sleeping children, including the eleven-year-old twins who had fallen asleep the moment they returned from fetching their grandmother. Smiling, he looked heavenward.

I hope Mary's father can see his handsome grandchildren from above.

Daniel closed his eyes. He thought it had been for a only moment, but when he opened them to see Sarah come out of the bedroom, the first hint of dawn was already glowing through the window.

"You must be exhausted, brother." Sarah stared at him with sympathy, then grinned with amusement. "The morning sun sheds light on your crown of glory, Daniel. Have those grey hairs been there long, or did this night's adventure frighten the color out of them?"

Daniel frowned. "I'm afraid my hair has been changing for some time now. Mary noticed it a year ago, much to my dismay."

"Well, I think it looks quite handsome on you. And I'm certain that Mary does not mind. You will always be a prince in her mind — grey hairs and all." Sarah gathered her shawl around her. "I must be going. Mother is still with Mary and Ephraim, but I am to look after Father Eaton. He's not been well, you know."

Daniel furrowed his eyebrows. "This is the first I have heard. What ails him, Sarah?"

"It started about a week ago. He was having discomfort in his chest and mother finally sent for Doctor Burk. He says 'tis edema of the lungs."

"Your mother sent for the doctor?" Daniel's eyes widened. "She truly must have been concerned. Your mother has enough medicinals to open her own apothecary."

Sarah gave a slight smile as she walked toward the front door. "It took a great deal of soul-searching before she put aside her pride and called Dr. Burk." She stopped and turned back to face him. "Speaking of treating patients, perhaps you should put up a shingle outside your front door. It could read, 'Daniel Lowe, Man Midwife.'" She gave him a mischievous smile.

"Very amusing. Delivering my son last night was a most frightening affair. Thank God your mother arrived to help with… whatever it is she does afterward." Daniel waved his hand in the air as if to drive away the thoughts of what might be involved. "I tell you, Sarah, I cannot fathom why men choose to become involved in this profession. 'Man Midwives,' indeed! It is quite appalling."

"Well," said Sarah, walking out the door, "I shall never be caught allowing a man to perform such indecency on *my* person."

She inhaled audibly. "I love this time of year. Leaves changing, breezes stirring." Sarah paused. "Autumn is when you and Mary first met, is it not?"

Daniel smiled as he stepped outside. "Of course — right after the surrender at Saratoga that October. I'll never forget Mary's face leaning over me in the woods. I swear I began to love her from that moment on." He looked off into the distance, remembering that desperate time some thirteen years past, when Mary discovered him in the woods. Alone and dying, Daniel had given up on life. But providence had different ideas as Mary nursed him back to health, eventually falling in love with the enemy soldier. It was the beginning of his new journey as an American.

"Well, you have certainly grown up since that time, little miss." He winked. It was the pet name he had given her then and used throughout the ensuing years. Until recently, that is, when Sarah had said she was no longer so little. "So, when is the noble Richard Beal going to ask you to be his wife? He is quite well situated with his dairy farm, after all. And I have seen him eyeing you at Sabbath services."

Sarah twisted her face into a sneer. "Really, Daniel, I should best remain unmarried rather than be bound to such a pompous bore." Sarah stared at the clear sky. "If I should ever marry anyone, Daniel, it will not be someone who smells of cheese." She closed her eyes tightly. This elicited a chuckle from her brother-in-law.

Sarah's eyes snapped open and she covered her mouth with her hands. "I'd best hurry home to check on Father Eaton."

She scurried down the path toward the Eaton farm.

"Sarah, be sure to stay on the main roads. The woods are not as safe as they used to be. Too many strangers about."

She looked back at him and waved. Daniel stared after her for a moment.

I am certain she'll be fine.

He yawned and walked back toward his cabin.

4

Unexpected

astening down the road, Sarah inhaled the cool autumn air and hummed a lullaby out loud. She was filled with the joy of once again becoming an aunt. Wishing to hurry home and check on her stepfather, she ignored Daniel's advice and cut through the woods.

I will get home much faster if I stay off the road. She grinned as she thought again about her brother-in-law having to deliver the child. *Poor Daniel — always put in situations where he is most uncomfortable!* Yet the outcome was successful and all was well with her sister Mary and the new baby. Life was worth celebrating!

Looking around to be sure no one was watching, she pulled off her confining linen cap and unwrapped her hair from its pins. As she headed through the woods in the direction of home, she did something she could never do in front of her mother. She began to dance.

As she twirled and swayed in the wind, her rhythmic movements brought her to laughter. Her long blonde hair swung like a silk curtain in the breeze. She pretended the trees were dance partners as she swirled from one to the next. Imagining she was attending the harvest celebration dance, she graciously curtsied to her fanciful suitors, shyly avoiding their intense stares. Sarah blushed at the thought of a suitor actually gazing at her.

When there was a slight clearing among the trees, she closed her eyes as she moved, caught up in the reverie of the moment. Dancing filled her with a sense of joy and freedom that was rare in the life of a farmwoman, and she embraced the moment with fervor.

I could dance all day like this.

Her eyes still closed, the dream shattered when someone grabbed her by the waist. As her eyes flew open she screamed as she came face to face with a vagabond. He had several days' growth of beard on his face and his clothing was both torn and stiff from mud. With one of his front teeth missing and a thick purple bruise around one eye, the man was a frightening spectacle. The stench of rum overpowered Sarah as the stranger began to sing a Scottish tune.

"All in the merrye month of May,
When greenbuds they were swellin',
Sweet William on his deathbed lay,
For love of Barbara Allen."

Nausea enveloped Sarah and her breathing grew uneven. She tried to pull away from the man's grip, but he held tight.

"What's the matter, miss?" The stranger slurred his words. "I thought you wanted to dance. I'll even sing another verse for you." He belted out another chorus.

"Please, sir, let me go!" Sarah twisted and turned to free herself, but he held her even closer.

Anger filled the vagrant's voice. "You're not goin' to ignore me like Barbara Allen did to Sweet William, now, are ya, miss?"

Her lips quivered uncontrollably and she choked from fear.

The repulsive stranger groped Sarah and she could sense his breathing quickening. His hands were aggressive and painful. "Please stop. Stop!" She screamed as loudly as she could. *No one will hear me. I am a fool for coming this way.*

"You feel most pleasurable, miss." His hands began to pull her gown upwards as he pushed Sarah against a tree.

"No!"

Then she heard another voice, and the click of a musket's hammer.

"Let the lady go, unless you're wantin' to be on *your* bloody deathbed."

The stranger released Sarah and turned to face his challenger. Sarah fell trembling onto the ground, covering her eyes with her hands.

"No harm intended, mate," the stranger slurred. "Jus' thought this woodland nymph wanted a dance partner is all."

"You'll be dancing your way to hell if you lay hand upon her again."

Sarah heard staggering footsteps crunching the autumn leaves. The sound diminished and the woods were soon quiet.

Too frightened to look up, dizziness consumed her, as well as a sick feeling that ran throughout her being.

"That man, that man." The words escaped from her lips. She felt someone's hand on her shoulder and her eyes flew open. "No!"

Then she realized who had saved her.

"Mr. Stearns." She began to sob.

He squatted down and looked upon her with concern. "Are you all right, miss? You're shivering so."

Sarah could not stop shaking. "Yes. Thank you kindly."

Although desperate to recover from the incident, she still heard the fear in her own voice and it startled her.

"Please, miss, can you stand?" Nathaniel gazed at her with tranquil blue eyes.

"Yes, sir." Unsteady on her feet, she attempted to rise. He gripped her arms as he steadied her efforts.

"Miss, you're trembling. Come with me."

Her rescuer led her through the woods. Disoriented, Sarah allowed him to guide her along the path. Walking numbly beside him, she noticed little as they walked several hundred yards. When they arrived at the one-room log cabin, Nathaniel helped her up the entry stairs, still glancing around.

"Don't want that ruffian following you." He took her inside and led her to a chair by the recently kindled hearth. "Here, miss, please sit."

She followed his instructions, staring into the glowing fire without speaking. He handed her a cup and she drank without asking what it was. The tart flavor of fresh apple cider startled her out of her stupor.

Looking up at him as if seeing him for the first time, she said quietly, "Thank you, Mr. Stearns."

Nathaniel gave a shy smile as he looked downward. "Please, call me Nathaniel. 'Mr. Stearns' sounds like my father."

"Oh. I am sorry." Her lips quivered. "I don't know what happened. I was dancing through the woods because I was so joyful, and the next thing I knew... that man... it was just like..." She could not go on as warm tears washed down her cheeks.

Nathaniel pulled up a chair next to her and reached out to squeeze her hand. "You're safe now."

"I should not have been dancing. God is punishing me for my foolishness." She had to confess to someone, and she preferred telling her neighbor rather than revealing her sin to her mother. In despair, she placed her free hand onto her head in shame. But her guilt deepened when she realized that her cap was gone and her hair undone. She gasped in horror.

"What must you think of me? My hair undone, looking like some... some..." She could not go on without using an unspeakable word, which would only add to her long list of transgressions.

"Looking like some free-spirited lady? Because that is what I see." He gazed at her for a moment. "It seems to me that you have always had some independent ideas." A slight grin tugged at his mouth.

Sarah's mouth trembled with remorse. "And now I have lost my cap. What will Mother say?" Staring out the window, she exhaled in utter despair.

"Is this what you're missing?" Nathaniel put his hand inside his shirt and pulled out Sarah's linen cap. He handed her the crumpled headpiece.

Her mouth opened in astonishment. "Oh my... I don't know how to express my gratitude... how to thank you..."

"I found it on the ground. But you can thank me by never going through the woods alone again, Miss Thomsen." His voice sounded so harsh. Sarah looked back at the fire and her lips trembled. "I just would not wish for anything dreadful to occur to you, miss," he said, his tone much softer.

Sarah's eyes met his. "Nor would I, sir. And I shall ne'er venture alone in the woods again." She tilted her head as she fingered the linen cap he had taken from his shirt. "This is not the first time you've concealed a treasure for me. Years ago 'twas a piece of bread."

Nathaniel's mouth broke into a grin. "Yes, that fateful day when the town fathers decided you must be punished for going to school." The mirth in his eyes soon faded, replaced with anger. "'Twas cruel putting you in the stocks. You were only a child. All you wanted to do was go to school."

"My mother was horrified," Sarah said sheepishly. "I think that I have spent most of my life exasperating her." She looked down at the cap in her hands and twisted the linen in her still-trembling fingers.

Nathaniel's eyes furrowed. "That is not true, miss. I remember your mother expressing her concern for you when you were ill with the grippe some years ago. She had to leave you in the nursing care of your sister whilst delivering my mother's youngest child. I shall never forget her speaking of her fair young daughter who brought the sun with her where e're she went." Sarah noticed him staring at her long blonde hair, and he quickly turned away.

Her cheeks grew warm. "Thank you, Mister... Nathaniel." Sarah's voice no longer tremulous, she fixed her eyes on her rescuer. "And please call me Sarah." Her eyes drawn to the window, she held her hand up to shield her eyes from the bright light. "You have no curtains to keep out the sun."

He looked at the floor. "No," he said sadly. "My mother could not leave them behind. She said they would remind her of this home — of our family." He paused and cleared his throat. "At least she is well cared for by my Aunt Abigail and her husband in Boston."

"Families can be such a blessing, can they not?" Compassion filled her voice as she spoke. Suddenly she remembered the urgency of returning home.

"Father Eaton!" Her eyes widened as she thought of her stepfather's health. "I must return home forthwith. He has been ill."

Sarah stood up from the chair and he stood as well. She handed the cup to Nathaniel.

"I cannot thank you enough for your assistance, sir."

"And I cannot let you walk by yourself. That ruffian may still be about. I'll go with you."

"Please." Her voice spoke in earnest. "Do not tell Father Eaton what has occurred. It would strain his lungs further."

"I shall speak no word of this — so long as you keep your word to me."

"I promise." She touched his arm gently then whisked her hand away with embarrassment. She quickly twisted her long hair and tucked it back inside her cap. "I am certain 'tis not very well done, but perhaps Father Eaton will not notice."

Nathaniel's eyes softened for a moment as he gazed at her.

"You still have a few locks of hair coming undone." He touched the loose strands and tried to tuck them under her cap. His face turned bright red. "Forgive me. I should not have taken such liberties." He rubbed his forehead and turned away.

Sarah's breathing quickened and she touched her hair where his hand had been. She could still feel the sensation of his fingers. Although calloused from hard work, his hands had surprised her with their gentleness.

"Thank you." Her voice quivered. "I would not wish to look disheveled."

Nathaniel looked back at her.

"I think you look perfect." He stared at Sarah for so long that her cheeks filled with warmth. Then he turned away abruptly. "Let us be off then."

Sarah's breath caught as she watched his muscular arm with the rolled up sleeve grab his musket once again. She swallowed hard as she followed him out the door.

He perused the landscape carefully as they started walking to the next farm.

"We must make haste, Sarah, so you can attend to your father."

Sarah glanced at his face that she had long admired with its high cheekbones and skin browned by the sun. And his hair — she had often dreamed of running her fingers through his dark blond locks that kept coming undone from their ribbon. And those lips that spoke so infrequently... if only she could touch them. Perhaps kiss them.

Sarah, you are filled with foolishness.

After several moments of walking in silence, Sarah finally conjured the courage to ask something that had long troubled her. "Nathaniel, might I inquire about your father? Has there been any word?"

He stared straight ahead, squinting in the early morning sunlight.

"There has been nothing. When I left him at West Point after the war ended, he was well. He asked me to hasten home to check on our family.

He said he feared for their well-being." He walked silently for several rods. When he spoke again, his voice was strained. "His fears were merited."

Sarah glanced at her companion. "I'm so sorry about Ethan. I know that many in Deer Run died of the fever that year. That must have been a terrible shock for you to come home from the war and see your brother's grave."

"Yes." He glanced at her as they walked side by side.

"But you've heard nothing from your father?"

"No."

"I shall pray he comes home to you." Her voice was an earnest whisper. Nathaniel scrutinized her.

"You do not think I am a mad man for believing he will still come home? The rest of the town seems to question my sanity on the matter."

Sarah stared at her shoes as she considered what to say next. "I think 'tis important to hold onto faith — to trust that God will lead your heart. If you still feel in your spirit that your father is alive, then you must wait for him."

Nathaniel stared at her, then grabbed at her arm and squeezed it. Without thinking, Sarah reached up to grab his hand, but before she could reach it, he pulled his away.

She stared at him in surprise.

So tenderhearted yet so distant.

She puzzled about his inconsistent behavior — on the one hand reaching out, on the other drawing away.

Sarah attempted a change of subject. "I saw you at the meeting-house this past Sabbath Day. Were you not inspired by the reverend's words from Scripture?"

"In all honesty, I cannot remember the verses."

She grinned. "In truth? I cannot remember them either. I'm afraid my mind was traveling elsewhere. I pray that God will forgive me… Why do you not speak with me at Sabbath meetings, Nathaniel? It appears that you avoid my person." It was a bold question. She tried to keep her tone light, lest she reveal disappointment in her voice.

Nathaniel was silent for a moment before speaking. "I just assumed that… since Mr. Beal has set his eyes upon you… he would likely not appreciate my detaining his lady friend with private conversation."

"You *assumed* that I was his lady friend? And what, might I ask, caused this false assumption, Nathaniel Stearns?"

His mouth opened in surprise. "Well… I was certain that his profitable business would be cause enough for your interest in the man. He is quite well off, you know."

"And he is quite willing to inform any person willing to listen about his desirable dairy cows that produce enough milk to feed the entire village of Deer Run. He does prattle on so." Her hand flew to her mouth and her cheeks burned with shame. "I apologize, Nathaniel. I am being unkind."

Her companion gave a slight smile but did not look at her. "May I assume then, that you would not be averse to a conversation with myself on occasion? Say perhaps, after a Sabbath meeting service?"

Sarah grinned. "Yes. That is something that you *may* assume."

They were now a few feet from the front door of the Eaton farmhouse. The sun had fully risen over the horizon and the cool autumn breeze rustled Nathaniel's hair. Sarah noticed for the first time that his blue eyes were the same shade as the clear sky. She was sad they had arrived at her home so quickly.

"Thank you again, Nathaniel. I cannot imagine how this day might have concluded without your help." She gazed at her hero and then curtsied slightly before disappearing behind her front door.

Sarah leaned her back against the inside of the door and closed her eyes. She felt her cap where Nathaniel's fingers had been and smiled.

Only two days until Sabbath. Two days before I see him again.

Husking

*I*t had been only two days, but for Nathaniel it seemed like two years. His brief encounter with Sarah quenched like a sip of water offered to a parched man. Parched and starving — and now he yearned for more sustenance.

So when Sabbath day finally arrived, and with it the chance to see her again, he rushed to get ready. He made sure his faded clothing was freshly washed, his face cleanly shaven, and his long hair neatly tied back. He hated to think about the way he looked the day he rescued Sarah from the vagabond. All he planned on doing that morning was hunt deer. He had not planned on coming face-to-face with a doe-eyed beauty.

When did I start to realize Sarah had grown up? A year ago?

He remembered that day when he noticed the lanky schoolgirl had bloomed into a young woman — an alluring, winsome lady who took his breath away. His eyes had fixed on Sarah with a look that undoubtedly signaled his desire to speak with her. He also recalled Richard Beal stepping in front of him with a glaring stare that spoke volumes to the smitten rival. After focusing his hostile gaze on Nathaniel, Richard sauntered toward Sarah in a possessive manner.

I thought she desired him.

Then an excitement ran through his spine.

Could she possibly desire me?

He could not even dwell on the thought. Merely imagining her responding to his affections stirred him deeply. His brief encounter with her two days prior helped him understand one thing: He was enamored by Sarah Thomsen.

The bell at the meetinghouse tolled, eliciting an extra beat to lurch in his heart. He took one last look in the broken looking glass and hurried out the door. *Calm yourself, man.*

As he approached the meetinghouse from a distance, Nathaniel's palms moistened. Except for the occasional night at the tavern where the ale loosened his tongue, he had long since fallen out of practice interacting with friends. Too many painful experiences had closed off that part of his life.

He drew in a deep breath. It was time to talk.

"Good day, Reverend Phillips." Nathaniel tipped his tricorne hat at the pastor greeting his congregants. The minister looked at him in surprise and smiled.

"And a good morning to you as well, Mr. Stearns," the reverend replied. He shook Nathaniel's hand.

The townsfolk also seemed uncertain about the change in his demeanor. Most greeted him in kind, but Nathaniel noticed that a few appeared wary in their reception of him. He saw Richard Beal glance his way, before turning toward Sarah to speak with her. Richard seemed unaware that Nathaniel was approaching him from behind. The red-haired man's words were heard by most in the vicinity — including Nathaniel.

"Look at him." Richard's voice bellowed across the crowd standing outside the meetinghouse. "Finally decided to open his mouth after all these years. I thought maybe his tongue got lost in the war." He smirked and shook his head.

Sarah glared at him.

"That is cruel, Richard, and a lie." She looked over his shoulder and stared at Nathaniel with a welcoming smile.

When Nathaniel set his eyes on the blonde-haired woman, he could not help but return her smile. He knew his cheeks were turning red by the warmth flooding them. Ignoring Richard's ill manners, Nathaniel took a deep breath and approached her.

"Good day, Sarah."

"Good day, Nathaniel." She gave him a slight curtsy. "I hope you are doing well this lovely Sabbath Day."

"I am now, thank you." Suddenly at a loss for words, Nathaniel stood there awkwardly.

Don't stand here like a fool, say something!

But before he could think of something meaningful to speak, Richard moved in closer to Sarah. A look of annoyance crossed her eyes, and she extricated herself from her childhood friend's blockade.

"Richard, will you not greet our neighbor?" Sarah's voice was sharp. Richard's feelings were evident in the downward turn of his mouth.

"Mr. Stearns."

"Mr. Beal." The two men looked at each other without smiling. The awkward moment was finally interrupted with the arrival of Daniel Lowe and several of his children.

"Good morning, brother." Sarah's words broke the tension. "Is my sister still at home recovering from the birth?"

"Yes, your mother is with her this morning. She says that Mary needs to rest."

Daniel surveyed the threesome and a slight smile crossed his face.

"Good day, gentlemen." He tipped his hat at the trio. "It is a fine day today, is it not?"

Sarah was not often speechless, but today was an exception. She blurted out, "Yes, it is." There was a long, awkward pause. When no one else spoke, Daniel finally did.

"Well… tonight at dusk I was planning a corn-husking at my barn. I have an abundant crop this year and could use many hands to do the task. What say all of you?"

Nathaniel did not know how to reply. He had not been invited to such an event in years, mostly because he had avoided anyone who might have requested his presence. But the thought of attending a husking with Sarah stirred pleasure in his heart — a long forgotten sensation. "I… I suppose I could assist you, Daniel."

A huge smile lit up Sarah's face.

Richard turned bright red, his skin approaching the same shade as his hair. "I shall be there." Richard seethed through his teeth.

"I shall come to help you, Daniel," Sarah said.

Daniel smiled at his sister-in-law and winked.

"Well then, it is agreed. Thank you, gentlemen. Sarah." He turned to his children. "Come now, let us gather to our seats." Picking up two-year-old Alice, he carried the blonde-haired child up the steps to the meetinghouse.

Sarah started up the stairs as well. Both Nathaniel and Richard attempted to accompany her, but they ended up bumping into each other.

"Forgive my awkwardness." Nathaniel smiled at Richard and moved past him. Then he proceeded up the steps to accompany Sarah. He glanced back to see Richard glowering at the bottom of the steps.

Once inside the building, Sarah sat next to her brother-in-law and helped with her nieces and nephews. Nathaniel sat in his usual seat across the congregation. It was not near Sarah, but he was able to look at her across the room.

The congregation began to sing, led by one of the selectman in the town who seemed to fancy himself a capable singer. What the song leader lacked in ability he made up for with enthusiasm. When the selectman reached a rather high note that was completely off key, Nathaniel did his best to keep a straight face. Glancing at Sarah, he saw her struggling to control a laugh. When they caught each other's eyes, they almost lost their resolve.

When the singing ended, Reverend Phillips picked up his Bible and placed it upon the podium. The topic was "Loving One's Neighbor."

Nathaniel glanced at Richard sitting several rows away. He saw the angry Mr. Beal with his arms pulled across his chest and his jaw working back and forth.

This sermon appears to be lost on him.

Since the weather was still warm, the door of the meetinghouse was left open. A mild autumn breeze gave the only hint of colder days ahead.

"The congregation will stay awake most assuredly when there is fresh air to stir their senses," the reverend would announce on many an occasion.

But with the door wide open, any of God's creatures had access to the building as well. On this occasion, it was a neighbor's hen that ambled into the meetinghouse right in the middle of the minister's message.

Sitting on her Aunt Sarah's lap, little Alice Lowe pointed and giggled at the wandering chicken. Sarah kissed her niece's cheek and whispered in the girl's ear. Nathaniel watched her interaction with the child and his heart warmed.

The intrusive fowl was not yet finished interrupting the service. She headed straight for the reverend's podium and leaped straight upward, settling herself onto the pages of the Bible, feathers rustling through the air. Alice screamed with delight. Sarah struggled to maintain a serious face, burying her giggles behind her niece's head.

One of the church members stood up, grabbed the chicken, and went out the door with the squawking bird. Moments later, the noisy fowl gave one last protest before ending its adventure.

Someone will have a nice lunch. Nathaniel attempted to keep a straight face.

The only congregant unruffled by the event was Reverend Phillips, who didn't miss a word of his sermon.

Every fall, corn-huskings were a time to socialize. Neighbors sat on chairs or benches in a circle around a large pile of corn. The tedious work was made more bearable by the joy of mingling with friends and neighbors. It was often a ritual of courtship as well, with single males and females sitting alternately, using the event as an excuse to have a closer look at a potential partner.

Nathaniel Stearns understood the implication well, and he anxiously hoped to sit next to a particular female at this husking. So he waited at the entrance to the Eaton farm for a glimpse of Sarah on her way to the event. His patience soon paid off. Once again, his heart beat with anticipation as he took in the sight of the young woman approaching. Her slender form, arrayed in a homespun linen dress that reached to the ground, kept his rapt attention with each step she took. He did not recall ever seeing her wear this walnut-dyed gown before. He knew he would have remembered the way it highlighted her brown eyes, as well as the way it draped across her figure. She carried a woolen shawl over one arm in anticipation of the cooler weather later on. He suddenly envied the woven piece that would later be wrapped around the woman.

"Good even', Sarah."

She smiled warmly. "Good even' to you, Nathaniel."

"Might I walk with you to your brother's home?"

"I was hoping you would." Sarah looked down at the ground, her cheeks turning a stunning shade of pink.

"I was hoping you'd welcome my company." He cleared his throat. "I certainly would not wish you to walk by yourself."

"Nor would I." She glanced at him. "I have kept my promise. I've not ventured through the woods alone again."

He looked at her but did not reply.

Sarah seemed to enjoy the crunching sound as she stomped her leather shoes through the layers of dried leaves covering the road. Nathaniel noticed the way she forced her feet to step on the thickest piles of the fallen foliage. Her enjoyment was infectious.

"I remember my sisters doing exactly that," he said with a laugh. "Making the loudest sound they could in the leaves filled them with mirth."

They walked side-by-side as he breathed in the smell of venison cooking over someone's hearth.

"Someone will be enjoying a fine meal tonight," Sarah said. "I only had time to give Father Eaton some stew before I left. Mother was called away for a birthing."

"How fares your father, Sarah?"

She gave a weak smile. "He is not as strong as he once was. I do worry leaving him. I was going to stay home when Mother was called away but he would not hear of it. 'A lass must have her husking time,' he said in his jovial way." Sarah's eyes watered. "I do not know what I will do if he leaves us. He has been the only father I've known."

Nathaniel's heart stirred with her concern. "I am certain Dr. Burk is taking fine care of your father. Please don't let this weigh on your heart."

Sarah wiped underneath her eyes with a rapid motion as though wanting to hide her distress. She took a deep breath.

"Nathaniel, do you remember my real father?"

The question took him by surprise. "Well, yes… a little. I think I was perhaps six or so when he died."

"What do you remember about him?"

Nathaniel had to search his thoughts. "If my memory serves me well, your father was a kind and amusing sort of fellow. Always smiling. And he loved to sing at Sabbath services. He always put his heart into the words of the music." Sarah listened without speaking. Nathaniel added, "And I think he had flaxen hair, like his youngest daughter."

"I wish that I had known him."

Nathaniel paused. "I wish that you had, as well."

"Do you think…"

"Do I think what?" Nathaniel stopped walking and turned to face her.

"Do you think my father will know me in heaven?" Her lips trembled.

Nathaniel struggled to keep his own emotions in check. He reached down and lifted her chin so that she faced him.

"Most assuredly." His voice was a whisper and his heart melted at the yearning he saw in her eyes. The yearning for a father who was no longer there, a father she would only see in eternity.

Lord, is that where my father is — in eternity? He pushed the thought from his mind.

A few tears rolled down her cheeks and Nathaniel brushed them away.

"Now then, let us be off to the corn-husking." He forced a lilt in his voice. "Your brother will think we were lost on the way."

Sarah shivered from the growing chill in the air. She readied her shawl to wrap it around her shoulders, but Nathaniel took it from her hands and placed it around her. His hands briefly rested on her upper arms in the motion and he resisted the urge to keep them there.

"Thank you, Nathaniel." Her voice sounded both vulnerable and alluring. He placed his hands behind his back to keep them from wrapping his arm protectively around her.

They walked the rest of the way in comfortable silence.

When they arrived at the Lowe farm, Sarah seemed surprised by the number of neighbors who were attending.

"This will be a bustling affair."

Daniel and the twins, Danny and James, were busy setting up a circle of chairs in the barn.

"I'll see if they need some help." Nathaniel left her side to go assist.

Sarah walked toward the house to see how her sister, Mary, was doing with the new baby. Children scurried around outside, laughing and playing games. When Sarah walked into the house, there was peaceful quiet.

Mary sat in a chair by the fire nursing Ephraim.

"Sarah! How good to see you! Come sit with me."

Sarah sat on a chair next to Mary and looked at the infant suckling. "He is beautiful, Mary." The infant wrapped his tiny fingers around his mother's index finger while he ate. Soft sighs escaped from the baby's mouth in between the swallows of milk. "I never tire of seeing a newborn."

Mary peered at her. "Perhaps one day, you will be looking at your own newborn."

Sarah looked up, suddenly self-conscious. "I do not know…"

Mary scrutinized Sarah. "Daniel told me what happened at the meetinghouse today. You and Richard… and Nathaniel." Mary's lips turned upward into a suspicious grin.

Sarah felt her cheeks burn with embarrassment. "'Twas nothing, Mary. Truly." She knew her protests would not fool her sister. "Well, all right, it was something, but not what you are thinking. What are you thinking?"

Mary laughed. "I am thinking that perhaps you'd best sally out to the barn before they start the husking without you."

Reaching over the baby, Sarah gave her sister a tentative hug and hurried out to the barn. Guests were taking their seats one by one, alternating by gender. Looking around for Nathaniel, she heard the voice of Richard. "Here, Sarah. I've saved you a seat!"

Sarah cringed. *Where is Nathaniel?*

Her heartbeat quickened as she glanced to and fro in the dim light. She remembered the way his hand felt on her chin and the gentleness of his fingers wiping away her tears. She touched her cheek and remembered the sensation. It still took her breath away.

"Sarah!" Richard's voice was impatient. Sarah could feel everyone's eyes looking at her.

Still unable to locate Nathaniel, she reluctantly sat down next to Richard. There was still an empty seat beside her for a moment, but her hopes of sitting next to Nathaniel were dashed when Caleb Rowe sat on the other side of her. Richard wore a smug look of victory, much to Sarah's annoyance.

Nathaniel helped Daniel carry a heavy-looking log for a few huskers to sit upon. After placing it on the ground he looked for Sarah, only to see her in between Caleb and Richard. Although disappointed, he would not give in to defeat. The night was just beginning.

The huge pile of corn was already set in place in the center of the circle, looking like the makings of a bonfire. But this mound would be consumed not by fire but by eager hands ready to strip the corn of its leaves.

"Are we ready then?" Daniel asked the group. Excited eyes in the circle met his and he gave the signal to begin.

Richard acted as if this were a life-or-death competition, grabbing as many ears as he could and shucking them with no regard to thoroughness. Many of his finished ears of corn still held layers of leaves as he tossed them into the corncrib.

Most of the shuckers enjoyed the merriment of the occasion, laughing and chatting with neighbors they usually only saw at Sabbath services.

Nathaniel watched Sarah laugh as the thin silk strips from the ears of corn flew everywhere. Most of the participants had extra "hair" from the corn hanging from their own locks. Nathaniel sat across the circle from Sarah, and as the pile of corn diminished in size, he was able to get a better view of her. He smiled at her as his hands stripped each cob of its covering.

And then the unexpected happened. Nathaniel tore off the leaves from one ear and instead of the expected yellow color, dark red buds of corn peered out from the husk. He could not believe his eyes. He stared at the cob without speaking.

Caleb Rowe was the first to notice. "He's got a lucky ear!" he shouted above the din. Everyone paused in their work and looked at Nathaniel holding the cob that signified good fortune.

"You lucky dog, Stearns! Now someone gets a kiss from ya!" Caleb threw his head back and laughed, slapping his knees.

Nathaniel took his eyes off the red ear of corn. He knew what he wanted to do — but could he kiss the woman of his choice right here and now? As if reading Nathaniel's mind, Daniel spoke up.

"It's true." Daniel seemed to be smothering a grin. "It's called a lucky ear because it earns you a kiss."

The whole group began to laugh and murmur about who the recipient of the kiss might be. The only one not laughing was Richard Beal.

"So choose your lucky lady." Daniel waved his hand around the circle. "We cannot go on until the deed is done, you know."

Nathaniel eased out of his seat and made his way over to Sarah. The young woman's brown eyes grew wide.

He removed several strands of corn silk from Sarah's hair and cap. He squatted down in front of her and leaned in toward her face. Her eyes dazzling in the flickering firelight, Nathaniel stared at her full lips that opened partway as if inviting him. He shook so much he feared he would fall over in his unsteady stance. But his lips reached hers in a sure and steady caress that lasted longer than he had intended. His heart beat with such power, he thought the whole crowd might hear it. His lips melted into the warmth of hers and he wanted to stay there forever. As he reluctantly pulled away, the group cheered their approval. All, that is, except Richard.

Sarah touched her fingers to her lips. She started to smile but then appeared to be too flustered to continue. She stared into his blue eyes, which held hers like a physical force. Neither seemed able to release their gaze.

"All right then, let's break up this red-eared courtship and get back to work," someone shouted. Everyone laughed and worked at once. Nathaniel stood up to return to his chair. He could feel Richard's hot glare upon him, but he did not care. The only sensation he wanted to think about was the softness of Sarah Thomsen's lips upon his own.

He continued shucking but with less enthusiasm. When he looked over at Sarah, he could see her cheeks were still flushed. She picked up another ear to remove the husk, but was interrupted by Richard, who blathered just inches from her face. He spoke to her with rapid words and twisted features and Sarah's face expressed her displeasure with the man sitting next to her. Nathaniel grew angry and intended to confront him, but Sarah stood up and went inside her sister's house.

Richard looked over at Nathaniel with ice-cold eyes. Nathaniel's gaze in return was equally chilly.

The two men resumed their husking, each gripping the corncobs with angry fervor. They often glanced at each other but continued working in silence.

It was late in the evening when the husking was complete. Daniel served up cider and apples to the hungry group and everyone partook with eager appetites. Little by little, the jovial neighbors strolled home with just the light of a nearly full moon to illuminate their path.

Nathaniel waited for Sarah to come out from the house, but Daniel met him instead.

"In light of Mr. Beal's ire, perhaps it would be best if I walked Sarah home. Best not to incite the man's anger by walking with her. I would not want Sarah to be caught in a lover's triangle." Daniel smiled at Nathaniel as he patted him on his shoulder.

Disapointment flooded Nathaniel's thoughts. He had hoped to taste the sweetness of Sarah's lips again this night.

"You are right, of course." With reluctance, he turned to leave but looked back as Daniel called his name.

"Remember, there is a harvest dance next Friday. I'm certain Sarah will want to go." Daniel grinned at him.

Nathaniel smiled. "I'm certain I'll be going as well."

uth Eaton was horrified at the suggestion.

"Sarah? Go to the harvest dance?" She dropped the wooden spoon into the stew she stirred over the hearth. "I'd sooner see her put back in the stocks!"

"Now, Ruth, you do na' mean that." Myles chided her as he put his arms around her waist. "I wouldna' mind dancing with you, Missus Eaton." He swayed her a few steps before she held her feet fast.

"Mr. Eaton! Have you gone mad? Your lungs, after all."

"My lungs will fare well enough, my dear." He stroked his burly, rough hands over her cheek. "Please, Ruth. Do not quarrel with me. This is what the young ones do now and Sarah is of an age. She needs to have her chance to be with friends."

"But dancing! Myles, you know how I feel about such frolicking."

"Ruth, they're only holdin' hands while they dance." He held his wife close. "We need to let her go."

Missus Eaton's stance against the harvest celebration dance began to soften. Her husband had a way of disarming her arguments with his soothing voice and embrace. After a moment of silence she relented.

"All right then. But either Daniel or James must accompany her there and then home again. If anyone thinks he will have his way with my daughter, he will have to face one of them. And both my sons know how to fire ball."

"There's my good Ruth." He gave her a hug before she squirmed out of his arms. She smoothed out the wrinkles from her gown and apron.

"Enough of this foolish embracing. If someone comes in they will wonder what we are about."

Myles Eaton gave his wife a mischievous grin. "We wouldna' want them supposin' any frolickin' was going on." He winked at her.

"Mister Eaton." Her voice filled with exasperation as she returned to her stew. "Now where did that spoon go…"

⌒─◦

Sarah listened to her parents' conversation from the next room. When she heard her mother swayed by her stepfather's argument, she was beside herself with relief and joy.

Finally, I can dance!

She was ready to burst with enthusiasm, but had to smother her desire to shout. If her mother knew she had been listening in, Sarah might not be allowed to attend the annual fall celebration after all.

Slipping into bed in her night shift, she pulled the covers up to her chin. She snuggled into the soft quilts and imagined herself moving to the music. Mostly, she envisioned swaying to the melodies flowing from the fiddles — while holding the hands of Nathaniel Stearns.

That Friday Sarah could not concentrate on her work. Her mother had assigned her several chores — enough to keep Sarah from dancing on her toes around the house — but her mind was already at the Beal home. Since that family had the largest parlor in Deer Run, it was often the site for such village-wide celebrations. The fact that it was to be held at Richard's home was the only drawback to the dance, but Sarah knew its location was probably one of the reasons her mother had agreed to let her attend.

When Sarah thought she could not stand one more moment of sewing, her mother released her to prepare for the dance. She leaped up from her chair, dropping the box of pins all over the wooden floor.

"Please forgive me, Mother." She scrambled onto her knees, picking up each small pin and placing it back into the wooden box.

Her mother exhaled a deep sigh. "Go on now, Sarah. Get your gown on lest you be late."

Sarah hurried up from the floor and hugged her parent. "Thank you, Mother!"

She almost tripped while running across the main room floor to her bedroom. As she closed the door behind her, her eyes caught the gown hanging on the hook on the far wall. She had struggled all week long to finish sewing the indigo-dyed dress. She wanted Nathaniel to be one of the first to see her wearing it.

Her hands trembled as she took off her linen apron and work attire and then removed the new gown from its anchor on the wall. Pulling it over her head as she drew it downward, the folds of soft wool draped to the floor like the rivulets of a waterfall. She went to the looking glass and gasped — she had never felt so lovely before. Blushing at the low bodice, she grabbed a lace kerchief and tucked it into place.

I do not want to look like a loose woman.

Sarah undid her long blonde hair and brushed the locks until they shone. She twisted it up in the back and secured it with a wooden hairpin that was a gift from her parents on her last birthday. Next, she picked up the bottle of lavender water — a gift from her sister Mary — and smoothed it on her neck and arms. Lastly, she took her church bonnet and placed it on her hair, allowing the long ribbons to drape onto her shoulders.

She twisted with annoyance at the constricting whalebone stays that wrapped around her bodice and made her stand straighter. She knew it was pointless to fight the body-clinging device that was tied tighter than usual. She sighed in exasperation but was forced to surrender to the confinement.

"I shall dance all night, despite these wretched stays." She started to pinch her cheeks to make them a brighter pink and then realized they were already red with anticipation. She took one last look in the mirror before heading for the main room. She had heard her brother James' voice, and she did not want to keep him waiting.

The looks on the faces of her parents and brother revealed their surprise — and admiration.

"Sarah." James spoke after a moment of staring. "You are truly a young woman now. What happened to that free-spirited wisp of a lass I knew not long ago?"

Her cheeks grew even warmer. "That lass has now grown. Come, let us hurry to the harvest dance."

Missus Eaton wrapped a shawl around Sarah's shoulders. "Remember, James, you must be sure she fares safely. Look sharp for vagabonds and drunkards."

"I shall, Mother. My little sister is safe with me — and my firelock," he said, holding up his musket.

The worried mother seemed satisfied. Mr. Eaton put his arms around his wife as Sarah and James headed for the door.

"She will be safe, Ruth — and she will be happy."

Sarah giggled as she walked out the door. *I am going to a dance!* It was difficult to contain her excitement.

The moon was full enough to give adequate light to the siblings' steps as they walked the path to the Beal home. The moonlight filtering through the trees cast a glow across her brother's face. *Nathaniel will look quite handsome in the moonlight.* She inhaled a deep breath and felt the pressure of the stays across her bodice. The tightness of her new dress made her feel the changes that had slowly occurred in her figure, now blooming into young womanhood.

The air was getting colder now, giving ever-greater hints of winter days to come. The fallen leaves crunched underfoot with the build up of frost on the dry fronds. Sarah closed her mouth so the bitter air did not freeze her teeth.

"So, Miss Sarah," said James, "you must be looking forward to the dance tonight. Especially since it is at Richard's home." He had a teasing look in his eye.

"I am very much looking forward to dancing… but not with Richard."

"Ah yes, I heard a rumor of late — that perhaps a certain other neighbor has taken a fancy to my younger sister."

Although embarrassed to be at the center of this rumor, Sarah smiled with obvious joy.

"Perhaps." She hugged her shawl ever closer.

James grinned ear-to-ear as he walked beside her. The moonlight revealed the deepening lines that thirty-five years of farm life had etched into the face of her brother. Despite his seeming lightheartedness, James continued to monitor the woods nearby. This former sergeant in the Continental army still took his responsibilities seriously.

Out of the stillness of the night, an owl hooted with a haunting note. The sound always startled Sarah, and she was grateful her brother was nearby. She sighed with relief when they arrived without incident at the Beal farm. The pungent scents of cow manure and cheese made it obvious when one was near the dairy.

"Ah, the scent of a celebration." Sarah saw that James smiled in jest when he spoke.

"Yes, 'tis sweet to the senses," she joked in return. "After a bit, we shall no longer smell it. Such a relief!"

"So, I shall return in a few hours to transport you back home." He took in the sight of his grown-up little sister. "Do watch yourself, Sarah. Stay away from the wolves that charm. Those dogs only want to devour the innocent for their own satisfaction."

James had never spoken to her in such a fashion before, and it brought tears to her eyes.

"Thank you, James," she whispered. Standing on her tiptoes, she gave him a quick kiss on his cheek. "I shall beware the dogs." She turned and went into the farmhouse where the musicians warmed up.

As she entered the open door of the Beal home, the up-close sounds of the fiddles were so intense she could feel the energy right to her bones. Sarah let the music flow through her, her foot fidgeting at the prospect of following the melodies. She was glad Father Eaton had shown her a few traditional dance steps, although his shortness of breath had soon forced them to halt the lesson. The little she had learned from her stepfather stayed in her memory, and she had practiced the moves at every opportunity.

Scanning the room, Sarah looked with anxious eyes for any sign of Nathaniel, but he was nowhere to be seen. She saw her good friend

Rachel and they hugged each other. The two were just getting into an animated conversation when Richard Beal sauntered over.

"Good even', ladies," he said. "Such a delight to see you both. And Sarah," he said, taking in the sight of her new dress, "I've not seen such a vision in blue before." He winked at her and Sarah tried not to make a face.

I shall not roll my eyes tonight.

"Thank you, Richard." Her voice carried a politeness she did not feel.

As she spoke to him, she glanced over Rachel's shoulder and caught a glimpse of the one she'd been waiting for. Nathaniel stood in the doorway, his eyes dancing at the sight of Sarah. She could not help but smile. He crossed the room with steps that seemed determined as he moved in next to her.

Richard's annoyance was obvious, but before he could object, Nathaniel spoke. "May I have the first dance, Sarah?"

Sarah's heart beat faster, even though she had not yet begun to swirl to the music.

She swallowed with difficulty. "Yes." The couple's eyes were fixed upon each other.

Putting out his right hand, he led Sarah out to the middle of the parlor as the two fiddles readied to begin. Other couples lined up in rows facing each other and awaited the first notes, anticipation filling each face. The music started, the tune of "Sweet Richard" permeating the large parlor with its slowly building melody. Sarah had some difficulty remembering which direction to move, but she soon caught on. She laughed at her mistakes and Nathaniel kept smiling, despite her occasional missteps — and sometimes because of them.

It was difficult for her to concentrate on the proper steps, so engrossed was she in taking in Nathaniel's appearance. His blond hair was pulled back with a black ribbon. She had never before seen the grey woolen waistcoat that enhanced his broad shoulders and narrowed in at his waist. His handsome features had her spellbound.

As the tempo increased, so did the gaiety of the evening. And then Sarah heard something she had not ever heard before — Nathaniel began to laugh. It took her by surprise, because she realized for the first time how foreign this simple pleasure must have become for the man. It made her both sad and joyful at the same time.

Each time a group of dancers met with hands held high, Sarah could feel the touch of Nathaniel's warm fingers all the way to her heart.

Is this what it feels like to be in love? Sarah was not sure, but she knew she had never experienced these sensations before.

When the song ended, everyone was breathless. As she gasped for air, Nathaniel held her hand a moment longer than necessary before releasing it.

"May I get you some cider, Sarah?"

"That would be perfect."

As he went to get the drink, his rival appeared next to her. "You have saved this next dance for me, have you not?" Richard's voice held a hint of irritation.

"Why, yes, I suppose so." Sarah did not know what to say. Nathaniel had not yet asked her to dance again, and it would not be polite to refuse her host. When Nathaniel brought her the warm drink, she took it gratefully and sipped the sweet liquid. The music was starting again. Richard took the cup from her hand and gave it to Nathaniel.

"I will dance with the lady now, if you do not mind, sir." Richard glared at Nathaniel as he took Sarah by the hand and brought her to the dance floor. Nathaniel stood on the side, watching.

Sarah did not smile but glanced often at Nathaniel, whose eyes were fixed upon her. When she missed an occasional step, a look of anger crossed Richard's face, but then he would force a smile that his eyes did not match.

When Sarah and Richard held hands in the dance steps, his fingers clung with force to hers. The only sensation Sarah felt in her heart was annoyance.

The song was less than three minutes long, but the reel felt like an eternity. When it ended at last, Sarah made an attempt to be courteous.

"Thank you, Richard, for the lovely dance."

Richard started to speak to her when another friend hurried to his side, speaking with earnest into his ear. Sarah caught a few of the words in the hushed conversation and surmised that a few drunken boys were outside causing a commotion.

"I am sorry, Sarah. I must attend to this matter, but I will return forthwith." He squeezed her hand and locked eyes with her before following the friend outside.

Sarah breathed a sigh of relief and walked off the dance floor. Nathaniel was waiting for her and handed her the now-cool cider.

"Thank you, Nathaniel. I was so thirsty."

She swallowed the refreshment and looked up at him. He was just a few inches taller than her, but his presence was powerful and protective. She felt sheltered, cared for, safe with him.

"Sarah, may I have this next dance? And every other dance this night?" His deep voice was barely above a whisper as he took her hand. His blue eyes glistened in the candlelight. She could not have refused him even if she had wanted to. And she had no desire to decline.

"Yes."

The fiddlers began to play "Maiden Lane." The music lured them to the dance floor. Although surrounded by dozens of other dancers, Sarah felt as if they were alone, gliding across the floor, the occasional touch of their hands sending shivers up her arm.

One fiddle would play the tune. Then it was echoed by the second, as if the strings of each were flirting with the other. The melody was hypnotic, wooing her to him as the notes continued their own dance of affection.

Sarah's cheeks flushed with heat, but only partly from the exertion. When the courtly tune ended, Sarah and Nathaniel could not take their eyes from each other. Her breaths matched his in their intensity. Nathaniel was the first to speak.

"Perhaps we could get some fresh air. 'Tis so warm in here."

"Yes, I am quite warm."

Nathaniel found Sarah's shawl hanging on a hook on the wall, and then they walked outside, where several other couples had escaped the heat.

They both inhaled the fresh air. When they exhaled, their breath was visible in clouds of vapor.

"Perhaps you need to wear your shawl, lest you get chilled." He placed it around her, wrapping her snugly in the woven wool. "There. We would not wish you to get ill."

They walked side-by-side with familiar comfort. Although they had become better acquainted only recently, Sarah felt as if they had been close companions her whole life.

"I apologize for my lack of skill. I must confess, this is the first time I've been allowed to attend a dance." She felt embarrassed to admit this.

"I thought you were very graceful." His eyes locked upon her face.

"You are far too generous," she said, looking away. She turned back to her companion with a questioning look. "You are quite adept at dancing."

Nathaniel stared down at the ground while they walked among the trees. At length, he spoke. "We used to have dances in the war camp when we were not facing battles the next day. Some of the ladies from the surrounding towns would join us and teach us the steps. It helped keep our minds from thinking about the war." His face became serious and he grew quiet. He seemed transported back to a time long ago, but then snapped back to the present after a moment.

"Well then, enough talk of war." He seemed to force a labored smile. Sarah stared at him. *What terrible memories he must have.*

"I'm so relieved that you returned home safely, Nathaniel." Her wide eyes enveloped him with affection.

He stopped walking and put his hands around her waist. She could hear his breathing quicken, and his gaze seemed to consume her. She reached up and touched his cheek.

"Sarah, I…" He did not go on. He leaned in toward her and sought her lips with his own. His lips caressed her with a hungered yet gentle desire.

Sarah put her hands on his cheeks and returned his kiss with a passion that surprised her. When they pulled away, they were both out of breath. She reveled in the feel of his warm breath on her face and the pleasant sensations his lips had birthed in her.

Her voice trembled. "Nathaniel…" Before either of them could speak another word, they were again embracing and kissing. His arms left Sarah feeling both helpless and elated.

Nathaniel stopped as suddenly as he had started. He stepped away from Sarah and turned around, leaving her hurt and confused.

"Have I done something wrong?" Tears emerged on the rims of her eyes, as Nathaniel turned back to face her.

"No." He walked back toward her. "No. You've done nothing wrong." He stroked her face and touched her lips with his fingers. "You are an unexpected joy." He put his arms around her and held her without kissing. "An unexpected joy." His voice was a whisper.

He nuzzled her with his lips again.

"We must return to the dance." There was reluctance in his voice.

He walked with his arm around her shoulders and led her back to the house. As they strolled along the moonlit path, Sarah thought she saw someone out of the corner of her eye. She glanced back to get a better view, but the silent figure disappeared into the shadows like a hungry cat on the prowl.

*S*arah lay in bed awake, dreaming of the dance.

She envisioned the thrill of Nathaniel's arms and the tender passion of his kiss. Her mind transported to just a few hours before, swirling through each dance with the ruggedly handsome man who now clung to her heart and soul. She breathed in and hugged the quilts up to her chin.

A tapping at her window startled her out of her reverie. She sat up abruptly in bed.

"Who goes there?" She kept her voice to a loud whisper, not wishing to awaken her parents.

"Sarah, open the window." It was Richard Beal.

What can he possibly want at this hour? Irritation vexed her spirit at such an unexpected and inappropriate intrusion.

Flinging the quilts aside, she pulled off the top cover and wrapped it around her shoulders. She shivered as the cold floorboards met her bare feet. Scurrying to the casement, she struggled to open the frozen window. She did not want to allow too much cold air in. Leaving only an inch or two to communicate with him, she bent down to the opening.

"Richard, why are you here? 'Tis freezing!"

"Sarah, I came to warn you."

"Warn me? Pray, of what?"

He paused, then took in a deep breath.

"You know that I have been your friend these many years. And I place your best interests above my own." He paused again. "'Tis my duty as your friend to speak the truth about Nathaniel Stearns."

Sarah took in a deep breath and tapped her fingers with impatience. "Your duty? As my friend? Please, Richard." Shivering, she reached to close the window.

"Sarah, I am telling you the truth. You must listen!" There was an unexpected sincerity in his voice that caught her off guard.

"The truth? Please explain yourself." She waited for him to finish, longing for the warmth of her quilts.

"I would be remiss in not telling you the story of Nathaniel — and Rebekah Lyon. Now she is Rebekah Bannister."

Sarah had difficulty swallowing when her throat dried and her breathing quickened.

"Yes. I know Rebekah." She remembered how sixteen-year-old Rebekah had an understanding with Nathaniel before he went to war. Sarah had heard how Nathaniel's heart had been broken a short time later when Rebekah married Timothy Bannister from nearby Williamston. Just a few months later, Rebekah delivered a baby boy. Although the couple said the child was born early, he was a large and healthy baby at birth, leaving many tongues to wag while fingers were counted. All this took place nearly ten years ago. Sarah remembered how sorry she was for Nathaniel that his childhood sweetheart had betrayed his affections.

"Of course I remember what happened between her and Nathaniel. How she threw his heart in the mire while he was fighting for our country." Sarah set her mouth in a firm line, ready to defend Nathaniel. She continued to shiver as she hugged the quilt closer around her shoulders.

Richard took in a deep breath.

"Sarah, that is not the whole story."

She tilted her head with annoyance. "What, pray tell, do you mean?"

"The child that Rebekah birthed was not her husband's." Richard's voice whispered at the window. "Before Nathaniel Stearns left for war, he forced himself upon Rebekah. Timothy Bannister rescued the poor girl from humiliation and the whipping post. The child is Nathaniel's." These last words were said in a louder, more agitated voice.

Sarah trembled as though her heart had been stabbed with a cold knife. When she was able to speak again, her voice was tight and measured.

"And how, Richard, do you know this to be true?" A strange feeling of weakness encompassed her.

"Timothy Bannister told me himself. He even pointed out the child's light hair and blue eyes. It's like the boy was spit from Nathaniel's mouth."

Sarah envisioned the ten-year-old Bannister boy. He was, indeed, similar to Nathaniel. Sarah's heart raced now and she struggled to speak.

Taking in a deep breath, she whispered, "I must go now." Closing the cold window frame, Sarah walked with stiff limbs back to her bed. With difficulty, she pulled the quilts up around her neck. She shivered with such force, nausea beset her. When she stopped shaking, numbness enveloped her thoughts. Her mind could not fathom this terrible report.

Slowly, the pieces of Richard's story began to filter through to Sarah's consciousness.

Rebekah's son is Nathaniel's.

But the words that truly haunted Sarah's thoughts were the ones that had sent chills throughout her body.

He forced himself upon Rebekah.

As the meaning of this phrase melted through from her mind to her heart, Sarah covered her mouth with both hands in an attempt to muffle her sobs.

8

Confrontation

or the first time in years, Nathaniel's nightmares were replaced by pleasant dreams.

As he pushed the warm covers away, the chilled morning air penetrated his thin linen shirt. He donned his leather breeches and a deerskin jacket while stoking the fire in the hearth back to life. Crouching by the growing embers, the warmth that radiated to his skin reminded him of the comfort he had found in Sarah's embrace the previous night. Staring at the golden flames brought a smile to the man's face.

"An unexpected joy..." His voice was an audible whisper.

Yet even as he basked in the pleasant reminiscences of the harvest dance, he wondered if it were too good to be true. He had been alone for so many years that he had long since given up hope of finding real love. His childhood affections had been dashed on the rocks of betrayal, while his only other attempt at love had been birthed by anger and lack of forgiveness. Ultimately, his hope for someone to share his life had died along the way. Until now.

"Sarah." The sound of her name rolled off his tongue with a hushed reverence. He closed his eyes and envisioned her lips upon his, lips that seemed as eager as his to join together. He squeezed his eyes shut, hoping the memory would remain. But soon his eyes flew open.

What if 'tis all a dream? What if her heart is not true toward me?

And then a darker thought crept into his conscious. It was the realization that there was something he needed to share with this woman who was wending her way into his soul. He could not risk her discovering his secret on her own. That would be unthinkable… unforgivable.

He pushed his stiffened limbs up away from the soothing fire.

After pouring himself some cider that had warmed over the fire, he guzzled it before walking out the door. His steps were determined. He was on a mission of confession.

Sarah had not slept all night. When the first rays of sun streaked through her window, her swollen eyes balked at the glare. Pushing the quilts off, she arose from her bed and pulled on her woolen stockings, linen petticoats, and gown. She moved as if in a trance, without any show of emotion.

Without speaking a word, she walked into the main room where her parents sat at the tableboard. They met her with expectant smiles — she had been so happy the night before upon her return — but frowned when they saw her countenance.

"Are you ill, Sarah?" Her mother stood up from the table.

Glancing upward, Sarah replied, "No." Looking at the pot of leftover green corn pudding, Sarah's stomach roiled.

"I think I am not hungry this morning, Mother."

"But this is one of your favorites." Missus Eaton appeared confused.

Sarah put on her shawl. "I think a walk would suit me well." Her parents stared at her without speaking as she left the house.

Walking in the chilly morning air, Sarah barely felt the cold. It was difficult for her to feel anything after Richard's visit last night. His message could not have been more hurtful than if he had slapped her across the face. But even physical pain would have been preferable to the pain of these frightening accusations — ones that involved a man who had embraced her heart as well as her arms.

Can this be true? Can I have completely misjudged Nathaniel?

There was only one way to find out so she headed straight for his cabin to confront him. Before she reached his property, which was adjacent to her father's, she saw Nathaniel himself walking toward her. Her heart raced at the sight of him, but she forced herself to be calm. He broke out into a grin when he saw her and she struggled to maintain her composure. She determined to find out the truth.

"Sarah." He took her in his arms and kissed her. A look of confusion crossed his eyes as she did not return his kiss. "Is all not well?" He brushed a strand of hair back from her face. She found it difficult to meet his eyes.

She struggled to find the words but began as boldly as she was able.

"There is something that I must know, Nathaniel."

"Yes, anything." His hands gripped her arms tighter.

"I must know…" It pained her to continue, but she took in a deep breath and spoke with resolve. "I must know about the child."

Nathaniel stiffened. His hands clenched her arms even tighter. "Who told you about the child?" His voice bore a distressed tone. Was it guilt?

Sarah's heart squeezed in pain. "So 'tis true?" She stepped away from him in horror. "You knew about the baby and did nothing? After forcing yourself on Rebekah?" Tears of sadness and confusion flowed down her cheeks.

"Forcing myself on Rebekah?" He shook his head as if to clear it. "I know not what you speak!"

"Rebekah's child. Timothy had to marry her to save her from disgrace. How could you?"

Nathaniel stood as if frozen before speaking. When he opened his mouth, the words were deliberate and wounded.

"So this is what you believe." He started to walk away and then turned back to face her. "Did I ever do anything to you to deserve this accusation? Did I not always treat you with the utmost regard, even when I had the opportunity to take advantage?" A deep hurt filled his saddened blue eyes. "I thought perhaps you were different, Sarah."

Shoulders slumped, he headed back in the direction of his cabin.

Sarah stood, speechless. Had she and Nathaniel really just said these hurtful words to each other? Dizzy and weak, she sat on a fallen log to get her bearings. Nathaniel was right — he had never betrayed her trust when they were together. But he had as much as admitted the child was his. What was she to think? She sat on the log for an hour or more and wept. When she thought there could be no more tears within her, she arose from the log with the weariness of one worn and old, beaten down by the cares of this world. She made her way back to her home with heaviness in her limbs and heart.

9

Truth

"Mary, we need you." Missus Eaton stood in the doorway at Mary and Daniel's house and burst into tears.

"Mother, come inside." Mary led her mother over to a chair. "Polly, please fetch your grandmother some warm tea." When Missus Eaton's tears subsided, she looked up at Mary.

"Myles and I are beside ourselves." Her lips quivered and her voice strained. "Ever since the night of the dance, Sarah has been inconsolable. She has not ceased crying and she will not eat. We do not know what to do."

Mary put her fingers to her lips. "She will not divulge her heart-ache? That does not sound like Sarah."

"Perhaps, she will confide in you, Mary. You have always been close." Missus Eaton pleaded with her daughter.

"I cannot imagine what grieves her heart so. The dance was three days ago." Mary set her mouth in a thin line. "The harvest is complete. I shall leave the children with Daniel. Ephraim can come with me. I shall try to get Sarah to reveal her pain so that we may help her." Touching her mother's hand with her own, she tried to reassure her. "I will do all that I can, with God's help. Please rest here for a bit and drink your tea. Perhaps Prissy can read to you. She is a fine student."

Grabbing her wool cape and picking up the baby, Mary walked out into the chilly air, hugging Ephraim close and covering him with the fabric. *Dear Lord, I need your wisdom. Show me how to help my sister who is grieving so.*

Arriving at the Eaton home, Mary noticed the somber mood of her stepfather, Myles.

"I am certain Sarah will be herself again, soon, Father Eaton." She gave him a brave smile of encouragement before knocking on Sarah's door. There was no answer, so Mary entered.

Sarah was not crying, but Mary had never seen her in such a state. Her hair was disheveled and matted. Dried tears left crusty streaks on her cheeks, and her eyes looked hollow and distant. Her little sister did not look at Mary, but stared out the window.

Mary tiptoed to the bed. "Sarah." Mary sat next to her still holding Ephraim. With her free hand, she smoothed Sarah's hair across her forehead, just as she had done for her little sister since birth. Mary prayed in her heart that the Lord would comfort Sarah and heal her of this unspoken pain.

Fresh tears began to spill from Sarah's eyes and she looked up.

"I do not know what to do… what to think." Sarah took a deep shuddering breath. "I feel like my life is over and I hurt so in my heart."

"Tell me what has happened, my sweet." Mary's voice attempted to soothe her. "You are breaking our hearts with your silence."

When Sarah seemed more composed she sat up in the bed. She noticed Ephraim and stroked his chubby cheek. Looking at the infant seemed to elicit a fresh river of tears. In between sobs, Sarah opened up to Mary about the wonderful dance, the visit by Richard with the terrible, unexpected news, and the angry words exchanged with Nathaniel.

Mary listened with wide eyes that grew ever wider when Sarah revealed the part about Nathaniel's child. She waited until Sarah had finished before speaking.

"Are you certain that Rebekah's son is Nathaniel's baby? I find this difficult to believe." Mary shook her head in doubt.

"He even asked me how I knew about the child." Sarah sobbed convulsively. "He as much as admitted his guilt. And does not the lad resemble Nathaniel with his flaxen hair?"

Mary furrowed her eyebrows. "Timothy Bannister has flaxen hair as well." She looked with sympathy at her sister. "Sarah, I do not know what the truth is. But it does seem that Richard may have cause to thwart your feelings for Nathaniel."

Sarah wiped her swollen eyes on her sleeve. "That's what I thought at first. But then," she said, sobbing again, "then when Nathaniel admitted he had a child, I knew Richard must be right."

Smoothing her sister's hair back from her face, Mary looked her straight in the eye. "Things are not always as they seem, little sister. And there is someone who can clear this matter up."

Mary leaned over and gave her sister a kiss on the cheek. "You, Miss Sarah, must promise me that you will wash off your face and get some of Mother's stew to eat. You must be famished. Please, do as I ask."

Sarah nodded and Mary left the room. She wrapped her cape around Ephraim to protect him from the chilly October air before she stepped outside. Her footsteps were sure and determined as she set out for the home of Rebekah Bannister. Mary knew Rebekah was a woman whose word could be trusted and she counted on her honesty today. Her sister's happiness depended on it.

A few flakes of snow wisped down from the clouds, reminding Mary of this season so many years ago when she fell in love with Daniel. Their journey to love was as precarious as Sarah and Nathaniel's. Mary hoped and prayed that the younger couple would have as happy an ending as their own.

Approaching the crudely built cabin, Mary heard at least two of Rebekah's children crying indoors. Mary knocked with hesitant hands at first and then harder when no one answered. A half-naked child opened the door and just stared at her.

"Who is it, John?" Mary heard the young mother's voice inside.

Mary peaked in past the portal. "Good day, Missus Bannister. 'Tis Mary Lowe, come for a visit."

"Ah, Missus Lowe, come in." Rebekah seemed pleased to see a friend. "Have a seat."

Mary sat on the log offered to her. Ephraim started to fuss and Mary placed him on her breast to nurse. Both women smiled at each other as they fed their infants. Mary glanced around the dimly lit cabin where three of Rebekah's children played with sticks and rocks on the floor.

The oldest child, Thomas, read a book by the window.

"Timothy's out huntin' game," Rebekah offered. "Perhaps he'll come back with a buck." A hopeful look emerged on her face. Mary noticed the worn lines already etching themselves around the younger woman's eyes.

"A buck would be a fine thing." Mary gave her a smile.

Rebekah tilted her head and furrowed her brows. "But you've not come to inquire about such things."

"No. I have not." Mary paused. "I have come to help my sister."

A look of concern spread across Rebekah's face. "Sarah? Is she not well?"

Mary paused before answering. "Her heart is ill with sadness. Perhaps you can help us."

Narrowing her eyes, Rebekah leaned closer to Mary. "I'll do what e're I can to help."

"I knew I could count on you." Mary glanced at the oldest child by the window. "Do you suppose Thomas could bring me some fresh milk from the barn?"

"Aye, of course. Thomas, fetch some milk from the cow."

After the ten-year-old left, Mary stared at Rebekah and spoke in a quiet tone. She explained the situation with Rebekah regarding Sarah, Nathaniel, and the words spoken by Richard Beal. At first Rebekah appeared embarrassed to recall the story, but when she heard what Richard said, her demeanor changed to outrage.

"Nathaniel never forced himself on me. And the child is Tim's — that I know for certain." She kept her voice low. "I was filled with sadness when Nathaniel left for war. Timothy came to comfort me. But his affections went too far. Soon, I knew that Thomas was on the way and Tim and I hastened to marry."

She focused her eyes on Mary. "Nathaniel never touched me in such a manner. And you can tell Sarah that." She paused. "It breaks my heart that Nathaniel has been wounded once again." Tears filled her eyes.

"The Bible says that the truth shall set us free. Perhaps this truth will allow him a chance to be free to love again." Mary squeezed Rebekah's hand.

"I do hope so." The younger woman brushed tears aside.

"Well, then, I must hasten home before the darkness sets in." She regarded Rebekah. "Thank you. I am most grateful to you."

The two women hugged, then Mary rewrapped the shawl around the now-sleeping Ephraim and stepped outside. Tim was just returning with a large deer draped over his shoulders.

"Got a fine one, Rebekah," the husband called to his wife.

The woman in the doorway smiled. "Aye, a fine one indeed."

Mary waved good-bye to the family and hurried down the road toward the Eaton farm.

Sarah plopped down on the stack of hay in the barn. Shame and embarrassment filled her thoughts yet there were questions that remained unanswered.

"So, Richard lied to me? He slandered Nathaniel?" She paused for a moment. "And I believed him…" She stared in disbelief at Mary.

Mary sat next to her on a milking stool, still holding Ephraim in her arms.

"According to Rebekah Bannister and she is privy to the truth."

Sarah gazed out the door of the barn, barely noticing the bellowing bovine waiting to be milked in the first stall. She set the milk bucket down on the floor and covered her face with her hands.

"What have I done?"

Mary reached over and squeezed her sister's arm. "I am certain if you explain this misunderstanding to Nathaniel…"

Sarah gave her a pointed look and spoke in an earnest whisper. "You did not hear the hurt in Nathaniel's voice, nor see the pain in his eyes with my accusations." Tears rolled down her cheeks. "I am certain he can never forgive me." She stood up with resignation and brushed pieces of straw from her gown. "I'd best milk Susie."

Mary stood and freed the milking stool for Sarah to use.

As she bent over to pick up the bucket, she wiped tears away from her face. "Besides, there is still the matter of the child Nathaniel spoke of. How do you explain this?"

"I cannot. But I do know there has to be an explanation. Please Sarah, try to make this right. Apologize for your part in this and ask for forgiveness."

Sarah looked down at the floor for a moment, then met her sister's eyes. "Do you think he can forgive me?"

Mary smiled and touched Sarah's arm. "All you can do is try."

The edges of Sarah's lips turned upward ever so briefly. For the first time in days, a glimmer of hope resided in her heart.

"I shall seek him out at Sabbath service next."

But when the bell tolled at the meetinghouse next Sabbath, Nathaniel was nowhere to be found. Sarah waited outside as long as she could before her mother called her to sit down in their pew.

The minister's sermon was lost on Sarah that day. She was so distracted and disheartened she did not even notice her friend Rachel waving to her at the noon break.

"Are you well, Sarah?" Rachel's voice echoed concern.

Sarah paused before answering. "No, Rachel. I am sick in my heart."

Rachel's eyebrows furrowed. "I've not noticed Nathaniel Stearns at service today." Rachel studied her friend with a focused gaze. "Does your sad manner have to do with him?"

"Yes," Sarah whispered. She fought back tears but soon lost the battle. "I do not know what to do."

Rachel did not pry for details. "I do not know what has occurred, but I saw how you gazed at each other at the dance that night. I think I understand your feelings." Rachel touched Sarah's hand. "Please know that I am praying for you."

"I am most grateful to you, Rachel."

When Richard approached Sarah to speak with her, she glared at him and walked away. He stood there with a wounded look on his face while she hurried back into the meetinghouse.

When the service ended a few hours later, Sarah excused herself from visiting with family and walked back home by herself. As she hung her cape on the wall peg, she turned around and noticed the family Bible on the chest of drawers.

How long has it been since I have read those words?

Walking to the dresser, she lifted the heavy volume and carried it over to the chair by the hearth.

Perhaps if I had spent more time listening to God's word, I would not have been so deceived by the words of a liar.

She sighed in despair, then opened up the volume to her mother's favorite, the book of Proverbs. These words of wisdom had been read to her by her parent for as long as she could remember. Sarah began to read from chapter 6.

"These six things doth the LORD hate: yea, seven are an abomination unto him: A proud look, a lying tongue, and hands that shed innocent blood, An heart that deviseth wicked imaginations, feet that be swift in running to mischief, a false witness that speaketh lies, and he that soweth discord among brethren."

She placed the large volume on her lap and stared into the fire. "And I have been a part of believing these wicked imaginations — and hurting Nathaniel's heart." She put one hand on her forehead and closed her eyes.

"Dear Lord, can You ever forgive me?" She paused and her lips trembled. "Can he ever forgive me?"

10

Winter

*S*arah breathed on her hands in an effort to warm them up. Snow fell with heavy flakes this morning and the long walk from the barn to the Eaton home was enough to allow her fingers to turn numb.

It had been two months now since she and Nathaniel had spoken words of anger and hurt to each other. While she yearned to ask him for forgiveness, he was absent from any of the usual events in Deer Run. And his vacant seat in the meetinghouse each Sabbath service only reinforced the emptiness in her heart.

She continued to leave fresh bread on his doorstep every Sabbath morning. The empty basket was always left behind for her to refill. But had it not been for the crumb-filled linen, she would not have been able to surmise if the inhabitant had indeed been nearby to consume the basket's contents.

Sarah had been so bold as to send a note of apology to Nathaniel and leave it in the doorjamb. The note was left there, unread, and unanswered. She found it a week later, lying in the dirt, smeared with mud.

Now, as she shook off flakes of snow from her gown, she tried to shake off the feeling of despair. Would she ever be able to speak to him again? She knew she did not deserve his pardon. But she knew she had to keep trying to obtain it. She owed him that much. She no longer dwelt on the possibility that he might have a child somewhere. Nothing mattered to her anymore — except that the man who still held her heart might forgive her from the vicious accusations she had hurled at him so mercilessly.

She continued to busy herself helping her parents. With her mother frequently away attending births and her stepfather's ill health, there was more than enough work to keep her hands busy.

But no amount of busyness could ever keep her from desiring reconciliation. She continued to pray that one day, she and Nathaniel would reunite. She knew that only God could heal his heart — and help him to forgive her.

<hr />

Nathaniel Stearns was still recovering from the binge of the previous night when someone pounded on his door.

"Enter at your leisure." Nathaniel's voice was boisterous. Dr. Burk walked in with a mischievous grin on his face.

"Ready for the big night?" Robert Burk looked as excited as a schoolboy.

"Big night? Of what do you speak?" Nathaniel rubbed his forehead trying to smooth away the throbbing pain.

"You know! The cockfight!" Robert threw his arms outward for the grand announcement.

A glimmer of recognition played across Nathaniel's mind. "Ah yes, the cockfight. I've heard of these but never seen one before." He scratched his head and his eyes narrowed. "So these fights are rife with excitement?"

"'Tis beyond exciting." Robert rubbed his hands together in anticipation. "They're bringing up the big winning cocks from New York for the event. Joe Pickrel is expecting hundreds to his tavern. Stocking up on ale and rum, he is."

Nathaniel shook his head in doubt. "I still don't get the uproar over a couple of roosters."

Robert's jaw dropped open. "Roosters?" He stared at his companion with askance. "You've not seen a fight like this before! And there's big money on the table. Blood sport and betting — what could be better?"

What could be better, indeed? Nathaniel could think of several things that might be more desirable, but he pushed them from his mind.

"All right then, let us be off." Still cloudy from last night's ale, he donned his jacket with fumbling hands and left for the tavern with his friend.

As they walked side-by-side, Nathaniel asked his companion a question that had long simmered in his mind.

"So, Missus Burk — she does not mind her husband spending so many hours at tavern with the men?"

Robert's eyes narrowed slightly; he stared straight ahead.

"Matilda has no say in the matter. Besides, she cannot silence her tongue long enough to consider her husband's need for some peace."

Nathaniel asked no further questions and they walked in silence until the distant sounds of chattering men met their ears. Anticipation filled Robert's eyes once again.

"Ah, the sound of peace."

The loud guffaws of the crowd at the tavern did not sound peaceful to Nathaniel, but he knew that once he took his first sips of ale, the clamor would soon diffuse into a numbing din. Working his way through the assembly of strangers visiting from far and wide, Nathaniel fought the desire to escape the fray. He'd promised the good doctor he would join him for the big event, and he would not desert him now.

After obtaining their tankards of beer, they forced their way outdoors to find the best possible location for viewing the fight. After Joe Pickrel had sold more ale in one night than he had all winter, the owners of the cocks brought out their birds in cages. When the crowd saw the fighting fowl, the men went wild with cheers.

"What happened to their combs?" Nathaniel shouted to Robert above the din.

"They dub them," Robert shouted back. "If they're not removed, the other cock grabs hold and tears them off."

Nathaniel had never seen such large, athletic-looking roosters before. These were not the kind seen in farmyards. These were angry-looking, fierce fighters. And when he noticed the gleaming metal spurs attached to their feet, he knew this weaponry was going to be deadly for one of them, if not both.

The sparring began as soon as they were released by their owners.

The crowd of men went wild with lust for the kill. The roosters did not disappoint, as each lunged and bit his feathered opponent. The men next to Nathaniel bumped into him time and again with enthusiastic arm throwing, trying to egg on their chosen champion. Ale spilled freely and saliva oozed from the boisterous fans' mouths as they shouted jeers or cheers, depending on the situation of their chosen fighter.

When one of the roosters made a wrong move, the other took full advantage of his misstep. With full intent to finish him off, the stronger cock dove and attacked the weaker with precise and repeated gouges. The blood began to flow and the men in the crowd drooled in their excitement.

An intense wave of nausea flooded Nathaniel. Flashes of scenes from the war appeared in his thoughts — yelling, screaming, blood flowing. His heart raced and a ringing filled his ears.

He pushed his way through the crowd, gasping for air. He ran over to the edge of the woods and held onto a tree trunk with trembling hands. He vomited for so long he thought he would surely die.

When the retching ceased, his thoughts were more clear than they had been in many weeks. His limbs trembling with weakness, he stepped back from the tree that had supported him and walked on unsteady legs back to his cabin.

The cold night air refreshed his spirit as he pushed away the thoughts of what he'd just witnessed in the tavern yard. He'd not seen such lust for blood since the war, and he had no desire to view it again.

He did not care if Robert understood why he had to leave. It was not important to him any longer to please a person. He knew he needed to please God and lately, he'd ignored the heavenly beckonings to his heart.

As he walked into his cabin and brushed the snow from his jacket, he set his eyes on the one treasure his mother had sent home with him from Boston. He picked up his Bible with trembling hands and opened it for the first time in years.

11

Samuel

With the arrival of February came the arrival of James and Hannah's new baby, Samuel. His blue eyes reflected the same color of his mother's and the baby's golden hair matched his father's. He was both beautiful and loved.

All seemed to be going well until two weeks after his birth. Through the window, Sarah saw ten-year-old Asa running toward their house. She hurried to answer.

"Aunt Sarah, is Grandmother here?" The boy's face was flushed and his breathing rapid.

"Yes, Asa, what is it?" Sarah's mother dried her hands on a cloth and approached the boy.

"Grandmother, please hasten to our home. Samuel is ill. Mother says to tell you he is vomiting." Tears welled in Asa's eyes.

"Vomiting? Not like all babies sometimes do?"

"No, nothing like that. It comes out everywhere..." The boy pointed to his mouth and nose and twisted his face in disgust.

"I see." She went to her medicine cabinet and took out the slippery elm. "Sarah, can you accompany me to their home? Just in case I need your assistance."

Sarah's brows furrowed. "Of course, Mother." She untied her apron and pulled her cape off its hook.

"Myles, Sarah and I must attend baby Samuel. Will you be all right?" She touched his arm.

"Aye, Missus Eaton. Go see to the child." He smiled and patted her hand.

Kissing her husband good-bye, Missus Eaton and Sarah left with Asa to go to James and Hannah's home — the old Thomsen homestead where Sarah had been born.

Sarah had never seen Asa so upset.

"So, how long has Samuel been ill, Asa?"

"A day or so, Aunt Sarah. But father said that last night he was in terrible straights. He thinks perhaps it is an unbalance… in the… miasmas, or some such thing." He shrugged. "Father said that's what the army doctor used to call such troubles when the weather changed."

Sarah noticed her mother looking down at the ground.

Mother is fearful. This is not like her.

A chill trickled down Sarah's back but she shook off the feeling of alarm that crept into her thoughts. *The baby will be fine. He must be fine.*

When they arrived, Sarah could hear the baby crying.

"Poor little one." Her mother spoke to no one in particular.

As they entered the front door, little Lydia stood alone sucking her thumb. She took her finger from her mouth. "Baby sick." She pointed at the screaming infant in Hannah's lap.

"Yes, dear." Sarah lifted the child in her arms and hugged her, rocking her in a gentle swaying motion. Lydia rested her head on Sarah's shoulders.

"We were up with him half the night, Mother." James ran his hand through his disheveled hair. "He could not keep any of his milk down."

Sarah had never seen James this distraught.

"None of the other children had this problem." Hannah had dark circles under her eyes and wet stains of vomit covered her gown.

"Let us try a small bit of slippery elm, Hannah." Missus Eaton placed a small amount of diluted elm bark on Hannah's breast so the child could nurse the medicine along with the milk. When the baby finished nursing and the milk appeared to be tolerated by the child for a long while, the grandmother sighed.

"There now. Perhaps that will help Samuel." Missus Eaton gathered up her things.

Sarah kissed Lydia and gave her to James. "There, little one. Give your father some hugs." James took the child and kissed her cheek.

The two women had just reached the door to return home when baby Samuel began to wretch and choke. He vomited every bit of milk once again.

Hannah began to cry. "You see? He loses it all." All the children watched in silence as they stood nearby the chair where Hannah sat with the baby.

"Perhaps Dr. Burk has another remedy that might help." Missus Eaton twisted the edge of her cape.

James's face blanched. "I shall send for him. Asa, please fetch the good doctor."

Sarah and her mother removed their capes and resumed helping the family.

"So, who would like some supper?" Sarah made an effort to smile and rally the three children. Peter, Matthew, and Lydia just stared at their aunt. No one moved. "Come now, let us sally to the tableboard. Come on." She guided the three to benches near the table and found some bowls to serve them soup, which had been simmering on the hearth. The children lingered over their food without speaking.

When Dr. Burk arrived at their home, all the children's eyes were glued to his face.

"Can you fix him, Dr. Burk?" Six-year-old Peter's eyes were wide.

"I shall try my very best." The doctor patted his red hair. With the whole family watching his every move, Dr. Burk inspected the infant. His brow furrowed deeply.

"He does seem a bit lethargic…" The doctor's voice trailed off.

When his examination was complete, he looked up and gave a reassuring smile. "I think he simply has a severe colic. Let us try giving him some water. Small bits at a time. That should settle his digestion."

Sarah breathed a sigh of relief at the familiar word.

"Send for me, should you need my assistance further." Walking toward the door, the doctor put his tricorne hat on his head and pulled the collar of his jacket a little higher against the cold. Sarah noticed a look of concern on his face as he glanced back at the infant before leaving.

Hannah was half asleep in the chair holding Samuel. The baby was no longer screaming as he had been upon their arrival.

He is so quiet.

A gnawing fear ate at her thoughts.

What if the baby dies?

She shook off the worry as quickly as it emerged and busied herself with serving supper to James and her mother. Hannah refused any food.

"Perhaps, Sarah, I will spend the night here to help with the child. Could you return home to see to Father Eaton's needs? And go ahead to Sabbath service in the morning without me."

"Of course, Mother." Sarah kissed all the children on their cheeks and then put her arm around her brother. "I shall pray for Samuel, James."

He looked at his sister and squeezed her arm. "Thank you, Sarah."

She put on her cape and walked over toward Hannah and the baby. Leaning over them, Sarah kissed Hannah first and then the top of Samuel's head. She did not realize she was crying until a tear from her eyes fell on the sleeping infant. She wiped her face off and headed for the door.

The next morning, Myles Eaton insisted on attending services with Sarah.

"Are you certain, Father Eaton? Are you strong enough today?"

"Aye, lass, I will manage. I want to be in prayer for young Samuel."

She kissed him on the cheek. "You are the dearest father one could have."

She tied the ribbon on her church bonnet and wrapped her wool cape around her shoulders. Although the air was bitter cold, the winter had been surprisingly free of abundant snow. An occasional flurry of white flakes had been all the residents of Deer Run had contended with this year, and everyone was grateful.

As Sarah and her father approached the meetinghouse, Sarah gave an audible gasp. For the first time in months, she saw Nathaniel. He was just disappearing into the door of the building when she noticed him. She felt her heart beat faster and her feet stopped moving.

Sarah felt Father Eaton squeeze her arm. "Perhaps today you will speak with someone." He winked at her and prodded her to walk up the stairs with him. They ascended the stairs one at a time to accommodate Father Eaton's weakened condition.

Sitting in their family seat, Sarah smiled at Mary and Daniel. Mary looked at Sarah and moved her eyes toward Nathaniel and then back to Sarah. Sarah nodded to her sister but avoided looking at Nathaniel.

It was halfway through the sermon before Sarah could stand it no longer. She glanced over at Nathaniel, and she thought perhaps he had been looking at her, but he turned away so fast she could not be sure.

She wanted to cry. She closed her eyes, the weight of Samuel's illness and the pain of her relationship with Nathaniel overwhelming her.

Dear Lord, I cannot bear these pains. You have said that You have borne our griefs and carried our sorrows. Please, dear Lord, I need You to do so now.

She swallowed back her tears and opened her eyes. At that moment she glanced back at Nathaniel. His eyes held hers for a brief moment, and they seemed tender and compassionate. He looked away again, but her heart held a glimmer of hope.

When morning service was finished, Sarah looked around for Nathaniel, but she could not find him. As if this day could not be any more difficult, she turned around to face Richard Beal, who confronted her before she could escape.

"Sarah, I need to converse with you."

"There is nothing that I wish to speak about with you, Richard." She tried to maintain her composure.

"Sarah, please listen. I found out that I was wrong about Nathaniel. Someone had told me the story and I thought it was important for you to know. I was trying to help you." His voice sounded sincere and earnest.

She lashed out in anger. "You thought that you could help by spreading gossip? How could you, Richard? How could you share such slander without a thought for the consequences?"

He shifted his feet without answering and fidgeted with his hat. Sarah glared at him. "I do not wish to converse with you further." She turned and walked away.

Her father was not feeling well, so he and Sarah went home early. When they arrived at their house, they found a scribbled note from her mother on the door. It read: Sarah, please hasten forthwith.

"Father Eaton, I must go to James and Hannah's."

Tears welled in his eyes. "Go, Sarah. They must need you. I'll see to my own dinner."

Sarah pecked his cheek and ran down the road toward her brother's home. Fear gripped at her heart.

When she arrived, the sadness was palpable. Everyone was crying. All except Hannah, who stared straight ahead while holding the still form of baby Samuel.

Grief choked Sarah. Tightness clenched around her throat and chest to the point she could not breathe. She forced herself to inhale, but when she exhaled, the sobbing was gut wrenching. The beautiful child Samuel was here no more.

Dr. Burk told James he would arrange for a small coffin to be delivered right away. As he left the premises, Sarah thought she saw tears on his cheeks.

Mary and Daniel were notified and the family gathered together to comfort one another. When the small wooden box was delivered, the baby's grandmother and a few of the village ladies helped dress the small body for burial.

First thing the next morning, Sarah and her family gathered to carry the remains of baby Samuel to the family graveyard. The littlest Thomsen would be laid to rest next to his grandfather James and his Uncle Asa.

Samuel's father, James, was inconsolable as he stared at the graves of these three family members. Sarah watched Mary cling to their brother.

How can there be comfort in such a loss?

Sarah and Daniel stood side by side at the grave when she sensed someone's presence. She turned to look up the hill and there stood Nathaniel Stearns, tears awash on his cheeks. She saw Daniel follow her gaze. When Nathaniel's eyes met hers, he quickly turned and walked away.

Sarah could not dwell on the incident as everyone walked back toward James and Hannah's home. Hannah walked alone with a blank look on her face and her arms tightly wrapped around herself. James put his arm around her, but she pulled away.

When they arrived at the cabin, Hannah sat on a chair near the fire and stared at the flames. Lydia walked over to her mother and crawled onto her lap. When the child leaned on her mother's breast, Sarah noticed Hannah wince. Mary seemed to notice as well.

"Hannah's milk pains her." Carrying Ephraim, Mary walked over to the silent woman.

"Hannah." Mary spoke in a whisper. "Ephraim is hungry. Would you like to feed him?"

Without hesitation, Hannah opened up her gown and began to nurse the infant. She winced at first, the pressure of her milk having built to the point of discomfort. But as her milk began to flow, so did her tears. Great sobs of grief poured from her mouth, the deep longing of a mother who has lost her child.

Only then did Hannah allow James to put his arms around her. And as the grieving parents cried together, Sarah watched and wept with them.

12

Forgiving

I t was late February when Daniel Lowe trod the path to the Stearns' farm.

Ever since he'd seen Nathaniel at the graveyard, he was compelled to go visit the reclusive veteran. As he remembered the abundant tears on Nathaniel's cheeks at the baby's burial, Daniel's curiosity piqued from this unexpected reaction.

More importantly, Daniel's concern for Sarah had grown with each passing week. His sister-in-law had long held a special place in his heart since he was rescued by the Thomsen's during the war. Sarah could never replace his own little sister, Polly, who died from smallpox long ago, but when he became part of the Thomsen family years later, Sarah had helped fill the void left when Polly died. And now Sarah seemed filled with a sadness foreign to her normally bright disposition. He'd never seen her in such despair and he knew the situation with Nathaniel was at the core of her grief. If there was anything he could do to help, he was willing to try.

The ground underfoot seemed less frozen than in years past. The wind still held a chill, however, and he clung to the woolen collar of his coat with chapped, bleeding hands. He knew it would not be long before it was time to plow again for the spring planting, and he was determined to visit Nathaniel before they were both busy in their fields.

Wonder if we'll have an early spring? That would be a welcome change. Perhaps the freezing rain of Candlemas Day portends it.

To take his mind off the cold, he spoke out loud the words of the Candlemas Poem for the celebration every February 2…

"If Candlemas Day be fair and bright,
Winter will have another fright;
But if it be dark with clouds and rain,
Winter is gone and will not come again."

Arriving finally at the farmhouse, he knocked on the door. Daniel waited only a moment before the appearance of Nathaniel, who was obviously surprised to see him.

"Come in, sir." Nathaniel opened the door wider.

"Thank you."

Nathaniel set another chair by the fire and pointed for Daniel to sit. "May I get you a drink?"

"Warm cider would be pleasant if you have some."

"I do." He ladled some of the rich amber liquid into a pewter tankard and handed it to Daniel. "There. That should warm your insides."

Daniel looked around and saw a few planting tools being oiled by his host. The hand hoes were strewn on the floor in a haphazard manner.

"The luxury of a single man," Daniel jested. "Cleaning field tools inside the cabin by a warm fire. Mary would throw the tools and me out the door should I attempt such a task indoors."

Nathaniel gave a self-conscious grin. "Yes, I suppose so. One of the only advantages to being single, I imagine."

Daniel thought he noticed a look of pain in his host's eyes, but Nathaniel quickly recovered with a labored smile. "So Daniel, what brings you here to my very humble abode?"

"I wanted to thank you for coming to the burial of my nephew, Samuel. It was very kind of you."

Nathaniel stared at the fire. "'Twas not kindness, sir." He paused and then looked back at Daniel. "I think 'twas guilt."

"Guilt?" He was perplexed.

"Yes." Nathaniel let out a deep breath but gave no further explanation.

It was Daniel's turn to inhale deeply. "But the other reason I have come is my concern for my sister-in-law."

Nathaniel looked up quickly with a furrowed brow. "Is she not well?"

"Her health is well enough... but her spirit suffers." Daniel was unsure how much to say but he proceeded. "She is heartsick over you, Nathaniel. And her guilt over what she said to you rules her thoughts day and night. I know that she has tried to make things right with you — she wishes to beg your forgiveness — but she has been unable to do so. You have managed to avoid her." There. The words were out.

Nathaniel's back stiffened and he sat up straight in his chair. "Yes. Well, I think that she has said enough hurtful slander about me to make me understand her heart. I'll never forget her accusations. Her words were undeserved arrows." Pain filled the young man's eyes and he set his jaw.

Compassion grew in Daniel's heart for the man.

"It is never fair to be unjustly accused. Neither is it fair to be unwilling to forgive."

Nathaniel shot an angry glance at Daniel. "Her words cut to my soul! She believed wretched lies with no thought for the truth!"

He stood up and walked across the room with his back to Daniel. When he turned around, his face was red. "I'm just supposed to drop all my pride and tell her all's well? Forgive her, just like that?"

Daniel studied him for a moment. "I know Someone who once said you must forgive a person not seven times, but seventy times seven."

Nathaniel's anger seemed to weaken. He turned his back to Daniel for several moments. When he turned again, his face twisted in pain.

"So I must forgive her. But how, on God's holy earth, can I ever trust her again?" He sat down hard on the wooden chair. "I have spent so many years guarding my affections from pain. Then, for just a brief time, I dare to open my heart once again, only to have it thrown off a cliff of lies and deception."

Daniel chose his words with care.

"I have known Sarah for most of her life. She has always been impetuous and headstrong — often blurting out words without thinking — but never with guile in her heart. Once she knows she can trust you, you will never find a young woman more faithful — or more loving. You will never find someone more willing to admit the error of her ways. And she is grievously sorrowed concerning this error she has made. I pray that you can forgive her."

Nathaniel leaned over in his chair for a long while. His hands were together and his mouth rested against them. After several moments passed, he spoke. "I, who judge so harshly the mote in Sarah's eye, do not consider the beam in my own."

Daniel was perplexed.

Nathaniel inhaled and began to speak.

"I told you, Daniel, how I went to the graveyard out of guilt." His words seemed to proceed with difficulty. "It was my guilt over not attending the burial of my own child that drew me there."

Daniel's jaw dropped open. Nathaniel continued.

"It all started the year after I went to war. I was seeing things in battle — terrible things — that I in my seventeen years had never before witnessed." He squeezed his eyes shut and rubbed them. "When I received the letter from Rebekah saying she was with child by Tim Bannister and they were getting married, I took leave of my senses. The other lads took me out and got me drunk, thinking they were helping me in my misery. They found a pretty girl in the town willing to comfort a lonely soldier. It was not long before I received word at the camp that she was with child."

Nathaniel paused for a moment, before going on.

"I hastened to marry the girl before we were sent to Yorktown, but by the time I returned to New York, they told me she had died in childbirth and the little lass she bore had died as well." Nathaniel fought back tears. "So… that is my shame. That is the beam of wood in my soul compared to the speck of dirt in Sarah's."

Both men sat in silence, then Daniel finally spoke.

"Sometimes, the most difficult person to forgive is our own self." He looked with sympathy at Nathaniel. "Have you told Sarah of this?"

"No. I was on my way to tell her the morning after the dance when she confronted me with her false accusations. After that, all the feelings we had for each other seemed lost in our hurt and misunderstanding."

"And yet, the feeling, the deep affection, still seems to be quite alive, at least with Sarah. Perhaps in your heart as well?"

Nathaniel did not answer.

"Perhaps I should leave you alone with the Healer of all hearts. I am certain He will show you what to do." Daniel stood up from his chair and extended his hand to Nathaniel.

Nathaniel gripped his offering of friendship. "Thank you. Thank you for listening."

"The older I get, the more I learn to listen much and speak less." Daniel smiled and patted him on the shoulder. "Be well, my friend."

He left Nathaniel sitting by the fire. As Daniel closed the door, he closed his eyes for a moment.

Lord, please comfort the man. Please help him — and Sarah.

13

Dyeing

*I*t was the first of March and Sarah still had not heard from Nathaniel. Their estrangement had now lasted over four months, although it seemed more like four years.

Mary invited Sarah over to help watch the children while she dyed some fabric. Sarah readily accepted the change of scenery, since she knew her mother would likely not be called away for a birthing. With no babies in Deer Run due, Sarah was not needed at home.

For the project, Daniel had set up the large washing kettle outdoors. A low fire under the kettle would help the color set in the material, while frequent stirring would even the tone.

"We're going to use saffron today, Sarah. It makes a rich yellow hue — soft as a sunrise and promising as a new day. I collected an abundance last October from my autumn crocus." Mary smiled with a cheerful expression, a stark contrast to Sarah's countenance.

"Why not just use onion skins for yellow, like Mother does?"

"Because, little sister, the yellow from the saffron will dazzle you with its hue. The onion color, well, 'tis somewhat plain."

"I suppose." Sarah absentmindedly drew a heart in the dirt with her shoe.

Mary went indoors for a moment and came out with several yards of home-woven white linen. Sarah sighed in exasperation.

"Linen? I thought we were dyeing wool. Mary, we shall be here all day. You know the color just sits on the fiber. It's as if the linen refuses to change."

Mary gave her a gentle smile. "Not unlike stubborn people, I dare say."

Sarah sat down wearily on a log and sighed. "I agree." She picked up a small stick on the ground and drew letters in the moist dirt.

"You know, Sarah, the beauty of linen is that once it accepts the new color into its fibers, it will never fade. It's as if it suddenly realizes it needed to transform to become more beautiful — more complete. But sometimes it takes patience on the part of the person stirring the pot of dye."

Sarah looked at her sister moving the stick through the thick solution of saffron and linen. A feeling of hopelessness overwhelmed Sarah. "If only Nathaniel were so easy to stir."

"A gentle stirring can soften even the strongest will — especially if the defenses of one's heart long to surrender."

Sarah shook her head. "Perhaps." *I am not so convinced.*

Polly came out of the house carrying a fussy Ephraim.

"Mother, the baby wants milk. I have tried everything else but he wants you."

"Let me stir the linen, Mary." Sarah rose abruptly from the log. She had come to help her sister and so far she had done nothing but feel despondent and lethargic. "I have sat long enough."

She took over managing the stick while Mary wiped her hands on her apron and took the baby from Polly. While Mary went inside to feed Ephraim, Sarah concentrated on the task.

It was difficult to stir the many pieces of linen in the kettle. It required persistence and strength, but she would not give up.

Lord, give me the strength that I need to persevere in dyeing this cloth, as well as in dying to my own selfish interests. I pray, dear Lord, that You would forgive me of the gossip that so easily took hold in my heart. The tongue truly is a "fire, a world of iniquity." How quickly it can start such a blaze of hurt when it is not tamed. Forgive me, God. And... I pray Nathaniel can find it in his heart to forgive me, as well.

She continued to stir the saffron-laced water. Soon enough, the color had soaked through the fibrous linen, transforming the fabric into a brilliant yellow.

Mary came out of the cabin and shut the door behind her. "Ephraim is asleep." Walking over to the kettle, she noticed the change in the linen. "I think 'tis complete. I'll get another stick and we can carry the pieces together over to the rope line."

The two women balanced one piece of linen at a time on the sticks and carried them over to the line strung between two trees. Laying the pieces across the rope, the large sections of linen dripped profusely on the ground but soon began to dry with the sunny, breezy weather. After carrying six pieces of linen to the line, the task was complete.

Mary stood back with her hands on her waist and a self-satisfied look on her face. "Now there is a lovely shade of yellow."

"'Tis beautiful, Mary. Much lovelier than from onion skins."

Just then, Daniel and the twins walked toward the cabin from the field. They were covered with dirt from plowing.

"Stay away from the linen with those hands," Mary called out.

Daniel gave her a mischievous grin, his teeth standing out against the dirt smeared on his face. He walked over to Mary and grabbed her waist and kissed her on the lips.

"Daniel!" Mary squirmed away from him, but she was laughing. "Go wash!" He continued to grin at her while going toward the basin.

Six-year-old Sally and three-year-old Alice were playing in the yard and they giggled when Daniel kissed their mother.

"He does that every day." Sally whispered her secret to Aunt Sarah.

"He does?" Sarah whispered back in pretended shock.

"Yes! And sometimes at night they kiss a very long time and then go to their room."

Sarah made every attempt to keep from laughing.

Mary had a frown on her face. "You are supposed to be sleeping at such times, Miss Sally."

Speaking in a louder tone, Sally gave a deep sigh. "Do you suppose someday someone will kiss me like that?"

Daniel overheard the six-year-old and narrowed his eyes while drying his face with a towel. "Well, Sally, if someone tries to kiss you, I daresay that he will have to get past three muskets to do so — mine and your brothers."

Sally started to cry. "Mother, Papa is going to shoot him!"

Mary narrowed her eyes at her husband. "Daniel, please!"

"All right then. I shall only beat him about the ears a bit."

Mary rolled her eyes and smiled. "I pity the poor suitor who woos one of your daughters, Daniel." She glanced at Sarah. "Come, let's go in for victuals."

The children hurried indoors and Sarah joined the hungry family for some gruel, salt pork, and cooked turnips. The supply of vegetables in the root cellar was becoming sparse. It would soon be time to plant the garden to replenish the stockpile.

"I'm going to have to plant more potatoes, carrots, and cabbage this year." Mary grinned at the growing twins who were almost twelve. "You boys are eating more and more each day."

"A man's appetite for working men, right, boys?" Daniel pointed his fork at the two, who seemed to inhale the food from their plates.

"It's a good thing Ephraim has a ways to go before he has a man's appetite." Mary shook her head in amazement. The twins' plates were almost empty already.

"Well, lads, time to return to the plow before Grandsire's oxen decide to take a long nap." Daniel made a pointed glance at Sally. "And I shall need to hurry back to do more kissing with your mother."

Danny and James groaned with embarrassment, but Sally grinned with enjoyment. After the three returned to the field, Sarah smiled at Mary and helped her remove the plates.

"You are blessed with an abundance of love."

Mary paused in clearing off the table. She reached out toward Sarah's hand and squeezed it. "You shall be as well."

Sarah did not answer but gave an appreciative look to her sister.

When the table was clear, they went outdoors to check on the linen. The air being so arid, the material was already dry.

Three-year-old Alice ran over to the hanging pieces draped across the clothesline. She made a game of hiding behind two sections, then pushing the two pieces open and sticking her small face out. "Look out window!" The child squealed with delight.

As Sarah watched her repeatedly play the window game, inspiration birthed an idea.

"Mary, would you mind if I took one of the pieces for my sewing? I would gladly exchange another piece of linen for it."

"Of course, you may have one. I was going to give you some linen anyway and you do not need to give me one in return." Mary gave her a quizzical look. "Any particular sewing project in mind?"

Sarah's hopes danced. "Perhaps."

Mary walked over to the clothesline and removed the largest piece. She folded the yardage and handed it to her.

"May this material be a blessing for you, dear sister." She hugged Sarah warmly.

"I'm certain it will be." Sarah waved good-bye and hurried off for home. She was anxious to see if Mary was right about the saffron bringing the promise of a new day.

14

Reconciling

athaniel could not forget Daniel Lowe's visit of a month ago. His words encouraging Nathaniel to forgive Sarah grated on his thoughts like unwashed wool on bare skin — uncomfortable yet welcome in their warmth.

The truth was Nathaniel longed to reconcile with Sarah. Pride was his enemy — holding onto the hurt as though it were some faithful companion. But he knew lack of forgiveness was a cold and lonely partner to cling to. And worse, he had no cause to judge Sarah. His own behavior in the past had forfeited his right to believe himself free of indiscretion.

"For all have sinned, and come short of the glory of God." *How could I have forgotten those words?*

What he had not forgotten was the warmth of Sarah's embrace and the softness of her kiss. The memories continued to invade his determination to forget her, but it had become a losing battle.

His thoughts filled with these musings on this early March morning. He finished the last gulps of warm cider in his tankard. He was not hungry for food yet but would eat later after preparing the field for planting corn. Standing by the hearth, he thought he heard a knock on the door.

Walking over to the door, he opened it slightly and then all the way.

"Sarah!" Surprise infused his voice and excitement saturated his being. Attempting to calm himself, he struggled to slow down his breathing. But nothing would slow down his pounding heart.

She looked embarrassed as she shyly met his eye.

"Good day, Nathaniel." Her words were barely above a whisper. "I've brought you something." The wind increased in intensity, causing the skirt of her gown to lurch to one side. She grabbed hold of her linen cap to keep it in place.

"Come inside, Sarah. The wind is strong this morning." She stepped indoors with some hesitation and stood there. Her feet shifted their position.

"I hope I'm not intruding." Her eyes glanced downward.

"No, of course not. Please, come sit." He pointed toward the hearth and she walked over to it. He noticed she was carrying something yellow in her hands, but he was not sure what it was. Of one thing he was certain — her presence chiseled away at his defenses. She wore his favorite walnut-dyed gown that draped so smoothly over her form. The scent of flowers that wafted as she walked by made him heady with desire.

He meandered with unsteady feet toward the hearth.

"May I get you something to drink?" His voice quivered.

She met his eyes. "No, but thank you kindly." Her rich brown eyes met his, once again arresting him with their beauty. Before he could get any words out, she spoke again. "The reason I have come is to bring you this." She unfolded the yellow piece of material. "I remember you said your mother took the curtain with her to Boston. It seemed as though — and perhaps I misread you — the yellow curtain she took had been a comfort to you. I thought perhaps this one might make you feel more at home, besides guarding your eyes from the bright sun." She looked out the window at the increasing clouds and gave a self-conscious laugh. "When there is a bright sun, that is."

"'Tis beautiful, Sarah." Much like its seamstress, he thought, but held his tongue. "I hope it was not too much trouble for you. I know how busy you are." He swallowed with difficulty.

"Oh no. Mary and I dyed the linen yesterday. It dried so fast, I was able to sew it together evening last."

"You sewed this last night?" He noticed the dark circles under her eyes. "I hope you were able to sleep well."

She turned away from his intense gaze. "Well enough." She stood up. "Let us see if this fits."

Nathaniel rose from his chair in an awkward manner and watched her go to the window. Thunder rumbled overhead causing them both to startle.

"No, there will certainly be no sunshine this morning." Sarah reached up to remove the curtain rod.

He watched her slender arms remove the wooden dowel from its pegs. Sliding her curtain over the rod, her long fingers manipulated the linen across the bar until the wood was sticking out on each side.

"Here, Sarah, let me help you hang that." He took the dowel from her hands as she reached upward to replace it on the pegs. In doing so, his fingers slid across her arms for a moment and he noticed her face turn red. Once again he felt his heart beat faster and his own cheeks grow warm.

Standing back from the window, he admired the linen curtains as well as the woman who had created them. A few strands of Sarah's blonde hair had come undone during the windy walk to his home, falling across her shoulders and back. He had to fight the desire to stroke them with his eager hands.

After a moment of silence, Sarah's mouth quivered. Nathaniel thought he saw tears brimming on her eyelids.

"Well then, I must sally home before the storm." She hurried to the door and stepped outside. The wind increased in intensity and Nathaniel hastened to follow. "Sarah!" he cried, but his voice was swallowed up by the haunting howl of the storm.

When Nathaniel looked southward at the trees in the distance, his breath caught in his throat. A powerful flow of wind was bending huge trees downward, almost to the ground.

"Sarah, wait!" She had already walked several yards and he ran after her. She stopped and screamed when a gust tore the cap from her head.

Running to her, he grabbed both of her arms. "Come inside, quickly." He half-carried her back to his cabin, fighting the powerful wind that tried to knock them both over. The rain pelted them before they reached the door.

The sound outdoors was frightening and terrible, the wind groaning in a sickening manner. Sarah stared at Nathaniel, her eyes wide with terror.

He searched for something to shield them and ran to the straw mattress on his bed and dragged it off the frame. "Sarah, hasten beneath this." She followed his directions. Once she was safely under the cushion, he crawled beneath the mattress next to her and held onto it tightly.

Nathaniel could feel her shivering with fright next to him as the storm raged. It was as if all nature battled on his doorstep to keep the change of seasons from occurring. He heard Sarah crying next to him. He wanted to hold her and comfort her, but he was concerned that the mattress might be torn away by the powerful winds if the roof did not hold.

When it seemed the storm would last forever, it finally relented. Everything was quiet except for Sarah whimpering next to him. Nathaniel threw off the mattress and smoothed down her disheveled hair.

"Are you safe?" Both his voice and hands trembled.

"Yes." Her voice was pinched and shaking. He drew the shivering woman into his arms and kissed the damp hair on her head. His hands quivered as his lips descended from her hair, down her cheek and then found their home on her lips. He could not get enough of her warm mouth that seemed to be just as eager to unite with his. His body longed to continue this embrace, but he forced himself to pull away from her intoxicating lips. He held her close to his chest.

"Nathaniel, I am so sorry." Sarah's face was half buried in his shirt.

He gently drew her away so he could face her and then touched her lips. "'Tis I who needs to make apology for my behavior and my stubborn heart." He paused. "And there is something that I must tell you before I lose myself again in your embrace."

He put his arms around her and held her next to him. And he told her the story he had shared with Daniel. About Rebekah, her betrayal, his drunken behavior, and subsequent indiscretion. And then he told her about his infant daughter — a baby he had never seen or held before she died.

"My daughter was buried without her father being there to mourn her short life."

Sarah pulled away from his arms, and he feared she would not forgive him. But he was wrong. Sarah's face was filled with compassion.

"My heart aches for you, Nathaniel. For all you have been through."

Her eyes searched his and she picked up his hand and kissed his fingers.

"I do not want your pity, Sarah." He pulled his hand away. Sarah touched his cheeks with moist hands.

"'Tis not my pity that you have Nathaniel." Tears welled in her eyes. "'Tis my heart you own. It is all yours."

Nathaniel relaxed and drew her close, all his defenses crumbling.

"I love you, Sarah. So completely. More than any other, you have taken my heart and woven it with yours. I feel incomplete without you."

"I love you, Nathaniel."

His warm lips met hers. As their kiss lingered, all the hurt and misunderstandings of the last months were replaced by the joy of a new-found love based on trust and faith.

It was the love Nathaniel had long desired.

Wedding

athaniel wasted no time in asking Sarah to be his wife and she accepted without hesitation. The only thing left to do was ask Myles Eaton for permission.

Although the village of Deer Run had much clean up to do from the devastating storm, Myles assured Nathaniel everyone would be willing to make time for a wedding. His future father-in-law seemed delighted with the news.

"'Tis marriage season, after all," he said to Nathaniel when he came to ask for Sarah's hand. "Nothing like a celebration to take our mind from the work. Besides, lad, I'm sure you're wantin' to get to the weddin' night soon enough." He winked at the future groom, who looked at the floor with a sheepish grin.

Myles' expression grew serious. "Now I'll be expecting you to take proper care of my dear Sarah, lad. She may not have been mine from birth, but she has been in my heart these many years, as much as one of my own daughters."

Nathaniel looked at Myles with gratitude. "I shall treat her as the treasure she is to me. Thank you for giving us your blessing."

"You're a fine and responsible lad, Nathaniel. You have an adventurous life ahead with your spirited new bride. And one filled with passion and love — as well as great faithfulness."

"Yes, sir. I thank you, sir."

"One more thing, Nathaniel — this has been on my heart of late —

should anything happen to me, please see to the well-being of Missus Eaton. I do not wish her to want for anything."

Myles was clearly serious, more sober than Nathaniel had ever seen him.

"I shall honor your request, sir. Your wife shall want for naught. Yet I pray that this promise need not be fulfilled for quite some time."

"Thank you, lad. I know that I can count on all of my sons."

Nathaniel gave a slight bow to his future father-in-law and hurried out the door, anxious to find Sarah. She was in the barn collecting eggs, and she almost dropped them when he came up behind her to lift her in the air.

She laughed. "Put me down." When he did so, he turned her toward himself and held her close.

"So, how would you like to become my wife in three weeks?" He grinned from ear to ear.

Sarah gave a humorous frown. "Why so long?" Bursting into a huge grin, she threw her arms around his neck. "Yes! I only wish it were three hours." His lips caressed hers in a slow and passionate yearning. His hands worked their way behind her back and he drew her close. "Or three minutes." Her voice was breathless. He kissed her again, consumed in the embrace. His breathing could not keep up with the pounding in his heart.

His whole body ached for her to stay, but Sarah pushed away from him, gripping his warm hands.

"Three weeks. I hope I can bear the wait." She kissed his trembling hands.

"I can bear it — so long as you are the treasure that I win at the end." He was still out of breath.

"You have already won my heart — soon I will be all yours."

He pulled her close and held her tight, rubbing the back of her head with a gentle rhythmic motion. He kissed the top of her forehead and stepped away.

"I'd best return home — before I forget we are not yet husband and wife."

Sarah looked at the straw on the barn floor and blushed. She met his gaze. "I look forward to being your wife, Nathaniel. I long for our wedding as well."

Nathaniel drew her close for one more kiss and then started toward home. He glanced back for one last look at his future wife.

"Three weeks." He grinned and hurried home.

Sarah was so busy the next few weeks she had little time to think about missing Nathaniel's embrace. But after blowing out the candle at night and gazing out of her bedroom window, she could think of little else. At length she would fall asleep, hugging her pillow, anxious for the time when her future husband would be the one in her arms every night.

The only shadow of concern that blighted her joy was a conversation she overheard at Sabbath service just before the wedding day. She was certain she heard one of Richard Beal's friends discuss a shivaree. As anxious as she was for her wedding night, the prospect of singing revelers outside her window interrupting their first night together filled her with embarrassment.

"Mary, what shall I do?" She confided her fears to her sister at Sabbath lunch. "I am mortified that Richard and his comrades might bother us."

Mary drew Daniel into the conversation and he looked at the ground for several moments before breaking out into a grin. "Do not fear, Sarah. We have a plan."

The wedding day arrived and the whole town gathered in the Eaton home for the ceremony. Although the main room was large, it would not fit the nearly two hundred guests, including all the children and teenagers. Adults crammed together as best they could while some stood on chairs in order to observe the nuptials.

Sarah wore the indigo blue dress she had sewn for the harvest dance. Nathaniel looked handsome to Sarah in his woolen waistcoat and breeches, which his mother had made for him a few months past. Although she could not be in Deer Run for the ceremony, his mother had sent a warm letter to Sarah, welcoming her into their family.

The ceremony was brief as they pledged to honor one another as man and wife. Nathaniel gripped Sarah's hands. She grinned so much her cheeks began to ache. As far as she was concerned, they were the only ones in the room, and when they kissed upon pronouncement of being made husband and wife, they had to be interrupted by the justice of the peace who declared that Nathaniel could now stop kissing his wife. Sarah's cheeks warmed with embarrassment. Glancing at her mother, Sarah noticed Missus Eaton was bright red after the extended kiss.

The celebrating began with the guests moving out to the barn for fiddling and dancing. Sarah's mother was overruled on the dancing by Myles, but she protested the frolicking by remaining in the house with several of the guests. Nathaniel and Sarah greeted their guests, thanking each for coming. Richard was not in the line of well-wishers, much to Sarah's relief.

When the fiddlers were warmed up and ready to strike the first notes of the opening song, Sarah was transported back to their first dance during the harvest. This time, Sarah allowed her thoughts to be consumed with this man who was now her husband. As they moved to the alluring melodies, the touch of his fingers on hers intoxicated her.

After several songs were played and the guests were caught up in the festive spirit, Nathaniel drew Sarah aside and whispered in her ear, "Are you ready to leave, Missus Stearns?" His breath in her ear sent shivers of pleasure through her.

"Yes. Quite ready, Mr. Stearns." His gaze held hers as they quietly left the barn.

"Wait here one moment, Sarah."

She saw her husband walk over to Daniel and speak to him. Daniel in turn walked inside the house where Mary had been feeding Ephraim. When Mary walked out of the house, her arms were empty and she and Daniel walked into the woods.

Nathaniel held Sarah's arm for a moment and looked after the couple disappearing into the darkening woods.

"What are we waiting for, Nathaniel?" Sarah whispered.

Her husband smiled at her. "You'll see." He kissed her then said, "All right. Now."

He led her toward the woods, making sure that some of the party-goers noticed them leaving.

They walked dozens of rods toward their home before Sarah felt Nathaniel pulling her aside into a thick grove of bushes. "Crouch down," he whispered. To Sarah's surprise, Mary and Daniel popped up from the grove and proceeded on the path toward the Stearns' home. Nathaniel looked at Sarah and held his finger against his lips.

They waited for several moments while some drunken revelers, led by Richard Beal, followed Daniel and Mary down the path.

Sarah's eyes grew wide. Nathaniel smothered his laughter. They waited until the revelers were out of sight before Nathaniel pulled on Sarah's arm. "Come now. 'Tis safe."

"Where are we going?" Confused, Sarah nonetheless followed her new husband.

Nathaniel winked at his new bride. "You'll see."

It appeared to Sarah they would be traveling a good distance to their destination, since he carried his musket.

"Not taking any chances of running into bear or wolves." He held onto Sarah's hand and waited for her to make her way through the underbrush. After what seemed to Sarah like an hour of hiking, they arrived. In the moonlight, the outline of an old structure revealed itself.

"I remember this place." She stared at the rough hideout made of bark and bent branches. "Mary hid Daniel here when he was wounded." The still-standing English wigwam fascinated Sarah.

Nathaniel drew her close to himself and kissed her. "This is also where they hid after their wedding."

Sarah covered her mouth in surprise and laughed. "My sister." She shook her head, barely containing her amusement. "And I always thought her to be so proper."

"Well, they were married, after all."

Sarah grinned. "I know. It just surprises me."

Nathaniel took her by the hand. "Come inside."

She followed him through the door and the aroma of lavender flooded her senses. Her eyes adjusted to the dim light. Sarah was grateful for the full moon that allowed several streams of soft white light to come through the holes in the walls.

"I know 'tis difficult to see, but Mary brought some quilts for us here." Nathaniel cleared his throat. He closed the door of the wigwam, removed his hat, and set his musket on the ground.

"She thinks of everything. How long have all of you been planning this?" Sarah wrapped her arms around herself, suddenly feeling awkward.

"After you spoke with Mary about the shivaree, Daniel came up with the idea. I thought it very clever." He approached her, his gaze wandering over her form. Gently pulling her arms downward, he removed the lace kerchief she had tucked into her bodice for modesty. His fingers stroked her neck and he swallowed with effort. His voice was husky. "I know that I do not want to be interrupted."

"Nor do I." Her voice whispered. Sarah stared with desire at her handsome husband. She watched him remove his waistcoat as the moonlight accented his high cheekbones. She stared with admiration at his chest that was visible through his shirt.

Her breathing quickened as his hands reached around her waist. She could feel the intensity in his fingers as they caressed her. He removed each pin from her hair one at a time and wove his fingers through her long locks as they came undone. Her waist-length tresses cascaded over her shoulders and back. His kisses were warm, moist, and persistent.

"Sarah, I am so in love with you. My wife…" He began to kiss her with a passion she had only dreamed of before now. He carefully placed her on one of the quilts and enfolded her with his love for the first time.

***

Daniel and Mary arrived at the Stearns cabin and stoked the fire in the hearth. Once it cast a brilliant glow around the room, Daniel looked at his wife. "Let us give our revelers a night to remember."

"Daniel, you are full of mischief."

He took her hand and stood with her in front of the curtained window. He knew their shadows would appear with the glow from the fireplace behind them, but their features would be obscure. Daniel drew Mary close, grinning from ear to ear.

"I suppose you will have to kiss me with passion, Missus Lowe."

"If I must, Mr. Lowe. 'Tis all for a good cause." She giggled as he began to caress and kiss her in front of the veiled window.

Soon he heard what he had been expecting — loud revelers singing with more than a hint of inebriation in their voices. As Daniel continued to kiss his wife, Mary jerked away.

"Mattie Groves! Daniel, that is an appalling song. I am embarrassed by these adulterous words."

Daniel reluctantly stopped kissing her and cleared his throat. He stomped with deliberate steps toward the door and opened it with force. The drunken singers had just begun to taunt the couple when they all stopped, their mouths dropping open.

"Mr. Lowe!" Richard swayed backward a step.

"Yes, Mr. Beal. And why, pray, are you disrupting my lovemaking with my wife?"

"I… I did not realize it was you, sir." He looked around for his friends, but they had run off into the woods.

Daniel closed the door behind himself and walked toward Richard, who was taking a few steps backward.

"And who exactly did you think you might be interrupting, Mr. Beal?" Daniel continued his slow walk toward the drunken man.

"Why, Sarah of course…"

"And you thought that song would be a proper serenade for my sister-in-law?"

Richard stood speechless. Daniel pulled back one arm and thrust a powerful fist into Richard's face. The younger man grabbed his nose in pain and looked horror-stricken to see blood on his hands. He ran off into the woods.

Daniel shook out his fist and strode back to the cabin.

Upon entering, he approached his wife. She looked at him with a curious expression. "What did you say, Daniel?"

"I merely encouraged the man to leave."

Mary looked doubtful and tilted her head. "You encouraged him?"

Daniel smiled and placed his arms snugly around his wife's waist.

"Now, where were we?"

He drew her toward the bed and Mary gasped. "This is not our bed, Daniel."

"It is right now." He grinned and laid her on the straw mattress. They embraced again, caught up in a love only made more passionate by the years.

16

Promises

Two days after Sarah and Nathaniel wed, Myles Eaton's health declined.

Everyone was called to gather at his bedside and, one by one, they came to say good-bye. Daniel's final visit with his father-in-law was more painful than he could have imagined. Except for the Thomsen family, Myles was Daniel's first friend in America. And looking at the previously strong, healthy man now shriveled and gasping for breath, Daniel's heart was grief stricken.

"Father Eaton." Daniel approached the dying man's bedside. "Perhaps we need to send for another doctor." He struggled to maintain his composure.

Myles gave a weak smile. "No, lad." His voice was little more than a whisper. "This body has seen its last good days." He continued to labor for each breath. "But you ... you must stay strong for this family."

Daniel rubbed his hand across his mouth, barely containing his trembling lips. He wanted to be strong, but his heart ached at the prospect of losing his friend.

"Father Eaton, you have been a faithful friend to me from the start. You trusted me when I did not deserve your trust. But even more than a friend, you were truly a father to me. How can I ever thank you?" Tears rolled down his cheeks.

Myles reached up and patted Daniel's cheeks. "You're a good lad, Daniel. And you have been as loved by me as any son by blood would have been. And you've been a good husband to Mary. I couldna' ask for anything more… I'm tired now, my friend." He closed his eyes.

Daniel's mouth contorted in its effort to remain composed. "Farewell, my friend." He squeezed Myles' hand and left the room, allowing Ruth Eaton and Mary to come in.

Mary reached out to touch Daniel's face. They squeezed each other's hand for a moment before she went inside the room to sit by her mother at the bedside. Daniel joined the others waiting in the main room.

After a few more minutes, Daniel heard the loud sobs of Mother Eaton, and knew their beloved parent was gone to be with his heavenly Father. Daniel, James, Dr. Burk, and a few of Myles' sons-in-law went into the room.

James put his arms around his mother. "You can wait outside. The men and I will lay him out."

Ruth Eaton stood up, determination on her tear-stained face.

"No, James. I shall stay and help." The men did not argue with her. Mary handed the linen shroud that was kept in the chest of drawers to Daniel. He took it without speaking and she left the room.

Each of the men took on their task of removing Myles' clothing. Dr. Burk and James began to clean the body with bayberry soap and water. Fighting back tears, Daniel picked up the razor and shaved the still, graying face. Ruth Eaton trimmed her husband's hair and smoothed it back with her fingers.

When the body was prepared, they lifted it into the shroud, inserting the arms into the sleeves. Then all the men except Daniel left the room. Mary and two of Myles' daughters came in and sewed the open areas of the shroud closed. When they arrived at the head, Ruth looked at the others. "I should like to say my final good-byes now."

Daniel and the women left the room to allow Ruth her privacy, knowing that once she said her good-bye, she would sew shut the last opening in the shroud.

The burial took place the next morning and Myles was laid to rest next to his first wife and one of their daughters, who had died in childbirth.

His other six daughters, their spouses, all the Thomsen children, and the myriad grandchildren from both families gathered to remember the man. As Daniel looked around at all the saddened faces, it struck him how the life of one simple farmer had affected the lives of so many here, as well as the villagers in Deer Run, who had benefited from his kind acts of generosity. Myles Eaton would be deeply missed and never forgotten.

Daniel and all the sons did not forget their promise to Myles to take care of Ruth Eaton. It was decided that James Lowe, one of Daniel and Mary's twins, would move in with his grandmother until Nathaniel could finish with the spring planting in his field. When the crops were in the ground, Sarah and Nathaniel would then move into the larger Eaton home from their one-room cabin. James could then move back home with his parents and Ruth Eaton would live with Sarah and Nathaniel.

Nathaniel would be the new caretaker for the Eaton livestock, and all the family would help Nathaniel harvest his crop in the fall. They were a family and they would be there for each other.

It was what Myles would have wanted. They would all honor his memory as well as honor their God.

Sarah lay awake in bed, unable to sleep. She glanced over at her still-sleeping husband lying next to her and smiled despite her tears of grief over the loss of her stepfather.

She carefully removed the quilt covering them both and pulled her linen night shift on over her head. Studying Nathaniel's face to be sure she had not awakened him, she threw her shawl over her shoulders and slipped outside.

Wiping the tears from her cheeks, she took in a deep breath of the cool April air. *Our last day in our first home.*

The thought made her sad as she realized they would no longer have the solitude of this one-room cabin — this small refuge from the world around them. But with the planting completed, it was time to gather their belongings and move in with her widowed mother. She did not begrudge the situation, merely lamented this loss of privacy.

Now I know why Mary and Daniel sought the quiet of the wigwam.

Staring out at the budding trees, she was swept up in the soft shades of pinks and oranges of the sunrise that signaled the start of a new day. The empty tips of the branches against the sky looked like thin fingers reaching out toward heaven, craving the touch of their Creator.

The heavens declare the glory of God; and the firmament sheweth his handywork. She hugged her shawl around herself, comforted by the words of David's psalm.

Staring out at the beauty of God's creation, she heard her husband open the door and walk toward her. She felt his strong arms wrap around her from behind as he hugged her close and kissed her cheek. "I thought you'd left me, Missus Stearns."

"And why would I do that, Mr. Stearns, when I am so much in love with my husband?" She clasped his arms closer around her.

"You've been crying." He kissed her wet cheek again.

As hard as she tried to control them, fresh tears flowed down her face. "I miss him so, Nathaniel."

"I know." He held her without speaking. Sarah broke the silence.

"As long as I can remember, I've been left behind. First my brothers Asa and James — and Asa never came back. Then Mary and Daniel moved to their cabin with the babies. Then my mother when she'd go to birthings. I have been so alone." Her lips trembled again. "And now, Father Eaton."

"You're not alone, Sarah. I am here."

She squeezed his arms. "You must promise me, Nathaniel, that you will never leave me. If 'tis in your power to keep me with you, I beg you to promise me you'll never leave."

She turned around in his arms to face him. Reaching up, she ran her fingers through his shoulder-length hair, pushing it back from his face and behind one ear. Her eyes sought his for the reassurance she craved.

He stroked her long blonde hair down the length of her back. His eyes were filled with love as they locked upon hers. "I promise you, Sarah. If 'tis in my power, I shall never leave you."

She reached up and kissed his cheeks.

"Today is our last day here, you know."

"Yes. But it does not mean we can never return to the cabin."

She looked up at him. "You mean, just the two of us?"

He caressed her back with gentle strokes that sent shivers of delight through her. "Most assuredly," he whispered as he kissed her with hungry lips that melted her sadness. As his warm embrace continued, her desire for her husband consumed her. She was swept away with his love.

When he was able to pause, he whispered next to her ear, "Let us go inside." He lifted her up in his muscular arms and carried her into the cabin, shutting the door firmly with one leg.

17

Affliction

aniel! Please hurry!" He saw Mary running toward him in the field.

Daniel sighed. His frame of mind was more dismal than it had been for years. He handed the reins of the oxen to Danny.

"Take these, son." Weariness and discouragement threatened to overwhelm his sense of well being. Ever since the terrible storm hit Deer Run two months ago, it was one thing after another. That storm had decimated both the newly plowed flax field as well as Mary's vegetable garden with fallen trees. Their food supply was already sparse. Now there would be a prolonged shortage.

Then influenza had struck first one, then all of their children. They were only now beginning to recover.

What could be wrong now?

He limped over toward his distraught wife. His war wound had long since healed, but it still caused him great discomfort. Enemy musket fire had shredded his leg muscle during that battle near Saratoga. Then infection set in, eating away much healthy tissue and leaving a deep scar along with a pronounced limp. Today, it hurt more than usual.

"What is it Mary?" He wiped the sweat off his brow with dirt-covered sleeves.

"I found something wretched in the chamber pot." Her lips trembled. "The children... the children have worms!"

Daniel's shoulders slumped in defeat. Placing his hands on his hips, he gazed for a few moments at the ground. Looking up, he made a pronouncement.

"Send James for Dr. Burk."

Mary's eyes widened. "Daniel, that will cost more than we have."

Daniel did not give in. "We will find a way. You know that he has the best medicinal for this." Without another word, he walked back over to the oxen, which were hooked to one more fallen log ready for hauling. He took the reins from Danny and resumed his work. Danny, meanwhile, returned to chopping the fallen trees into firewood.

Mary turned back toward their cabin.

Daniel's mind was now distracted from his task. Ever since he had decided to stay behind in America, his biggest fear was that he would not be able to provide for his family. In England, he had a sure future with a comfortable inheritance, enough money to support any number of children that he and his wife might have. When he became an American, all that financial security was lost. His father had been quick to point that out when he visited Daniel's family seven years prior.

Daniel had been so excited when he heard his father was coming to America. Angry tears stung his eyes as he recalled conversations with his only living parent.

"Come home, Daniel," his father pleaded. "We will make up an acceptable excuse for you with the King's army. You will be recommissioned as an officer after we tell them you were wounded and unable to return from the wilderness in America. Rejoin with them and they will assign you an easy post in England. You can raise the boys there. They can go to the finest schools."

His father's plans did not include bringing Mary or the girls, however. They would stay behind in America, supported by Daniel's father, who would send an allowance to them.

"Mary is lovely enough, but you know she is not gentry. She would not fit in with our family."

Daniel found his father's words demeaning. He bristled at the memory, then hurried the oxen along at a faster pace.

How many more days to clear this field? Exhaustion overwhelmed him.

It was time to break for the noon meal. Although it was only May, the sun beat down as though it were mid summer. He squinted as he put the oxen in the shade and gave them each a bucket of water.

"Let's sally home," he yelled over to Danny.

When the two arrived back at the cabin, Dr. Burk was peering into three-year-old Alice's mouth. Mary held Ephraim in her arms, bouncing him to keep him content.

"Good day, Daniel." Robert Burk nodded at him.

"Good day, Robert." Embarrassment burned Daniel's cheeks with heat at the thought of calling the doctor for such an ailment. Worms could mean only one thing to Daniel — bad and inadequate food.

Dr. Burk finished examining Alice. "It looks like most of the children are suffering from vermiforms, Daniel."

Fancy name for worms. A wave of disgust flooded Daniel's thoughts. Dr. Burk continued speaking. Since Daniel was head of the household, the doctor directed the instructions to him.

"I'll leave you a sufficient supply of Carolina Pink to make some tea. But first give them calomel to evacuate their bowels. That will make the tea more effective. Give a cupful in the morning and at night. You may add milk and sugar so they will ingest it more readily."

Daniel took the vial of powdered root from the doctor.

"Thank you." He stood there and rubbed the back of his neck in an awkward manner.

"I will put this on your account, Daniel. Perhaps — if you are soon done with removing your trees — you can take a turn chopping firewood for me."

Relief infused Daniel.

"Yes, I should be done with my field in a fortnight. Thank you." He shook hands with the doctor.

"Good day, Daniel. Mary." He bowed and left.

Daniel stared for a moment at the man who had affection for his wife years ago when they were young.

Mary must be wishing she had waited for Robert after the war and married him.

"I'm hungry, Mother." Tears rolled down Alice's thin cheeks.

Mary set the bowls on the table and served up a thin soup. She had made fresh bread that morning, which would make it seem like stomachs were full.

At least the corn crop was bountiful last year.

Daniel was quiet throughout the meal, watching each of his children devour every bite. He noticed the lack of new vegetables in the stew.

Blasted storm.

He was still hungry when the meal was complete, but he pushed away from the tableboard.

"Another fine meal, Missus Lowe." He forced a smile.

"Thank you, Daniel." Her voice was quiet. Then her eyes brightened. "Perhaps the boys can go rabbit hunting tonight."

Daniel leaned over and kissed her on the cheek.

"That is an excellent idea, Missus Lowe." His mouth attempted to smile, but his heart was vacant of joy. "Come, lads, let's return to the field. It should go faster with the three of us."

$$\backsim$$

The next day, purging the children's intestines with the calomel consumed every moment. By nightfall, Daniel saw Mary finally sit down, a nauseated look on her face.

"I do not think I can clean out the chamber pot one more time. I feel ill."

Daniel looked at his wife with pity. He had been in the field all day but knew his wife was exhausted.

"Rest, Mary. I will make the root tea for the children." He looked at the twelve-year-old twins. "Perhaps you'd best drink some yourselves." The boys scrunched up their noses but did not object.

Pouring the steaming concoction into the cups, he added a spoon of sugar to each and a generous serving of milk.

"There, Miss Alice. I will serve you your tea."

After taking a sip, she made a face. "It tastes funny, Papa."

Polly stepped in to help. "Oh, it looks fine and sweet, Alice. Watch how I drink mine."

It was obviously bitter tasting to her, but she drank every drop and said, "Sweet and delicious!"

Daniel looked at his oldest daughter with gratitude. The ten-year-old encouraged the others to "drink it quickly — the faster you swallow, the sweeter the flavor," making a game out of the treatment.

All the children appeared exhausted from the long day. Alice began to yawn.

"To bed." He hurried them all under their quilts. All four girls shared a large bed. Since it was getting warmer, the twins went to the barn and slept on the hay.

Daniel checked on Mary and found her nursing Ephraim in bed. He stared at the beauty of his wife feeding their son.

The child soon fell asleep.

"Can you set Ephraim in his cradle, Daniel?" Mary yawned.

He picked up the drowsy eight-month-old and laid him carefully in his wooden bed. Daniel rocked the cradle for a moment to ensure the child would stay asleep.

Creeping back toward their bed, Daniel removed his shirt and crawled in beside his wife. He drew next to her and kissed her shoulder.

"I am so tired, Daniel."

Disappointment flooded him, but he smothered his desires.

"All right then. Perhaps tomorrow." Before he finished the sentence, Mary was in a sound sleep.

In the morning, Mary awoke with a fever. It might have seemed like nothing serious but she cried in pain when she turned onto her breast. Looking down, Daniel saw a large red area.

"Daniel." Her voice shook. "This is so painful. Please send someone for my mother."

After sending Danny on the errand, he brought her some water. She gulped it down and then pulled the quilt over herself. Her skin flushed from illness and she moaned in discomfort.

"Please fix the tea for the children." Her teeth chattered.

"I shall. Then Polly will give it to everyone while I stay with you."

He looked out their window. "What is taking Danny so long?" he said under his breath.

After what seemed an interminable amount of time, Danny returned, but the news was not good.

"Grandmother is attending a birth in Williamston. Aunt Sarah says we must send for the doctor."

Daniel did not hesitate. "Yes, hasten to get him, Danny."

Mary's reddened eyes widened.

"Daniel…" He covered her lips with two fingers.

"This is not the time to object. You need help, Mary."

Just then, Sarah arrived from the Eaton farm.

"I've brought you some of Mother's medicinals, Mary. I was not certain what you needed and Danny did not say what was wrong."

Mary showed Sarah her inflamed breast and Sarah's eyes grew wide. She looked at Daniel and visibly swallowed. "Have you sent for Dr. Burk?"

"Yes."

The doctor arrived within moments and Daniel showed him into the bedroom. Ephraim woke up and started to cry.

"I shall take him to the main room and see if he wants some gruel." Sarah picked up the frightened infant and left, closing the door behind her.

As ill as Mary was, Daniel watched her attempt to cover her breast with the blanket. Daniel grasped her hand and kissed her cheek. His voice spoke softly. "You must let the doctor look, Mary."

"I really must see the infection, Mary." Dr. Burk's voice was calm but insistent.

Mary kept herself covered with the blanket as best she could. The doctor narrowed his eyes.

"'Tis a bule with a gathering of pus — an infection in the milk ducts. I saw it many times during the war." He looked up at Daniel. "I apprenticed under several doctors whilst in the army."

"During the war? I am confused…" Her fever was returning, and her cheeks were bright red.

"Yes, we had many new mothers there in the camps… Anyway, we must drain the infection, otherwise it will spread."

Daniel swallowed with difficulty and his voice sounded tight. "Yes, whatever is necessary." He held Mary's hand while the doctor unfolded the cloth that held his lancets.

Mary shut her eyes tightly, squeezing a few tears down her cheeks. Daniel's mouth trembled as he kissed her hand. "I shall stay with you, Mary."

"Thank you," she whispered.

Mary shuddered as the sharp knife sliced into the tender flesh. Her tears poured out without restraint. The lancet hit the center of the infection and pus drained out freely.

"I am sorry, Mary. I would not do this were it not necessary." The doctor's hands trembled.

Daniel fought back tears while stroking the hair back from Mary's damp forehead.

When Dr. Burk finished draining the abscess, he reassumed his professional demeanor. "'Tis necessary to change the dressing twice a day," he told Daniel. "And I'm sure her mother has a supply of teas that will help with her healing."

After cleaning off his lancet, Dr. Burk gathered his supplies and put them back in his leather pack.

Daniel wiped his face and rose from the bed.

"I shall be by your home in a day or two to chop that firewood for you." He shifted his feet, feeling ill at ease.

"That is most agreeable to me, Daniel." He glanced over at Mary. "Rest well, Mary. Let your sister help out for a day or two so you can recover."

She tried to smile. "Thank you, Robert."

The doctor cleared his throat. "Well then, I shall leave you to recover."

Daniel followed him outdoors.

"She should do well, Daniel." He patted him firmly on his upper arm.

"Thank you, Robert. I cannot thank you enough." He combed his hand nervously through his hair.

The doctor started to walk away and then turned back toward Daniel.

"You do know what a blessed man you are, do you not?" Dr. Burk's face contorted with emotion.

Daniel looked at Robert. He saw a successful doctor with everything he could hope for in the way of earthly riches. But Daniel, like the rest of the residents of Deer Run, knew that Robert's blessings did not extend to happiness in his marriage.

"Yes," Daniel replied. "Yes, I am a blessed man."

18

Temptation

When Daniel knew Mary was recovering well from her illness, he kept good on his promise to work for Dr. Burk.

"See to the needs of your mother and the little ones," he said to the twins. "Danny, make sure the fire is tended, and help with the wood chopping. James, see to the animals and whatever else your mother needs. She is still weakened."

"Yes, Father." The boys nodded with sober looks on their faces. The twelve-year-olds were not often left in charge.

He took a moment to study the twins more closely. They were almost as tall as Mary and their faces were starting to take on their father's angular jaw. It would not be long before hair would begin growing on those cheeks.

Where have the years gone?

"Well then. I expect you will make me proud." He patted them both on their shoulders, picked up his axe from the woodpile, and left for the Burk home.

It was a two-mile walk to their large homestead. Robert Burk had taken over the home after the war. His parents died while he was away and his younger siblings were sent to live with relatives. Robert once confided to Daniel that he was anxious to fill up the now empty rooms with a family of his own. After he took Matilda Howard for his wife following the war, it seemed as if Robert's dream would be fulfilled. But there was great disparity between the dream and the reality. The couple remained childless and Robert spent more time at the tavern than any other husband in Deer Run.

Daniel pondered this unhappy tale as he approached their home. Dr. Burk was just leaving, his satchel over his shoulder.

"Injury at the Lyon's place." Robert spoke in a nonchalant manner. "Be back after a bit. Thank you for coming, Daniel."

"Hope it's nothing serious, Robert."

"Probably not. I'll find out." The doctor led his horse out of the barn and looked back at Daniel. "The well's over there," he said, pointing. "It'll be a hot one today." Riding off, he waved at Daniel.

Daniel turned toward the woodpile sitting in the sun to dry. Although it was still May, the summer heat seemed intent on forcing its way into the atmosphere ahead of the calendar.

This was a job he was well used to. Ever since he chopped his way through the forests of New York and Canada during the war, his muscles had strengthened for the task. The cold winters in Massachusetts only increased his skill and stamina, as wood was a constant and necessary commodity. He was grateful he could exchange this work for the medical care provided by Robert Burk.

After only a few minutes of chopping, the sweat on his back made his linen shirt cling to his skin. He unbuttoned the front, allowing more air to reach his skin. As he continued the tedious task, he heard the door of the house open.

"Good day, Daniel." Matilda walked toward him carrying a tankard. "I've brought you something to drink to quench your thirst."

"Thank you, Matilda." He took the tankard from her hands and tried not to appear startled at her revealing bodice. He turned his eyes away, anxious to drink what he thought would be cider. Instead, he tasted rum.

"I did not realize this was rum." He handed the tankard back to her. "I'm sorry, but this will sap my energy in this heat. But I thank you for the refreshment. I'll just drink water from the well."

"Oh, I am sorry, Daniel. Robert always requests rum. No matter. Let me bring you some cider. But first I shall bring you some water to help cool you off." She gave him a flirtatious smile and walked over to the well. Daniel stared after her for a moment. Matilda's face would not be described by most as beautiful, but her allure was in her well-endowed form. And she had never shied away from flaunting her figure with revealing bodices — far more revealing than most of the God-fearing women in Deer Run. But even by Matilda's usual standards, today's sheer bodice left little to Daniel's imagination.

Best keep your mind on your job. He continued working, forcing himself to look at the wood.

When she returned with a bucket of water, she set it on the ground, exposing more of her décolletage when she leaned over. She handed him a cup.

"My, 'tis very warm already." She put her hand in the bucket of water and poured some on her neck. It dripped down the front of her dress. He could not help but notice her voluptuous form as the wet material clung to it. Daniel swallowed with difficulty.

"Excuse me." He cleared his throat and returned to chopping the wood. He hoisted the axe high in the air, thrusting harsh blows onto the logs.

Matilda appeared to watch him closely and then sauntered over to where he worked. He could hear the rustle of her gown approaching.

"I heard your wife has been ill."

Daniel stopped chopping for a moment.

"Yes, but she is recovering."

Matilda drew her mouth into a pucker and then smiled.

"It must have been difficult for you. I am certain you are a man of many needs."

Daniel squinted in the sun and only glanced at Matilda. "As I said, she is recovering well."

Matilda took in a slow deep breath. "Well, Robert will be gone for some time and I am out of firewood. He often forgets that I have needs as well as his patients. Perhaps… when you have chopped several logs, you could bring them in to my hearth for me."

Daniel stopped for a moment. That seemed a reasonable request.

"I can do that for you, Matilda."

She smiled. "Thank you, Daniel." She sidled back to her house with an occasional glance back at him.

He wiped the sweat from his brow. *Keep working.*

After another hour of work, he looked with satisfaction at the growing pile of chopped maple. *I'll just carry these inside for her.*

He fit a half dozen logs in his arms and walked toward the house.

Matilda sat in a chair drinking some wine. She rose from her chair the moment he entered.

"Let me help you, Daniel." She moved toward him and grabbed some of the logs from his arms.

"I am fine, Matilda, truly."

"Nonsense. Even a man with arms as strong as yours needs help sometimes."

She leaned over to set the logs next to the hearth. Standing above her Daniel received an eyeful as her bodice had opened up completely. He swallowed hard.

"I'd best get back to the wood pile." He could feel the sweat increasing on his face and he knew it was not just the weather.

"Oh but wait, Daniel. You must let me check your hands for splinters. All this chopping… even a man of your strength can be undone by a mere sliver of wood."

Grabbing his hand she leaned toward his leg with hers. His breathing became rapid and an unsettling warmth flooded him.

"Why look, Daniel." She caressed the tip of his finger. "Here's a splinter right here." She began to surreptitiously move his hand toward her breast.

Flustered, he pulled his hand away and moved away from her. "I am finished here."

He stumbled on the threshold as he hurried out the door. Picking up his axe from the woodpile, he did not even look back toward the Burk home as he raced toward the road.

He ran halfway home before he stopped to catch his breath.

What just happened? He rubbed his head and face. He knew Matilda to be flirtatious with other men, but he never imagined this scenario. The words of the book of Proverbs filled his thoughts. *For the commandment is a lamp; and the law is light; and reproofs of instruction are the way of life: to keep thee from the evil woman, from the flattery of the tongue of a strange woman. Lust not after her beauty in thine heart;*

neither let her take thee with her eyelids.

Daniel was out of breath and covered with sweat by the time he arrived home. Mary sat in the chair nursing Ephraim.

"Done so soon, Daniel? Was enough chopped to pay the account?" She seemed annoyed and tired.

"No," he said, exasperated. "Perhaps there can be another way to pay the debt." He took a cup of cider Polly handed him.

"Another way? I dare say we have little to offer the man in return for all he has done." Irritation filled Mary's eyes.

Anger surged through Daniel as he glared at his wife. He glanced over at his daughter. "Polly, can you manage helping your mother without the boys the rest of the day?"

"Yes, Papa. Priscilla and I can see to the little ones."

Five-year-old Sally put her hands on her hips. "I am not so little." She had a defiant look on her face.

Daniel smiled despite his ire.

"Well then, young ladies one and all, take care of your mother whilst we are gone." He left the cabin without speaking to Mary.

Daniel found the twins in the barn, cleaning out the dirty straw.

"Lads, come with me. And bring your own axes."

Danny and James looked at each other in surprise but followed their father.

"Where are we going?" James' voice was full of anticipation.

"We will work at Dr. Burk's chopping wood." He paused. "And whilst we are there, you are not to speak to Missus Burk. Or look at her."

James looked at Danny in confusion. Danny shrugged his shoulders.

Arriving at the homestead, Daniel pointed to the pile of wood. "There is our work for the day."

Just then, Missus Burk came out of her home, but she seemed taken aback by the presence of the boys. And Danny and James appeared to be shocked by the sight of Missus Burk's abundant bosom. Both boys stared far too long before they heard their father clear his throat loudly. They looked down at the ground.

"I see you have brought your sons with you." Her voice was low and held a hint of disappointment.

"Yes, Missus Burk. The lads will help me do the chopping. All day." His words were pointed and the meaning clear.

"I see. You know where the well is, should you need it." She turned and walked with strident steps back to the house.

He put his hands on the boys' shoulders. "Let us set to work."

The boys continued looking at the ground while their father led them over to the woodpile. After several hours, they had worked their way through most of the pile.

"There." Daniel wiped the sweat from his brow. "We are done for today. That should pay some of the account."

He led the boys back down the path home. Although weary, he needed to talk to his sons, now on the verge of manhood.

"Do you remember the story of Joseph and Pharaoh's wife?"

James turned red. "You mean, when she grabbed his clothes and tried to kiss him?"

Daniel grinned. "Your mind seems to wander during many a Sabbath sermon, James. It seems miraculous that you paid such close attention to the reverend that day."

Danny laughed and playfully punched his brother.

"There will be times when you must decide to do what Joseph did." Daniel continued in a more sober tone. "There will be times you are tempted by your flesh. At those moments, the best thing you can do is simply run away."

James looked at his father with a serious expression. "And that's what you did today, is it not?"

Daniel put his arm around James' shoulder, which was damp with sweat.

"I see you understand the situation — and that you are wiser than your years, son."

They walked the rest of the way in silence. Daniel understood this was a time of change in their conversations. They would not just be discussing the teachings in the Bible — they would be discussing what it meant to be a man. The boys would learn that a man is one who seeks to please God and not the lusts of the heart.

19

Harmony

aniel had not been back to work at Dr. Burk's for three days. Mary tried to be understanding, but she was getting anxious about their medical account. There were few ways they could pay off their bill, and Mary was at a loss to understand Daniel's hesitancy.

"Must you do the plowing today, Daniel? 'Tis already too late to plant a decent flax crop. Would it not be wiser to take a turn at the doctor's?"

Daniel's eyes narrowed. "I will see to the business of our farm, Missus Lowe." He finished his tankard of cider and slammed the door on the way to the barn.

Polly and Priscilla's eyes opened wide with fear. Their parents were rarely at odds and the recent tension was palpable.

Mary lowered her eyes and fought back warm tears.

"Back to work, girls." Mary cleaned up Alice from her breakfast. Danny and James were just finished eating as well. They looked at each other and, without speaking, appeared to come to a decision.

James began. "Mother, I think perhaps we should tell you something." He paused. "'Tis about the situation at the doctor's."

Mary met his eyes with a look of confusion. "Situation? Whatever do you mean?" She stood up straight while lifting Alice from the bench.

James shifted in his seat. "Well, Missus Burk — perhaps she is warmer than most ladies — but she does not cover as much of herself as you do."

Danny flashed his brother an annoyed look. Mary's eyes widened.

"Quit beating about the bush, James." Danny looked with earnest at his mother. "She was all but falling out of her gown is what she was. And I think she was making Father quite uneasy."

"I see." Mary was beginning to see the situation with clarity. "Thank you, boys." She walked over to the window. "It looks like your father has left for the field. Polly, I'll be in my room for a moment."

Mary went to her room and sat on the bed. She did not often have time alone to pray these days, but she would make time today.

Father in heaven, I have misjudged my husband terribly. Please forgive me… and I pray that he can forgive me as well. Dear Lord, this account weighs heavy on my heart. Show me what to do so Daniel need not return to that house to work. Help us, Lord.

When she opened her eyes, they rested on a pile of material stacked on the chest of drawers.

No, Lord! Not the linen!

But she could not shake the impression that this was the answer to their need. She thought of all the hours she had spent spinning and weaving the flax into this fine material. She had plans to make the girls new gowns and the boys new shirts. They were already outgrowing their clothes from last year.

How will I clothe them, Lord? And we have no crop of flax this year because of the storm. What will we do?

She felt a soothing presence as she recalled the words she knew well from Scripture.

And why take ye thought for raiment? Consider the lilies of the field, how they grow; they toil not, neither do they spin: And yet I say unto you, That even Solomon in all his glory was not arrayed like one of these. Wherefore, if God so clothe the grass of the field, which to day is, and to morrow is cast into the oven, shall he not much more clothe you, O ye of little faith?… For your heavenly Father knoweth that ye have need of all these things.

The words of Jesus touched the deep fear in her heart.

"And I must seek first the kingdom of God and his righteousness; and all these things shall be added unto me." Mary spoke this verse out loud.

She stood up, defeated in her own desires yet determined to follow God's. Picking up the pile of linen, she went into the main room.

"Polly, I just finished nursing Ephraim. Are you able to manage the household if I run an important errand? The boys will be about should you require their help."

The ten-year-old smiled at her. "Yes, Mother. You know I can manage."

Mary fought back tears. "I can always trust you, Polly." She smoothed her hand across the girl's hair and kissed her. "I shall return forthwith."

She kissed the other children and left on her errand, determined to settle the medical account as well as settle something with Matilda.

Walking at a fast pace, Mary traversed the two miles. She saw Matilda working in her garden and approached the woman. She noticed Matilda wore a somewhat modest gown this morning.

At least she is wearing her stays today rather than being loose. Mary forced vindictive thoughts out of her mind.

"Such a surprise to see you, Mary. I thought you were not well."

"I am quite well now, thank you." Mary gave her a pleasant yet guarded smile.

"Come inside for some refreshment." Matilda seemed genuinely pleased to have company.

Walking inside the large home, Mary was impressed by the orderliness. The fine furniture was without stain and there were no pieces of clothing strewn about.

Unlike my home with seven children.

As clean as it appeared, however, it felt cold and lonely.

"Please have a seat." Matilda pointed to a leather-covered chair.

"Such a comfortable place to sit."

"Yes. It does not get used much. It belongs to my husband… but he is not often here to enjoy it." Matilda glanced downward.

"Well, I am certain he is quite busy with his practice."

Matilda looked up with a pained expression. "Yes. His practice… and other things."

Mary was anxious to get to the reasons for her visit.

"So… I have come to settle our account with your husband. There are seventeen yards of linen here that should pay the fees." She handed the woven material to Matilda with reluctance.

The woman's eyes grew wide. "'Tis lovely." She looked at Mary with surprise. "Are you certain? This is a most generous length of linen. This would, of course, settle the account."

"Then it's done." Mary swallowed with difficulty. "And… my husband will no longer be coming here to chop wood."

Matilda glanced at Mary, then looked away. After a moment she spoke.

"You are well-loved by your husband, Mary. And you have seven children to bear witness."

"Yes." Mary looked at the woman for the first time with some compassion. "Perhaps one day, you shall bear a child."

Matilda had a pained expression on her face. "One must share a common bed with a consort if one is to bear a child."

Matilda's blatant admission shocked Mary. Neither spoke for a few moments. Matilda finally broke the silence.

"I was with child once."

"What happened?" Mary stared at her in astonishment.

Matilda looked at her with flushed cheeks. "It was before the war ended. I was seeing a young man who was home on leave. One thing led to another and I knew there was a child on the way. He said he doubted it was his and he wanted nothing to do with me." Tears welled in her eyes. "That's when my mother took me to someone in another town — a lady with some medicinals. The plants would kill my baby."

Tears rolled down Matilda's cheeks. "It was horrible. The woman said it would be easy but it was not. I suffered so. And when the child came out, I could see its little hands and feet." At this memory, she began to sob.

Mary was speechless. At length, she reached out and squeezed Matilda's hand.

The woman resumed her story. "After Robert and I married, I longed to carry a child again. But it did not happen. And then, when Robert was visiting the tavern one evening, who should be there but my baby's father. He told Robert everything. My husband was humiliated. Since then, we have never shared a bed."

Mary did not know what to say, so she prayed for wisdom.

"Perhaps, if you apologized to Robert, he could forgive you."

Matilda looked doubtful. "I think it is far too late," she whispered. There was a look of resignation and hopelessness on her face.

"With God, all things are possible, Matilda."

Matilda shook her head. "My doubt is greater than my faith." She stared out the window with a vacant look. It appeared the visit was over.

"I shall be on my way." Mary stood up. "I hope the linen will be to your satisfaction."

Matilda gave a half-hearted smile. "'Tis far finer than anything I've ever woven."

She walked Mary to the door and waved good-bye.

Mary just started walking away when she whipped around to face Matilda once more.

"Oh, and one more thing." Mary smiled sweetly. "Do not ever go near my husband again." She stared directly into Matilda's wide eyes before turning around to walk home.

Mary could not get to the corn field fast enough. She needed to make amends to her husband. Seeing him from a distance, she noticed he had removed his shirt in the heat of the day.

She waved at him and called his name.

"Mary." He seemed baffled by her presence but pleased.

She walked right up to him and couldn't help but admire his muscular arms glistening with sweat. Her arms wrapped around his waist, and he smiled as he returned the embrace.

"And to what do I owe this pleasure, Missus Lowe." He felt so warm next to her.

"I owe you an apology, Daniel. The boys told me about Matilda — how she dressed. It was quite clear what had occurred."

Daniel looked down at Mary and gave an appreciative grin. "There is no woman who excites me more than my wife." He drew the length of her body close to himself and his moist lips met hers. Their kiss became more passionate and she could feel her breathing quicken. He began to caress her and she shivered with delight.

She gave him a mischievous grin. "The wigwam is not far from here."

"No. It is not."

He took her by the hand and they hurried to their destination.

20

Announcements

June was a special month for Sarah. Not only was she turning twenty, but there was new life growing inside her.

She had suspected for several weeks now and was anxious to tell Nathaniel, but she didn't want to get his hopes up too soon. She knew of many women who had lost their unborn babies early in a pregnancy. Nathaniel had suffered so much loss already. Sarah feared disappointing him if all did not go well.

As her body began changing, however, she knew her husband would notice, so Sarah decided to give him the news on her birthday. It would be her gift to him.

The whole family would be coming over later that day, so Sarah wanted to tell him first thing this morning, while they were alone.

"Nathaniel." Whispering to her sleeping husband, she moved his hair away from his face. He opened one sleepy eye and grinned. His tanned face crinkled with delight as he reached over to his wife.

Drawing her close, he nuzzled her hair and whispered next to her ear, "Happy birthday, my love." When he started kissing her neck, she giggled from the enticing feel of his lips. Soon the announcement of the expected child became lost in a moment of passionate affection.

It can wait till later.

But later brought with it the business of the day — breakfast, milking, baking. And Nathaniel had to tend to the sheep and pigs, as well as the oxen that everyone in the family used for plowing. Sarah wanted the moment of the announcement to be unhurried so they could savor the news together and rejoice in the expected child. But there was much work to do, and the news would have to wait.

The whole family was expected at the Eaton farm for the celebration. From the moment Widow Eaton had gotten up that morning, she directed the many preparations for the meal. While chopping up the parsnips and carrots for the stew, Sarah's mother looked at her with suspicion.

"Are you well, Sarah?"

Sarah did not look at her.

"Of course, Mother, why do you ask?"

"Well, I know a woman with child when I see one."

Sarah gasped.

"Mother!" She put a finger to her lips to gesture a hushed voice. "I've not spoken to my husband yet. Please, do not say anything. I want to surprise him when we are alone. Before I tell the family."

"I've noticed your change in appetite and your pale countenance. Men do not notice these things, but we midwives see all the signs. Do not fear, I shall not spoil your surprise." Tears welling in her eyes, she hugged Sarah. "'Twill be a joy to have new life in our home once again."

"I am so happy, Mother. And I cannot wait to tell Nathaniel. I was going to this morning, but… we were otherwise engaged." Sarah's cheeks grew warm.

"So when is the child expected?"

"I believe in December."

Ruth Eaton looked surprised. "You are that far along?"

Sarah felt heat rise in her cheeks again. "Yes, I believe this little one has been with us since right after our wedding." Sarah's eyes became moist. "I must confess, I do not understand why being with child causes me to cry so often. 'Tis most disconcerting."

Widow Eaton grinned. "It somehow disturbs the humors in our body and causes us to be melancholic. We women must just accept it." Widow Eaton's voice carried a matter-of-fact tone.

Wiping away rivulets of tears from her face, Sarah sniffed.

"Well, enough of the melancholy. I have work to do." She went back to kneading the bread dough, banging it with her fists and rolling it in the flour.

Sarah expected Nathaniel to come in from feeding the livestock, but over an hour went by with no sign of him.

"He must have been delayed." Sarah peered down the path to the field where he should have been feeding the pigs. "I wonder what's taking so long. The others will be here soon."

Just then her husband turned the bend from behind the barn, covered in muck and a scowl on his face. He shook his head in disgust when he saw Sarah watching him.

"Blasted pigs somehow got out of the enclosure. It took me all this time to round up the little buggers. I have to get this foul smell off me."

As he stood outside removing the dirty clothes, Sarah caught a whiff of the pig manure, sending her stomach into a tumult of nausea. She fought back the urge to vomit.

"I'll get you some clean clothes." Feeling weak at the knees, she held her stomach as she went to the chest of drawers in their room. She took slow, deep breaths and the queasiness ebbed. Grabbing a clean shirt and breeches for her husband, she handed them to her mother.

"Can you give these to Nathaniel? I'm afraid the smell will overwhelm me."

Widow Eaton had a sympathetic look on her face. "Of course."

Disappointment filled Sarah — she would not have time to speak with her husband before the family arrived. But she was relieved she'd not lost her breakfast right in front of him.

She heard James and Hannah and their children arrive at the door. Sarah straightened out her clothing and looked in the mirror. By pinching her cheeks, it would be difficult for anyone to tell how pale her skin really was.

Everyone talked excitedly in the main room, so Sarah joined them.

Hannah seemed more ebullient than she had been in many months. Still recovering from the death of baby Samuel, her grief had been obvious to all. But today, she seemed different. Happier.

Nathaniel came inside from his cleanup. He grinned at his wife and kissed her. "Perhaps I should have kissed you several moments ago —

before I washed." He gave her a teasing look.

Sarah made a face. "I truly love you, dear husband… but not that much." She grinned and laughed when he kissed her again.

Mary and Daniel walked in the door accompanied by their children.

"What's all this kissing going on here?" Daniel said, feigning gruffness. "You'd think you naughty young people were married or something."

The large group of siblings and cousins chatted and laughed. The other women joined Widow Eaton and Sarah in setting out the food that soon covered the tableboard. Roast duck, stew, cheese, freshly baked bread, and a huge bowlful of ripe wild strawberries covered with milk and sugar elicited hungry looks from everyone. The chattering children were so excited that Widow Eaton had to raise her voice to get everyone's attention.

"Please, may we bow our heads and ask the good Lord to bless this bountiful meal?"

Everyone became quiet and bowed their heads. James began the prayer.

"Dear heavenly Father, we are humbled by Your goodness and provision for our families. We are grateful for the lives of all who are still here as well as those who have gone on before us." He paused and sniffed. "And we are so grateful for Sarah, whose birth we celebrate today. And we thank You, dear Lord, for the new life that grows inside Hannah. For all these blessings, we give You thanks. Amen."

It took a moment before the announcement in the prayer sank in. Hannah was expecting!

Everyone spoke at once and all the women gathered around Hannah and kissed her warmly, expressing their joy. Sarah was excited for Hannah, but she fought back tears of disappointment. She had been so anxious to share her news with her husband and then her family. But after all the heartache Hannah and James had been through with the death of their infant, Sarah could not spoil their special moment of joy. Her news would have to wait.

The abundant food stirred choruses of approval from the group. The twins stood at the tableboard with spoons in hand, ready to dive in. Their father gave them a warning look.

"Not too much, lads." Daniel kept his voice low.

But Widow Eaton and Sarah had prepared enough food to feed everyone, even the hungriest of participants. No one would go hungry.

Sarah's appetite was the only one that seemed lacking. In fact, the more she took in the sight of so much food, the sicker she felt. She struggled to maintain her composure as she felt a wave of acid in her throat. "Excuse me." She ran out the door and toward the barn.

Sitting on a bale of hay, she closed her eyes and took in slow breaths, praying the sensation would stop. When it ceased, she put her face in her hands and wept.

"Sarah?" Her husband sat next to her and placed his arms around her shoulders. "What's wrong?"

"I wanted it to be so special." Her words came in gasps between her sobs.

"What? You wanted what to be so special?" He stroked her hair away from her face.

"I wanted just you and me to have a joyful moment to celebrate by ourselves when I told you the news. Instead, I just feel horrible and ill, and I do not wish to spoil Hannah's excitement either." Her distress seemed to escalate the more she talked.

Nathaniel lifted her chin so her eyes met his. He seemed to struggle to maintain his own emotions.

"Sarah, is it true? Do you carry our child?"

Wiping the tears from her face, she whispered, "Yes."

It took him a moment to speak. "So, I am to be a father?" He swallowed back tears. Sarah knew how much this meant to her husband. It was as if all the years of loneliness, without his family, were suddenly forgotten. This new life was a new beginning of hope.

Sarah took his hand and placed it on her rounded belly. "Your child lives here. And though I feel ill, I am joyful that I carry your son or daughter." She stroked his cheek. "I am so in love with you, Nathaniel."

He wrapped his arms around her, his tears moistening her sleeve.

"Thank you, Sarah. You cannot fathom my great love for you." He held her for a moment and then suddenly held her at arm's length with a look of concern. "Was I holding you too tight?" Panic infused his voice.

Despite her tears, she laughed. "No. Please hold me again."

He put his arms around her in a more cautious manner than usual. She pulled them around herself in a tighter embrace. "You shall not hurt us."

He relaxed and gripped her for a moment longer.

"Let us share our good news." His excited grin made him look like a schoolboy.

"But what about Hannah? I do not wish to take away from her joy."

He held her chin up to look at him. "This will add to her joy." He took her hand and led her back to the house where the noisy group still celebrated.

Sarah walked with hesitation behind her husband. He stopped and put his arm around her waist.

"You've never seemed so shy before, Sarah."

"I've never been with child before. I do not know what to say."

"Then let me speak for us both." His strong arms guided her back to the house. When they came in the door, everyone stopped talking.

Mary looked with concern at her little sister. "Are you all right, Sarah?"

Nathaniel answered. "She is more than all right." He paused and wrapped his arm around her. Sarah could feel the trembling in his fingers as he stroked her shoulder. "My wife is with child."

Everyone's face shone with the joy of the announcement.

"My littlest sister, going to be a mother. Here, here!" James raised his cider tankard to the new parents.

Hannah was the first to hurry toward her sister-in-law and give her a hug. "We shall carry our little ones together." She gripped both of Sarah's arms and grinned.

As the whole group of siblings hurried over to celebrate the news, Sarah noticed her mother look heavenward.

"Dear Lord, I hope their father James can see his children." Ruth Eaton closed her eyes and smiled.

21

Heroes

July 4, 1791 — the fifteenth birthday of America — and the weather befit the day. It was intensely hot and filled with potential for enthusiastic celebration.

Sarah wiped the sweat off her forehead for at least the tenth time, trying to keep the liquid from ruining the letter she was writing. She was sending out yet one more inquiry about the possible location of her missing father-in-law. She hurried to complete this latest communication before she and Nathaniel would leave for the town square.

She focused on her efforts to write, despite the uncomfortable heat.

Dear Sir,

I am making inquiries into the possible whereabouts of a soldier from the Continental army who was last seen at West Point, New York, in spring of 1783. His name is Sgt. Benjamin Stearns. When last reported, he was uninjured and on his way home to Deer Run in the state of Massachusetts, but he has not been heard from since. His family is most anxious to learn of his whereabouts.

Should you have any knowledge of this man, please do us the honor of a reply. We are grateful for any assistance you can provide.

Your most humble servant,

Sarah left the signature blank so that Nathaniel could complete that portion. She would take the letter to the post rider tomorrow and send it off to yet another captain of the state militia, this time in Boston. Previous communications to militias in New York had gone unanswered. Perhaps Boston would hold the answer. There was renewed urgency in their search now that Benjamin Stearns had a grandchild on the way.

Another drop of sweat rolled off Sarah's face, marring the parchment. She dabbed at the wetness with her sleeve and sighed with exasperation.

"Well, 'tis almost perfect."

The door to their bedroom opened and her husband emerged wearing his Continental army uniform. The rich blue wool brought out the sapphire in his eyes. He wiped at the white facing along the front, attempting to remove any possible vestiges of dirt. Deftly whisking the strings of his green epaulette, he encouraged the braided strands to lay flat down his left shoulder. His face was somber.

"Does this look all right?" His brows furrowed while Sarah's face erupted with pleasure.

"You have never looked more handsome, Corporal Stearns." She stood up and walked over to get a closer look. "I do not think anyone will notice that I had to add extra wool to the shoulders." She smoothed the material along his upper arms. "You will be the most dashing militiaman of all during the muster."

Nathaniel wrapped his arms around her waist.

"I do not feel dashing — just warm. The heat from this jacket brings back memories of summer battles." He removed the jacket for a few moments to cool off. "Thank you, Sarah." He leaned down to kiss his wife and then glanced over at the table. "I see you've completed another letter?"

"Yes, it just requires your signature."

Her husband shook his head. "I wish you could sign for me. Yours is a far sight more pleasurable to read than my scrawl. Leaving school at age eleven did not much help my writing skills."

"Your signature is the important one, Nathaniel. I am just your scribe." She smiled at him. "Besides, the measure of a man is not his ability to perform such a task. You are wise, sensible, hard working, and so kind." She touched his cheek. "And you are so loved by your wife."

He finished signing the letter and looked up at her with a mischievous grin. Taking her into his arms, he drew her close.

"Your mother is away at a birthing. Perhaps we could have our own celebration here before we go into town."

She giggled and pushed him away.

"We are late already, Mr. Stearns. Please release your wife!"

He did so with reluctantance but held onto her for a moment longer. "Later then?"

"Perhaps." She batted her eyelashes and stroked the skin near his lips.

He grinned while putting the uniform back on. "Later then."

She gave him a brief kiss as they walked out the door, carrying the fruit, bread, and cheeses they would take to the picnic.

They placed their hats in a position to shield their eyes from the late afternoon sun. Sarah placed one hand on her belly, smoothing the material over her growing baby. She noticed Nathaniel watching the gentle movement of her fingers.

"Someday, the birthing your mother will be attending will be yours."

Sarah looked at him with affection. "I cannot wait to give you our child, Nathaniel. I hope he looks just like you."

"Well, if 'tis a lass, I hope she will favor her mother." His smile warmed her heart.

"Be it lad or lass, I hope the child has your blue eyes. They remind me of the summer sky."

Nathaniel leaned down to kiss her while they walked. "Mother Eaton seems to be doing more births in Williamston of late." He adjusted the collar of his coat.

"Ever since Widow Baxter died, Mother has had to divide her practice between that town and ours. I fear she is working too hard."

"Perhaps Deer Run needs another midwife. There seems to be no shortage of growing families here."

"No." Sarah smiled. "Not as long as the husbands in Deer Run remain so affectionate."

Approaching the town square, they heard the voices of laughter as the festivities had begun. Children played tag, older boys competed in races, and the men tested their skills at wrestling.

"I do not know why anyone wishes to get hotter in such weather." Shaking her head, Sarah looked with surprise at the sweating athletes intent upon proving their physical prowess.

"You do look very warm, Sarah. Let us find a place in the shade where you can rest." He led her to one of the town square sitting logs that was overhung by a huge chestnut tree. The branches spread far and wide and there was a soft and welcoming breeze.

"Thank you, Nathaniel. Look, there's Mary and Daniel."

Mary saw Sarah at the same moment and walked over to the shade with a squirming Ephraim in her arms. "Good day, Sarah and Nathaniel. May we join you? Ephraim is nigh ready to leap from my arms."

Sarah laughed. "Please, come sit."

The men exchanged greetings. "Let us get the ladies some cider." Daniel wiped the sweat off his forehead with his sleeve. "I could use some myself in this heat." Nathaniel leaned over his wife and kissed her. Looking back at her for a moment, he grinned before joining in conversation with Daniel.

Mary looked with amusement at Sarah. "My, such a change you have wrought in Nathaniel Stearns, my dear sister."

She gave Sarah a hug, all the while monitoring Ephraim's attempts at holding onto the log. "What do you mean?"

"Do you not see? The man is smitten with you. I've never seen such a transformation from one so withdrawn to one so enamored."

Sarah gave a weak smile. "Do you truly believe so, Mary? I am ever fraught with the feeling that I am not as good as… others in his past. I feel sometimes that I am just… a replacement."

"Well, if that man is not completely in love with you, then I cannot imagine what affection he could be feigning." Mary seemed surprised. "Sarah, do you truly fear he lacks devotion to you? Because I surely do not see that in his eyes."

Sarah looked down at her hands in her lap. "I've no cause to feel this way on Nathaniel's part. He is a most affectionate husband. I feel the fear is within me — an uncertainty that lives in my heart, keeping me from believing that he could truly treasure me."

Mary reached over to cover Sarah's hands with her own.

"Sarah, none of us feels completely good, or even worthy of the love in our lives. But just as God loves us for who we are — despite our faults and weaknesses — so can our earthly husbands love us truly and completely." Mary glanced over at their husbands, who were carefully carrying tankards of cider across the green to their wives. "Look at them guarding the refreshment for us. Just as they tenderly care for us — protecting us, shielding us from harm."

"I know you are right. I just wish that my heart was in accord with my thoughts." Sarah forced a smile as her husband approached and took the cider he brought for her. "Thank you, my love."

Nathaniel smiled at Sarah and placed his hand on her shoulder. "Looks like the muster is beginning." There was disappointment in his voice. "I'd best be lining up." He picked up his musket and walked with hesitant steps toward the militia preparing to march in formation.

"Nathaniel looks quite handsome in his uniform." Mary began to nurse Ephraim. "Is this the first time he has mustered since the war ended?"

"Yes. I found his uniform in an old trunk after we were married. I offered to widen the shoulders for him. I guess he no longer had an excuse to remain apart from the veterans." Sarah looked with sadness at her husband. "He does not seem well content."

Daniel watched the former Continental soldiers lining up on the green, under the direction of his brother-in-law, Sergeant James Thomsen. "I can understand his misgivings." Swallowing a long gulp of the cider, Daniel stared at the veterans, yet his gaze seemed far removed from the festivities.

Sarah looked at her brother-in-law with sympathy, imagining the conflicted feelings that arose in his thoughts every Fourth of July. It was on this day thirteen years ago that the former British soldier had lain down his allegiance to his mother country and embraced the freedom of America. But that heartrending decision had cost him his family in England as well as the trust of some Americans, despite his obvious commitment to his new country.

Will he ever feel accepted as an American?

She saw Mary reach up and squeeze her husband's hand with affectionate understanding. Daniel looked down at his wife and gave her a grateful smile.

They don't even need to speak a word. Their love is so complete, they can read each other's thoughts. I hope Nathaniel and I can be like that... someday.

Sarah wistfully gazed over at Nathaniel, who was executing the maneuvers commanded by her brother James. Her husband's movements appeared stilted and uncomfortable. Sarah's heart ached from the look of misery on his face. But her compassionate thoughts were interrupted by shouts from the crowd.

"Fight! Fight!"

The children of Deer Run were in an uproar as a crowd gathered in a smokescreen of dust. There was so much commotion even James was distracted from leading the militia, and he abruptly dismissed the veterans.

Adults rushed to the center of the fray, with Daniel in the lead. When he got to the center of the fight and found twelve-year-old Danny in the thick of it, he assumed a military bearing.

"Halt!" Daniel yelled at the enraged youngsters. As the punches continued, he and another parent dragged the two fist-slingers apart. Both boys were bleeding from the nose and the older boy, of about fourteen, was holding his hand over a swollen eye. Danny's eyes blazed with anger and he attempted to lunge at the other boy again.

"As you were, sir!" Daniel yanked Danny to the ground. The two boys stared with hatred at each other. "Who started this?"

Neither boy said a word. With everything now quiet, the anguished cries of eight-year-old Priscilla Lowe reached the ears of the crowd. Mary handed Ephraim to Sarah and wrapped her arms around her crying daughter.

Ten-year-old Polly was enraged. "It was him what started it." She pointed an accusing finger at the older boy with the swollen eye. "He was making Priscilla cry!"

The older boy's father looked at his son while holding him by the scruff of his neck. "That true?" The boy looked down but did not say a word. "Apologize to the miss. Now!" He slapped his son's ears in anger.

The boy winced. "Sorry." It was obvious the sentiment was not heartfelt. Daniel's jaw clenched.

"You boys shake hands now and be done." The two fighters glared at each other and shook hands with such a grip that it seemed to continue their battle rather than reconcile it. The fathers drew them apart.

Mary took Ephraim back from Sarah and put one arm around Priscilla's shoulder as they all walked back to the shade of the chestnut tree. Sarah saw that Danny's nose was still bleeding and took off her apron to use as a bandage. By the look on his face, the injury was far more than physical.

"What happened, Danny?" Sarah dabbed at the blood.

"Nothin', Aunt Sarah." The boy was near tears.

Daniel came up to his oldest son and began to lecture.

"Could you not have avoided a fight in the middle of celebrating the birth of our country?"

"Our country?" Danny glared at his father.

Daniel's eyes narrowed.

"What is your meaning, sir?" Daniel worked his jaw.

"Perhaps I would not be fighting if my father were not a Redcoat!"

Daniel's face froze, his eyes wounded and fixed straight ahead. By now James and his family had arrived for the family gathering and he walked over toward his nephew. By the look on James' countenance, he had heard every word spoken between the father and son.

"Danny, come walk with me." James took him by the shoulder and led him toward the woods. As they walked side by side, James spoke with earnest to Danny, although the group under the tree could not hear the conversation. It was obvious by Danny's intent demeanor that the veteran soldier, James Thomsen, was having an impact on his nephew.

Mary was near tears as she hugged and consoled Priscilla. "Tell me what happened, Prissy."

"I was just speaking of Papa, and that big boy said, 'PaPAH, PaPAH! Why do you not say 'Father' like the rest of us Americans?' He kept laughing at me and then called Papa a 'lobsterback' — whatever that is. He was so wretched." Priscilla cried again.

Polly put her hands on her hips. "I wanted to punch him in the nose myself, but Danny beat me to it."

Daniel sat on the log, his shoulders slumping. "It's like the war never ended." He stared off into the distance.

Nathaniel regarded his brother-in-law.

"That's not true, Daniel. It has ended and the two countries are at peace. And you are part of our family here in America. You are an American."

"Nathaniel is right," Sarah added. "And you have just as much right to be an American as those born here."

Daniel attempted to smile but his eyes betrayed his sadness.

"And now, my own son thinks I am the enemy." His voice was strained and his eyes filled with hopelessness while he clutched his hands together and held them to his lips. Mary placed one hand on his shoulder and squeezed the tightened muscle in his arm. Ephraim grasped onto Daniel's hair, which was pulled back by a ribbon, and tugged on it while laughing. Daniel leaned over to the infant and kissed him. "I shall enjoy your affection while you have no knowledge of my past, dear boy." He picked up his youngest child and held him close. Sarah thought she saw a tear in the corner of Daniel's eye.

She felt her husband pulling something from her hair. Looking up at his hand, Sarah saw dangling from his fingers a long flower pod that had fallen off the spreading tree branches. The chestnut was bursting with the furry blooms.

"Catkins." Nathaniel smiled. "They are everywhere. Filling the field with promise of future abundance. We shall enjoy the sustenance of chestnuts come fall."

Sarah smiled at him, then focused on Daniel.

"Our futures are all filled with the promise of new birth and renewed hope for peace. Time will heal," she said reassuringly.

Dusk was approaching and it was almost time for the reading of the Declaration of Independence.

"Where is James?" Mary looked around for her brother. "He shall be late for the reading."

Just then James and Danny emerged from the woods. When Sarah looked at her nephew, she could tell he had been crying. James had his hand around the boy's shoulders and he good-naturedly patted

Danny's back before walking over to the steps of the meetinghouse to prepare for the recitation.

Still sitting on the log and holding Ephraim, Daniel avoided Danny's gaze. The twelve-year-old approached his father and without speaking, sat next to him. Mary reached over and took Ephraim from Daniel's arms so the older son and his father could talk.

Young Danny swallowed with difficulty and spoke in a quiet voice to his father. "Is it true what Uncle James said?"

Daniel did not meet his son's eyes. "Is what true?"

Danny drew in a deep breath. "Is it true that you saved Mother's life and… killed a Redcoat? Is that how you own that scar?" Danny's eyes were wide with amazement.

"Yes, it is true." Daniel rubbed his right cheek over the long thin scar that resulted from the knife-wielding intruder's attack so many years before.

"So, you are a hero then. Is that not so?" Danny's eyes filled with tears.

Daniel met his oldest son's eyes. "If a hero means that I would give my life for someone that I love, then yes, I am a hero. I would die for your mother, or you, if need be. I would do so gladly to protect you."

Danny had another question that seemed to sit with urgency on his lips. With the same boldness birthed from the blood of his English-born parent, he pressed onward.

"Father, why did you become an American?"

Daniel looked with contemplation at his firstborn, and then gazed across the town green and stared at a huge spreading chestnut tree.

"See that tree, Danny? When chestnuts grow in the forest, they become cramped and confined — unable to spread out and grow. They are not free to thrive in the way God intended them to." Daniel put his arm around Danny's shoulder and pointed at the branches. "Those limbs are strong and healthy. They fulfill their purpose by being given the freedom they require to fulfill their destiny. Here in America, I could fulfill my destiny with your mother. And with you."

Daniel held his son close as they watched James Thomsen rise to the top step of the meetinghouse. And as the veteran of the Continental army began the speech that commemorated the birth of the fledgling

America, Sarah's eyes welled with tears at the powerful love that a father and son had for each other that would bridge a gap of misunderstanding. It was a love that could bring hope to a world of hurt.

And as Nathaniel held Sarah in his arms while listening to the words of Thomas Jefferson that so inspired the nation to fight for liberty, she held hope that the hurt in her own heart would heal. That her years of feeling unworthy of love would be healed and nurtured by the God Who loved her — and the husband who now held her safely in his heart.

It could be her own liberation from fear.

22

Dreams

hat was that?

Nathaniel heard a familiar explosion — musket fire. His heart raced and sweat began to form on his brow.

Here we go again. Both excitement and trepidation consumed him.

Poising in a crouched position, his moist hands gripped the fire-arm's wooden stock. He knew he needed to wait but his limbs longed to surge forward. And then he saw his comrades bursting out of one trench after another, pressing toward the top of the hill.

Gunfire was everywhere but he did not feel any pain. He moved like a machine, fast, with one intent — to kill. As he mounted the top of the ridge, a gunner aimed his firelock at him. But Nathaniel was ready and set his sights on the man and fired at close range. The enemy marksman never had a chance. Blood splattered across Nathaniel's face, but he did not stop long enough to wipe it off. Thrusting his bayonet at a fleeing man, he then plunged the blade over and over, each encounter bringing a sense of deep satisfaction. A wide-eyed man, trying desperately to escape the fray, was his next victim. Nathaniel held him down by the throat and squeezed the life out of the man. A sense of relief flooded Nathaniel.

"Nathaniel!"

Rubbing his eyes, Nathaniel awakened to the dreaded realization that his nightmares had returned. Sarah sat wide-eyed in bed staring at him with horror.

Ever since the Fourth of July celebration, the war had once again come back to plague his sleep. Marching with the militia, listening to military commands, firing the thirteen-round salute to the original thirteen colonies — it all brought back the visions of war. His nights once again testified to unhealed wounds.

"Sarah." He wiped the sweat from his brow. Tears welled in his eyes as he looked at the terror on her face. "I'm so sorry." Breathing hard from the dream, he felt light-headed.

"Are you all right?" Her lips trembled.

Shaking, he propped himself up on one elbow and touched her. "Are you?" He caressed her arm, ashamed of what he must have been doing. "Please forgive me."

His wife leaned over and kissed him. "There is nothing to forgive. You were having a nightmare."

Nathaniel feared asking her, but he needed to know. "Sarah, what was I doing?"

Her eyes grew wide and she touched his face.

"When I first awoke, I heard you screaming in anger. Then your arms acted as if you were stabbing someone. And then…" She paused and swallowed. "Then you were gripping the pillow as though killing someone. The look on your face — it frightened me." Tears rolled down her cheeks.

"I didn't hurt you, did I?" Terror gripped him.

She smiled despite the tears and stroked his hair. "No. You never hurt me. You never would."

Nathaniel exhaled with relief and drew her toward him. He wrapped his arms around her and embraced her. Kissing her cheek, he struggled to hold back the tears. His dear, loving wife curled up beside him, and they went back to sleep.

When morning arrived, neither of them spoke of the nightmare, but it was never far from Nathaniel's thoughts. Watching Sarah put on her linen gown over her shift, he noticed her growing belly. It made him both joyous and fearful.

What if I should injure her in one of my dreams? The thought was too distressing to entertain for long.

Sarah seemed more affectionate than usual this morning. It was as if she understood the pain of his memories. Looking at her smiling and touching him at every opportunity — a gentle rub on his shoulder, a caress to his cheek, visible tokens of comfort and reassurance — he loved her all the more for her understanding. And he cherished her even more for her passionate commitment to a husband so deeply scarred by war.

Widow Eaton interrupted his thoughts at the breakfast table.

"We'll have to hurry to get chores done." She wiped the spilled corn gruel that stuck to the wooden table. "Mary is freed from cooking on her birthday. Sarah and I must hasten there and begin the feast."

"I almost forgot." Nathaniel swallowed the last of his cider. "I'd best get to the barn and feed the stock. It'll be another steamy August day today, by the feel of it."

Sarah leaned over and kissed his cheek before he stood up. "Do not work too hard, my love."

He placed his hand gently on her belly and then held her close to himself for a moment. "Thank you, Sarah." Standing up, he grabbed one last piece of bread from the table to eat on his way to the barn.

The sun scorched the earth when Nathaniel, Sarah, and Widow Eaton began the mile-long walk to the Lowe farm. Sarah's straw bonnet protected her eyes, but Nathaniel noticed her cheeks flushed with the heat. Strands of moist hair escaped her hat, causing her to blow a puff of air upward for relief from the annoying locks.

"Do you need to sit for a moment, Sarah?" Nathaniel said with concern.

"No, I am well enough. It will just be pleasant to get in the shade of a tree." Her smile reassured him and he took one of her arms to guide her on the path. As they neared Mary and Daniel's home, the sound of children laughing filled the air.

"Look at him!" Sally Lowe squealed with delight. "Ephraim's walking!"

Sure enough, the adventurous eleven-month-old was taking his first steps in the front yard.

Mary smiled, hands on hips as she watched her youngest child. "Wants to keep up with the big ones, he does. Welcome, everyone!"

"Happy birthday, Mary!" Sarah said, giving her sister a quick hug. Mary held her close and looked down at Sarah's growing belly.

"I cannot hold you so close anymore."

"Now you know how I have felt trying to hold you close these many years." They laughed, and then the women went inside to begin the food preparations.

Nathaniel saw Daniel near the woodpile chopping a supply of oak. He waved at his brother-in-law in greeting and walked toward him.

"Good day, Daniel."

Daniel smiled. "How do you fare?"

"Well enough. Can I help you with the chopping?"

"You can make a stack against the barn."

"Of course." Nathaniel leaned down to stack a pile in the crook of his arms.

"And how is your wife faring? She seems to be doing well."

Nathaniel smiled. "She is." He grew sober. "I don't know what I would do without her." He piled the logs one upon another and became quiet.

Daniel stared at him. "Well, I have never seen my sister-in-law so content before. You must be doing her good as well." He wiped a dirty sleeve across his forehead.

"I hope that is so."

Daniel stopped chopping wood for a moment. "You seem thoughtful. What weighs on your heart?"

"My dreams — nightmares from the pit of hell."

Daniel paused before speaking. "You mean nightmares from war?"

"Was not war hell?" Anguish gripped at Nathaniel's spirit. He felt vulnerable sharing this secret he had guarded for years.

"Yes, it most certainly was. Let us sit for a bit." Wiping the sweat from his brow, Daniel studied him. "So what sets them off for you?"

Nathaniel's eyebrows shot up and he looked with surprise at his brother-in-law. "You know these dreams?"

Daniel rubbed the back of his head and looked down at his feet. "They have been my unwelcome companion these many years." Both men sat there without speaking for several minutes. Nathaniel broke the silence.

"I suppose I forget that you, too, were in the war. That you might have haunting visions in the night as well."

Daniel nodded his head and looked off into the distance. He found a tankard of cider on the ground and drank a large gulp.

"It was the Fourth of July," Nathaniel began. "The marching, the feel of my uniform, the musket fire — it brought it all back." He wiped the sweat off his neck. "These dreams have visited me almost every night since then. But last night... 'twas the worst." He looked up at the tree branch overhanging the barn and blinked several times. "I was back at Yorktown. It was as if my friend had just been killed — there was fresh rage in my heart. I was so full of the desire to avenge that the bloodlust consumed me. I found I was taking pleasure in killing. But the worst part was, I woke Sarah. She had a look of terror in her eyes... I will never forget." At this, tears began to roll from his eyes.

He continued. "I asked her what I had been doing in my dream and she said I looked like I was killing someone. She had to have been horrified."

"What did she say?"

"She said that she knew I was just having a nightmare. When I asked her if I had hurt her, she said no." Nathaniel looked over at Daniel with fear. "But what if I ever do hurt her? What if I hurt our child? I could never forgive myself." Wiping the tears away, he dared to ask Daniel a pointed question. "Have you ever hurt Mary?"

Daniel put his hand on Nathaniel's shoulder. "No, I have not. But I understand the fear because it has often visited my thoughts as well. Mary, too, has understood about the nightmares. I know this only makes us love our wives even more, does it not?"

"Yes." Nathaniel wiped off his face with shaking hands.

"Our brother-in-law James suffers as well."

Nathaniel was surprised. "I did not know."

"I think most of us carry these scars in us. The wretched memories of the unthinkable that we've seen — as well as knowing there is a devil inside us that can carry out the ungodly task of war. It is a frightening monster that lays hidden in our hearts. Any God-fearing man understands it is a demon we wish to quell — especially when we are in the arms of our wives. But with God's help, that demon has no power over you… or your loved ones."

Nathaniel was perplexed. "Yet you say you still suffer from these dreams."

"Yes. But they lessen each year. I have prayed that God would deliver me from these visions of war. I go to the Bible each time they try to come back. And I pray the psalm of David. 'Have mercy upon me, O LORD; for I am weak: O LORD, heal me; for my bones are vexed.' King David was a warrior. I get comfort in reading the psalms."

They sat there in silence for several moments, still healing from the scars that ran so deep.

"Thank you for speaking of this." Nathaniel stared at the ground. "I needed to unburden my heart with someone who shares my secret — someone who understands the diabolical dreams."

"We veterans share much in common, regardless of the army we fought for." Daniel gave a rueful grin. "I remember a friend long ago from the French War suffering nightmares. I suppose a hundred years from now, should wars still be waged, others will suffer as well." He patted Nathaniel's shoulder. "I shall pray for you, Nathaniel. Perhaps you can pray for me as well."

Desperation for the Lord's help overwhelmed him. "Can we pray together… now?"

"Of course."

And as kindred soldiers from the Revolution — one a Redcoat and one a Rebel — bowed their heads together, Nathaniel realized they were now united as more than members of a family. They now shared the bond of trusting for God's healing from the residual wounds of war.

23

Comfort

*S*arah noticed Mary seemed quieter than usual. On a day of celebration, this was not typical for her sister.

"Mary." Sarah encircled her sister's shoulder. "You do not despair about being another year older, do you?"

Mary seemed surprised at the question.

"No, pray tell, why do you ask?" Mary gave a slight smile but her eyes seemed less bright than her words.

Sarah squeezed her arm and scrutinized her.

"We have been sisters far too long for you to attempt to deceive me. What weighs so on your heart?" Sarah's words became softer and her eyes locked onto Mary's with concern.

Mary looked downward as she picked up a doll that had fallen onto the wooden floor. After Mary retrieved the toy, Sarah noticed her sister's eyes glistened.

"'Tis nothing." Mary swiped at the tears that began falling. "I know that God will provide. It's just been… a difficult year."

Sarah's eyes narrowed. "What can we do to help? Please let us assist you in some way. Whatever it might be. Please."

Mary paused before speaking. "'Tis too great a need and it cannot be met short of a miracle." She picked up a broom and began sweeping the floor without saying anything further.

Widow Eaton came in from the barn carrying two headless, plucked chickens, their feathers still clinging to her gown.

"These hens gave me a fit with their fluttering ways, but they succumbed to the skills of the huntress at last." Sarah and Mary smiled at their mother's playful words. It was a sign to them that she was healing from the loss of her husband.

"I'll take those, Mother." Sarah took the limp fowl from the widow's hands and began to prepare the meat for the stew. Widow Eaton grabbed the knife and began slicing the carrots, onions, and turnips.

"Please sit, Mary. 'Tis your birthday. The one day of the year you need not cook." Widow Eaton grinned at her older daughter.

Mary looked around helplessly and sat on a chair. "I do not know how not to help. Sarah should be the one sitting." She pointed to her sister's growing belly.

Sarah grinned. "Well, I am quite able to help with the cooking. After all, this child still has four months to go. I am not so large yet."

"Not so large as I was." A small smile worked its way on the sides of Mary's lips. She was rocking in the wooden chair, slowly starting to relax.

"That is because you carried two babies." Sarah looked up from her work and smirked. "I am quite certain this is only one."

Polly came into the house, carrying a squirming Ephraim. "Mother, he smells most foul."

Mary laughed. "So much for relaxing on my birthday. Come, you precious, smelly child." Ephraim resisted her efforts to submit to the diaper change. "This child bears his father's strong will. He will cultivate a few gray hairs on our heads, I fear." She kissed his chubby cheeks after the change was complete. "But I love you so, my son — even if you are a rascal!" Ephraim laughed when she set him outside to play with the others.

"Ah, here come James and Hannah!" Mary greeted them at the doorway and invited them in.

"Happy birthday, Mary." James gave his sister a hug. "I think I shall join the gentlemen outside." He looked at his mother and Sarah and tipped his tricorne hat. "Ladies," he said with mock formality. Looking at Sarah, he feigned a shocked expression and pointed toward her belly. "I fear Missus Stearns has already consumed half the dinner all by herself!"

Sarah scrunched her face and threw a turnip straight at him. Ducking from the vegetable, he laughed and ran outdoors.

"Men!" Sarah shook her head and tried not to laugh. "They make us fat and then bemuse themselves with our predicament." Mary and Hannah laughed. Widow Eaton tried to resist breaking into a smile but she lost the effort.

"True enough." Their mother began to hum under her breath while chopping the vegetables.

Hannah walked over to Mary and gave her sister-in-law a hug.

"I have an unexpected gift for you, Mary." She had been holding a large bundle in her arms and proceeded to untie the wrapping. "I happened to be in the loft a few days ago looking for spindle supplies. As I was searching, I made a choice discovery. Look!"

Hannah's eyes beamed as she held out a huge bolt of woven linen. "I could not believe it. You must have stored it in the loft your last year at the Thomsen homestead. When you moved, you forgot 'twas there."

Mary stared without speaking at the precious yards of sun-bleached woven flax. Tears washed down her cheeks as she stroked the soft material.

"We had an abundant harvest the year I carried the twins. There was so much flax to weave. I remember storing some upstairs in the loft, but it slipped my mind." Mary sat back down in the rocking chair, her tears of relief dropping onto the huge folded pile.

Sarah wiped her hands off and walked over to her sister. Clasping her fingers across her sister's, she stared into Mary's eyes, fighting back her own tears. "Is this your miracle?" she whispered.

Mary nodded with trembling lips. "Yes."

They hugged and Sarah thanked God in her heart for this answer to her sister's need — a miracle of comfort and provision.

⌒⌒◦

The celebration for Mary's birthday had lasted for several hours, and Sarah, Nathaniel, and Widow Eaton did not arrive home until dusk. Weary but content, they all crawled into their beds that night after the stock had been tended to.

The late-August air was oppressive. Windows were left open in an attempt to encourage a spare breeze to provide some measure of relief. However, despite Sarah's efforts to remain cool, her thin night shift clung to her skin, adhered by profuse sweat. Sarah drifted off into a restless sleep for a brief time before a sound outdoors startled her awake.

Rising from bed as quickly as her belly would allow, she stared out the window looking for the source of the sound. Her moist hands squeezed the wooden sill so hard her fingers began to slip.

I know I heard twigs cracking. Her heart lurched in an odd rhythm. She feared the loudness of her breathing might alert someone to her presence.

"Sarah?"

She jumped with fear and held her chest as if trying to keep her heart contained within.

"Nathaniel!" She barely managed to let his name escape from her tight throat. "I think someone may be outside." Her quivering voice betrayed her intense fear.

Her husband hurried to the window. Peering into the moonlit yard, he grinned. "'Tis only raccoons lumbering towards the woods. You can come back to bed." He swept her long single braid back from her shoulder and kissed her on the cheek. Terror still gripped her as he led her back to their comfortable mattress.

Lying back down did not lessen the intensity of her breathing, nor did it calm the fear that seemed to consume her. Nathaniel stroked her cheek.

"'Tis all right, Sarah. No one is there." His reassuring voice did not calm her.

Her eyes widened with fright.

"Is the bar across the door?" She gripped the edges of her pillow.

Concern shrouded his countenance.

"Yes. I checked it before we retired." He stroked her tense arm. "You are fraught with fear, Sarah." He pulled her closer to himself and stroked her eyebrow. "You have a fawn's eyes. So wide and lovely." He smiled. "Do try to be calm."

Instead, the weight of her terror forced tears from her brown eyes.

"Sarah, what is wrong?" He pulled her yet closer to himself, wrapping one large hand protectively across her shoulder while the other rested on their baby. "Do you fear having our child?"

She shook her head and tried to speak, but the words choked in her throat. Finally, she calmed enough to coax out a few garbled phrases.

"That man." The words almost spit out of her mouth. "That man."

Nathaniel's eyes narrowed.

"What man?" His face looked confused.

Bit by bit, Sarah revealed the tale that she'd never shared with another person — the story of the intruder who had attacked her sister so long ago.

She struggled to reveal the events of that night. Not quite seven years old at the time, Sarah was home alone with her sister Mary. Their mother was away attending a childbirth while Daniel and Aunt Prudence's servants were sleeping in the barn. Mary had gone to the door to answer a knock, thinking it was her mother. Instead, a deserter from the British army entered and attempted to rape Mary. Terrified, Sarah hid underneath the bed. At the first opportunity, she escaped and went for help. Daniel saved their lives and killed the intruder. But while Mary's bruises were more obvious, Sarah's unseen trauma from that night lingered in her spirit, causing moments of intense fear and panic. Those occasional episodes remained into adulthood.

"I've been afraid to be alone at night since that time." Sarah's voice sounded dull and exhausted from telling the story. "And sometimes, when I think there is a noise outside, I am certain that someone is there. Even when my mind tells me 'tis not so, my heart is consumed by the thought." Tears rolled down her face while her body quivered from the resurgence of the terror that hid in her spirit.

Nathaniel looked at her with shock and sadness. He stroked her dampened hair away from her forehead. "My poor Sarah."

She noticed his lip trembling in the moonlight shining through the window. "Nathaniel, I know 'tis warm, but can you hold me close?" She looked up at him, pleading for comfort.

"Of course." Drawing her to himself, he nuzzled her cheeks and forehead. Sarah could feel her husband's tears trickle onto her face, blending with her own.

"I love you, Sarah." His voice broke. He continued to stroke her hair as she started to calm in his arms. Then an unexpected sound emerged from his lips. He began to sing softly to her. It was a warm, melodic sound that soothed her in the deepest depths of her despair.

> *"The Lord my shepherd is, I shall be well supplied,*
> *Since He is mine and I am His, what can I want beside?*
> *He leads me to the place, where heavenly pasture grows.*
> *Where living waters gently pass, and full salvation flows.*
> *If e'er I go astray, he doth my soul reclaim,*
> *And guides me in His own right way, for His most holy name.*
> *While he affords his aid, I cannot yield to fear;*
> *Though I should walk through death's dark shade, my shepherd's*
> *with me there."*

Nathaniel continued to caress her when he was finished singing.

Sarah had never felt so loved. Not only had God sent her such a caring husband with whom she felt safe to share her terrifying memory, but Nathaniel had sung her favorite song of comfort. And she had never even told him that "Aylesbury" was her favorite hymn.

24

Companion

*D*aniel stood at the edge of the drenched cornfield and pursed his lips.

We'll be fortunate to get half a yield this year.

His head drooping low, he sighed as he turned back toward his house. It was almost time to leave for the meetinghouse. He knew he needed to go to Sabbath service today, but his heart was not in it. He would rather make an attempt to harvest as much of the waterlogged corn as possible. Today was cloudy but free of rain — an overcast day as dreary and despondent as his spirits.

I'd best not raise the ire of the constable by working my field on the Sabbath. He pushed aside the bitter thought.

Trudging through the mud toward home, he looked up as he heard the voice of his youngest daughter in the distance.

He strained to see from a distance, but as he got closer to the child, his eyes widened with alarm.

"Get away from that dog!" Daniel screamed at the three-year-old.

Alice looked confused.

"Why, Papa? He's my friend." She continued to stroke the dog's muddied and disheveled fur.

Daniel approached his daughter with angry steps. His face hot and nostrils flaring, he grabbed Alice away from the dog. Setting her down several feet away, he picked up a rock and threw it at the thin animal. The canine scurried into the woods, tail tucked beneath her bony body.

"Mangy cur," Daniel muttered under his breath

Alice's lips trembled and abundant tears flowed down her cheeks.

"Papa." She spoke between sobs. "He is a sweet dog."

Daniel bent down to his daughter and put his large hands on her small shoulders.

"Alice, we cannot keep a dog. They eat far too much. Besides, they are dangerous."

She looked at him with pain-filled eyes. "He was kind to me."

Six-year-old Sally approached them. "Papa, that dog was hungry."

"Well now, there is the trouble, is it not? We have too many mouths to feed as it is." As soon as the words were out, he regretted their message. "That is not what I meant to say. We just do not have enough food to feed a mangy dog."

Sally looked at her father with pleading eyes.

"He is not mangy, Papa. And I will share my food with him."

"Enough, Sally. We will not keep a dog."

Sally looked forlornly at him, took her sister's hand without speaking, and walked back to the farmhouse.

Daniel watched his daughters walk away and felt a pang of guilt.

How could I say we have too many children to feed? Which one would I not choose to be in our family? God forgive me.

He knew God would forgive him, but could his daughters? He rubbed the back of his head and returned to the morning chores. He was almost finished feeding the pigs and he knew Mary would soon have everyone ready for Sabbath service. He measured out the corn for the swine, making sure he did not give too much.

"Wretched rain." He mumbled under his breath.

Mary walked out of the house carrying Ephraim. Daniel looked at his wife and made a vain attempt at smiling. The halfhearted grin did not go unnoticed by his wife.

"Your face looks as somber as those of your daughters, Daniel." Mary approached him, but Daniel turned away to stare off into the distance.

"We cannot keep a dog, Mary."

"They said you were upset and that we do not have enough food for a dog."

"Well, we do not. And we certainly do not need a wolf hanging around here."

"A wolf?" Mary's eyebrows raised.

"Well… it was not a wolf… but they are just the same." His mouth tightened in stubborn determination. Mary touched his face with tender fingers.

"Daniel, you know 'tis not the same." She drew his face to look at hers. "Do your memories of war cloud your thinking?" Her voice was soft and understanding but he pulled her hand down.

"Do not try to dissuade me, Missus Lowe. Dogs can be just as dangerous as wolves. And we do not have victuals to spare." He stepped away from his wife. "Where are the others? We will be late."

Mary's face turned red and she looked away.

"I shall call them." She returned to the house and reappeared a moment later with their seven children. Alice still struggled not to cry as her sister Polly held her hand. Prissy held Sally's hand and they all walked without speaking. The twins struggled to keep up behind their father's quick and determined steps. Despite Daniel's limp, he was moving faster today than usual.

The mile-long walk to the meetinghouse was quiet, except for the sound of the engorged river in the distance. The severe September storms had pushed the river levels out of their banks, and the rumble of water gave an ominous feel to an already overcast day.

Arriving at the meetinghouse, Daniel tipped his hat politely to neighbors and family members, but he spoke few words. He directed his family into their pew and sat down with a thud. His heart felt as heavy as his limbs.

He noticed Danny and James staring at him. He tried to appear lighthearted to his boys, but he knew his expression belied his feelings. The weight of feeding his large family while fearing the lack of provision overwhelmed him.

God, where are You? How will we make it through this winter? The flax crop was a complete loss. And now the corn is soaked before harvest. You said You would provide, but I see it not. Even the pigs look scrawny.

The singing began, stirring Daniel's despairing thoughts back to the service. He sang the lyrics without feeling, his voice stilted and dull. After the morning sermon was finished and they were dismissed for lunch, Daniel rose from his seat.

Hannah, Sarah, and Mary conversed together. Daniel noticed Mary occasionally looked at him with concern and hurt in her eyes. He wanted to set things right. He wanted to put his arms around her and feel like a confident, loving husband. But in truth, he felt like a failure.

Polly and Prissy set the blanket out on the damp ground, and Mary took out the simple lunch foods: bread, cheese, nuts, and some dried berries harvested from the woods. The salt pork was nearly gone and there would not be more until the next pig-killing in November. Everyone ate with enthusiasm except Daniel. He picked at the bread, putting small pieces into his mouth. The fresh dough tasted bitter to him.

"Are you not hungry, Daniel?"

He glanced at his wife whose wide green eyes filled with worry "Not so hungry. But the bread is delicious." He shifted on the blanket.

She looked downward and ate berries, one at a time.

After the meager meal was finished, Mary began to talk with Hannah, who had walked over to visit. The sisters-in-law, who had been close friends since childhood, stood together and chatted. Hannah's belly was getting larger and Daniel looked at his brother-in-law James in the distance, speaking with Nathaniel.

Daniel knew that James' fields had not been destroyed by the spring storm that devastated his flax field. And somehow, James had managed to harvest most of his corn before the heavy rains began. This knowledge only served to deepen Daniel's despair.

James manages with a large family, but he was born a farmer. He knows the land and the stock. I have neither his ability nor his natural foresight for farming. My lack of skills will be my family's ruination.

His despondent musings were interrupted by Mary's frightened plea.

"Where is Alice? I've looked everywhere for her and she's nowhere to be seen" Mary bit her lip and gripped her apron.

"I thought she was with Prissy." Panic rose in Polly's voice.

"She said she would relieve herself behind the meetinghouse," Prissy said, wide-eyed. "But when I went to find her, she was gone."

Daniel jumped to his feet.

"Danny, James, go look in the chestnut tree. She is always longing to climb it. If she is not there, look in the woods behind the meetinghouse." He fought back the panic in his thoughts and attempted to speak in a measured tone. "Sally, when did you last see her?"

Sally's lips quivered. "I do not know. Perhaps a few moments ago? She said she wanted to find some food in the woods."

Guilt gripped at Daniel's heart.

"Dear Lord, what have I done?" He looked off toward the woods, the section nearest the swollen river.

Mary's tears washed freely down her cheeks.

"Daniel," she sobbed. "The river." She looked at him with raw fear. "That river took my father's life."

By now, the whole town had gathered around the family as word of the missing child quickly spread.

Sarah put her arm around Mary, and Hannah gathered the young ones together.

"Children, sit on this blanket and we shall tell stories from the Bible." Hannah pulled her youngest daughter, Lydia, next to her under one arm, and held Sally Lowe under the other, attempting to comfort the distraught sister.

Daniel came over to Mary. His eyes filled with pain as he took her hands. "I will find our daughter." He kissed her trembling hands as he fought back his own tears. "I am so sorry. I know this is my fault." Daniel noticed Sarah stare at him quizzically but she did not say anything.

James gathered the men.

"Robert, you take a group to the west and search the woods. Tim, gather a few men and head for the north. Reuben, take the southern trail and spread out. Daniel, Nathaniel, and I will head east—toward the river. And remember, she will be frightened. Call her name over and over and then listen sharp. Alice is only three and has a small voice."

The men nodded in agreement, their faces somber. They set out without delay, determined to find the missing girl.

The women and older children gathered around Mary. They held hands and prayed that the child would be discovered unharmed.

Daniel heard them praying as he set out with his two brothers-in-law. *Dear Lord, please hear our prayers.*

He was beset with fear and guilt.

"This is completely my fault." He focused on the path while walking with James and Nathaniel.

"Your fault?" Nathaniel asked. "Pray tell, why?"

Daniel inhaled deeply and painfully. His throat constricted making his words unclear.

"Because... I said we had too many children to feed. I said it in anger — I did not mean it. But, of course, she does not know that. And now Alice thinks she must go to the woods to find food. I am a fool."

James stopped the hurried trio.

"Let us pray for God's guidance. He will lead our steps if we trust Him."

The men paused and prayed. Grief overwhelmed Daniel and he wept.

When James finished praying, he put his arm around his brother-in-law. "We shall find her, Daniel."

The muscles in Daniel's face twisted in pain. "Alice is named after my mother."

James looked at him with sympathy and repeated the encouraging words. "We shall find her. Come. Let us hasten."

The threesome headed east toward the roaring sound of the river. *Dear God, do not let her fall in.*

They sidestepped the numerous ferns in their path and slipped on a few wet rocks.

"Alice!" Despite their shouts, the thunder of the water a hundred yards ahead drowned out their voices.

On a normal trek through the woods, the searchers would have traversed the incline with ease. But today, their anxious hearts had all the men short of breath.

"What was that?" Nathaniel stopped abruptly.

"I heard nothing." James scanned the woods.

"I must be imagining. I thought I heard a dog bark."

He started to walk again but Daniel stopped him, hope filling his spirit for the first time.

"A dog, you say?" They all stopped again and called Alice's name, louder this time.

In the distance, they all heard it — the muffled bark of a dog.

The three men hurried toward the sound without speaking. The river was getting more thunderous in its tenor, and the men searched through the thick beech and chestnuts, looking for any sign of the child. As they approached the edge of the river, there upon a huge grey rock lay the large muddy dog from earlier that morning. The dog stared at them and wagged her tail. And curled up next to her was a sleeping Alice.

"Alice." Daniel cried the name more than spoke it.

He hurried over toward the child and picked her up with trembling hands. Her eyes opened and she looked around, bewildered and confused.

"Papa, I fell asleep." She rubbed her eyes and yawned.

"Yes." He smiled and wept. "Yes, you did." He clutched her to him.

Alice pushed back from his shoulder. "I looked for food but the dog stopped me. I got sleepy."

Nathaniel stepped up on the rock where the dog was lying. The disheveled animal put her ears back and thumped her tail. Nathaniel scratched behind her ear and she rolled over onto her back and wagged her tail faster. The rescuer stared down on the other side of the rock and looked at the others in amazement.

"One more step…" Nathaniel did not finish the sentence.

Daniel shivered at the thought of how near his daughter had come to falling over the rock — and into the raging river.

Thank you, Lord. I do not deserve Your mercy, but I am humbled and grateful.

"Papa, can we keep the dog? He's my friend." Alice placed small fingers on her father's face.

Daniel stared at the filthy, skinny animal.

"You have your mother's compassion, Alice." He smiled. "I must have looked this wretched when she found me. Yes, Alice. We can keep the dog."

He carried Alice over toward the rock and squatted down. She reached out toward the animal and the dog licked her fingers.

"Well… dog, I suppose you've earned your keep." Daniel took some bread from his pocket and put it in front of the starving animal. She eagerly swooped it into her mouth and swallowed it in one gulp. "You'd best come home with us now."

The dog responded to the word "home" and followed the three men. Daniel did not let go of Alice the entire walk home, nor the rest of the day except for allowing Mary to smother her lost daughter with kisses and admonitions to never go in the woods alone again.

The dog never left Daniel's and Alice's side the rest of the day. Alice decided to call her new dog Sunny.

"He kept me warm like the sun." She explained the name to her father that night while he tucked her into bed.

"Then Sunny it is." He touched Alice's nose playfully. Sally spoke up.

"Does she not know that Sunny is a she?" Sally had a wise, older sister look on her face.

"I am certain she will realize soon enough." Daniel brushed Sally's hair back from her forehead. His demeanor became serious. "Sally, I must apologize for my harsh words this morning. I was wrong to say what I did — about too many mouths to feed. Please forgive me."

Sally took her father's hand and kissed it. "I love you, Papa."

Daniel leaned over to kiss his daughter's cheek.

"I love you too, Sally. More than you will ever know."

He touched Alice's blonde head once more before releasing her to her nighttime slumber. Standing up from the bed the girls shared, he limped with weariness to the chair by the hearth. He sat down utterly exhausted and started to close his eyes — until he felt soft hair on his fingers. Looking down, Daniel saw Sunny resting her chin on his uninjured thigh. The dog stared up at her new master with liquid eyes.

The weight of the day's events flooded his emotions with repentance and relief. Looking down at the dog — an animal that had before now filled him with fear — he placed his hand on Sunny's head.

"Thank you." As tears of gratitude flowed from Daniel's eyes, the dog gratefully licked Daniel's hand.

ary watched Daniel shift in his chair by the hearth. She knew he was disappointed by a fruitless day of hunting — but he seemed unusually troubled.

"What is it, Daniel?"

He shook his head and frowned. "Would you not think that near a village called Deer Run, the bucks would be found in abundance?"

"Maybe they do not wish to be killed." Sally gave her six-year-old rationale to explain the situation.

Mary smiled at the girl. "Now that is sound reasoning, Sally." Mary added another log to the hearth. "At least the woodpile is not able to avoid the axe on its own."

Daniel did not smile at Mary's attempt to lighten the mood. He rubbed his jaw and his eyes looked pained.

"What weighs on you, Daniel?" Mary walked toward him and brushed his hair back from his damp brow. She noticed a few more gray hairs sprouting among his long dark brown locks. She kissed the top of his head.

"My tooth. It's pained me all day."

"Let me get you some hazelnut oil." Mary went to the medicine cupboard and poured some of the substance on an old cloth and brought it to her husband. "There now, bite down on this."

Putting the oily cloth against the tooth he bit down. He immediately stretched out his legs in pain and his hands clenched the arms of the wooden chair. Mary saw his eyes closed tight and she covered his hand with her own.

"I'm so sorry, Daniel." She had not seen him in this much pain since he'd been wounded in the war.

His hands relaxed and he looked at her with moist eyes.

"I will recover, I'm sure." He removed the cloth from his mouth. "I just need to get some sleep. The boys and I must rise before dawn. Those deer cannot hide from us forever." He rose from the chair and headed for their room.

Lord, please help him recover. Her silent prayer was followed by the girls arguing about which of them would get to hug Sunny first before going to bed.

"He likes me best," Alice cried.

"She likes all of us. And Sunny is a lass, not a lad!" Sally had her hands on her hips, lecturing the younger girl.

Mary looked at them with exasperation.

"Hush! To bed!" Mary ushered them over to their shared bed, where Polly and Prissy were already reading their books. Alice gave Sunny one last hug before jumping up on the straw-filled mattress. Mary covered the girls with several quilts.

"These should keep you all warm."

Prissy pulled away from Sally's feet.

"Your feet are freezing, Sally!"

Mary smiled at the four snuggled under the blankets.

"They shall warm up soon. Let us pray for your papa, that his tooth feels better."

All the girls closed their eyes and folded their hands in prayer.

"Dear Lord," Mary prayed. "Please watch over Papa and provide comfort in his time of need. We pray that you would help him sleep without pain — and provide relief for his tooth. Amen."

"Amen," all four girls echoed their response.

Mary leaned over to kiss each girl, and then walking over to the hearth, placed another thick log on the fire. She pulled the quilts higher over the twins' shoulders as they slept on the floor near the hearth.

"My exhausted hunters." She watched them sleep in peaceful repose.

They will be men soon. She sighed.

She patted Sunny on the head as the dog slept between the boys.

"Good night, sweet rescuer." The dog thumped her tail.

After checking that the door was barred, she went to their bedroom and quietly closed the door. Placing more wood on the smaller hearth in their room, Mary then checked on Ephraim, who was sound asleep in his cradle.

"Dear little one." She stroked his head with care so as not to disturb him.

Looking over at Daniel, she was relieved to see he was sound asleep in their bed.

Thank you Lord, for answering our prayer. Please bless him with sleep this night.

Removing her shawl and gown, she shivered as she crawled under the covers. She tried to fight the gnawing fear that beset her thoughts.

Please, dear Lord, heal his tooth.

She was asleep by the time her head reached the feather pillow.

Daniel awoke long before dawn, moaning in pain. Mary sat up in bed and hurried to get the rum. She brought the bottle to him and he shook his head with vehemance.

"I cannot drink spirits when I need to hunt."

"You cannot hunt when you are writhing in pain. Please, Daniel, drink."

He reluctantly took the bottle from her and swallowed a mouthful. Handing it back to her, he fell back onto the pillow and held his jaw, a look of hopelessness on his face.

"We shall never get through this winter. It's October already." Tears slipped from the corners of his eyes, as he tossed and turned from the persistent agony.

Mary looked at him with a resolute expression.

"Danny and James will hunt today. They know what to do — you've taught your sons well, Daniel."

He paused long enough to look at her in disbelief.

"They have never hunted alone before — not for deer." His voice sounded garbled from the swelling of infection.

"There is always a first time. You have often said so yourself." She looked at him with sympathy and kissed him before checking on the still-sleeping baby in the cradle. Mary threw her shawl over her linen night shift. Walking over to the door, she looked back at her still-writhing husband and hurried to wake the twins.

The twelve-year-olds were already up, serving themselves some of the simmering corn gruel from the kettle.

"Good, lads, you're already up. Your father is not well; his tooth vexes him sorely. Before you leave on the hunt — which you must do alone this time — go fetch Dr. Burk."

The boys looked at each other in surprise.

"Hunt deer alone?" Danny gulped down the last bites of gruel. "Come on, James. Let's hasten to the doctor's."

Before leaving with his brother, James looked with concern at his mother.

"Will Father be all right?"

Mary put on a brave smile. "I'm certain he will."

The boys left and Mary closed the wooden door as fast as she was able to keep out the cold morning air. Leaning back against the door, she closed her eyes and whispered a prayer that the certainty she had expressed to her sons would indeed be so.

She returned to her bedroom and dressed as fast as she could. She was grateful for the long woolen stockings bringing warmth to her freezing feet.

"Daniel." Sitting on the edge of the bed, she spoke in a soft voice so as not to wake Ephraim in the cradle. "I've sent for Dr. Burk."

Her husband's eyes flew open.

"No! We cannot afford to pay him." He slumped back down onto the bed, overwhelmed by the toothache. The rum, it seemed, had not even started to bring relief.

"We cannot afford to lose you, Daniel." Tears stung at her eyes. "The boys have already left to fetch him."

Standing, she walked with determination to the other room. The girls were beginning to awaken.

Mary gave some stale bread and milk to Sunny, who lapped up the offering.

"Polly, can you go milk Hepsibah for me? I'm waiting for the doctor to tend your father." Polly yawned and rubbed her eyes.

"Yes, Mother." The oldest girl put on her clothes and grabbed the milk bucket.

"Take Sunny with you. The sun has not yet risen."

Polly and Sunny went out the door to head for the barn. The other girls rose without enthusiasm from under the warm quilts and put on their garments as fast as their small hands could manage. Mary helped Alice tie her apron strings in the back.

"Where is Sunny?" The sleepy child yawned.

"She is helping Polly with the milking."

No sooner were the girls dressed than Danny and James burst through the front door, accompanied by Dr. Burk. The physician looked disheveled and had dark circles under his eyes. He looked at the bustling of activity in the Lowe home and spoke with admiration.

"I do not know how you accomplish all that you do, Mary. You have a fine family."

Mary thought she heard a hint of sadness in his voice. His eyes glistened with melancholy.

"Thank you, Robert. 'Tis a fine thing you have done to bring relief for my husband at such an hour. His tooth ails him much. I fear for his health."

"The boys told me of his distress. I've brought my tools. Hopefully, I can bring Daniel some relief. We had many soldiers in camp that suffered much of this ailment so I have experience in drawing teeth."

Mary shivered.

"Do as you must, Robert." She led him to the bedroom where Daniel lay. "I've given him some rum but to no avail." She fought back tears as she saw her husband moaning and grimacing in bed.

Dr. Burk rested his hand for a moment on hers.

"I'm certain I can help him, Mary." Removing his hand from hers, Dr. Burk strode to the patient's bedside and greeted Daniel. He was in too much pain to exchange pleasantries.

Ephraim awoke and Mary picked him up from his cradle and whisked the toddler from the room. She could not bear the thought of staying for a tooth extraction.

Mary sat down by the fire and began to nurse Ephraim. Polly had come in with the fresh bucket of milk and she began serving gruel and milk to her sisters. They were just beginning to eat the porridge when there came a loud scream from the bedroom.

They all jumped with fright. The four girls had wide, fearful eyes and Alice and Sally both started to cry.

"What is Dr. Burk doing to Papa?" Great tears fell from Sally's eyes.

Mary's mouth trembled despite her attempt to appear brave.

"He is drawing his tooth. This will make Papa better." She spoke matter-of-factly, but her heart broke for Daniel.

Lord, please relieve his pain!

Mary sniffed back the tears begging to emerge. She was relieved that no more screams were heard from the bedroom.

After several more anxious moments, Dr. Burk came out of the room, his hands bloodied and shaking.

"That was a nasty one." He spoke to no one in particular.

Before the doctor turned her way, Mary pulled her gown over her breast and sat Ephraim up in her lap.

"Will… will he be all right?" The words came out with difficulty.

"Yes, he should be fine. I've packed the hole in his mouth with some linen that you can remove tomorrow, and I'll leave you some medicinals he should rinse with twice a day. 'Twill not hurt to keep giving him rum when the pain is this severe." He looked at Mary. "He'll do well. What husband could not thrive when he is so well loved?" The doctor gave a melancholic smile and started for the door.

Mary stood, still holding her youngest.

"About the payment, Robert, I…"

The doctor put up his hand to stop her.

"You already paid excessively with the generous yardage of linen. I do believe you have a credit with us." He smiled and briefly touched her hand. "Go see to your husband." He put on his felt hat and hurried outdoors. Mary ran to the open door.

"Thank you, Robert." Her voice carried to him on the wind. He turned and tipped his hat to her.

Closing the door, she looked at four sets of worried eyes.

"Dr. Burk says Papa will be just fine. And I believe him. Polly please feed Ephraim some gruel while I attend to your father."

She set the sleepy toddler down and Prissy walked the boy over to the table.

Mary tiptoed into the bedroom and looked at her weakened husband lying on the bed. He looked at her with tortured eyes. He tried to speak but she held one finger against her lips.

"Do not speak, Daniel." Stroking his hair back from his head, she looked at his bloodied cheek. "I'm so sorry you are in such pain."

Tears began to pour from her eyes. Daniel reached up and wiped them away. He tried to speak to her, but the packing in his mouth prevented him.

"Let me get the basin to clean your face." She gathered a basin and warm water from the small kettle over their fire. She gingerly patted away the drying blood, and he winced when she got too close to the painful area. "I'll stop now. We can clean it better later."

Daniel held her fingers to his lips and kept them there until he slept. She slowly pulled her fingers away and he did not awaken. She kissed his head and pulled the quilts up to his chin for warmth. "Sleep well, my love."

Tiptoeing to the door, she left the room and prayed a grateful word of thanksgiving to the God who provided for her husband's care.

⌒◦

It was late afternoon before Mary heard the boys return from their day of hunting. Their voices were excited and Mary's heart filled with hope.

Opening the front door, she gasped. There on an old blanket lay the largest buck she'd ever seen.

"Danny! James! A fine hunt, I see!" She could not stop smiling as she trudged over through the strong wind, holding her shawl close about her shoulders. She stared at the unmoving creature, amazed at its beauty even in death. There was one shot from a musket ball near its heart.

"He went down quickly. We did not need to pursue." James seemed to stand taller as he spoke.

"Well done, boys."

"How is father?" Danny blew on his hands to warm them.

"Better." Relief filled Mary's voice. "He still rests in bed. Come tell him your victory before you dress the carcass."

The boys dragged the dead animal toward the barn, each pulling a corner of the blanket.

Mary shivered and went back indoors.

"Did they get one, Mother?" Polly was anxious for the news.

"Yes, Polly. A very large one."

The girl smiled in relief and returned to her reading.

Walking into the bedroom, Mary could not hold back her joy.

"Daniel." Her voice whispered with excitement. He opened his sleepy eyes.

"Such news!" Before she could speak further, there was a knock on the door and the excited twins entered.

"You tell him, James. 'Twas your ball that got him." Danny grinned from ear to ear.

James appeared hesitant at first, but the excitement was too much to contain.

"I shot a deer, Father — a buck almost as big as this room. We shall have meat for weeks now." The boy stood there proudly.

A weak smile appeared on Daniel's pale face. He spoke with difficulty, but all three understood his garbled message. "Well done, lads."

"Thank you, Father." James gave a slight bow.

"How do you fare, sir?" Danny looked with concern at the dried blood caked on his father's face.

Daniel tried to smile but then grimaced. Mary spoke for him.

"He fares far better than this morning." She grinned at the two boys.

The recovering patient motioned for the boys to come over to him. With weakened arms, he pulled both boys down and hugged them.

Releasing his grip, they stood up.

"Thank you." Daniel's speech was somewhat distorted, but his meaning was clear.

"You are welcome, Father. Rest now." Danny said and the two boys walked toward the door.

They look so much taller. Mary's heart swelled with pride.

Daniel took Mary's hand and squeezed it. He gave a slight smile and brought her fingers to his lips. She took her other hand and stroked his cheek that was not in pain.

"We are blessed with the most wonderful sons. They are just like their father." She nuzzled his cheek. "You'd best get well soon, my husband. I want to kiss those lips again."

Looking at him with a sly glance, she got up to leave. He teasingly pulled her down toward him and fondled her with clumsy hands. Mary laughed in surprise and pulled away.

"Is the rum clouding your judgment, Mr. Lowe? I have work to do. And you have healing to do. We shall discuss your passions another time." Mary giggled as she removed his hands. Smoothing the folds of her gown, she walked to the door. Reaching for the doorknob, she turned back to her husband.

"I do love you, Daniel — most passionately."

"I love you, Mary."

He closed his eyes and drifted off again into slumber.

Mary stared for a moment at the man who had won her heart so many years ago. It still belonged completely to him.

"Thank you, Lord." She blew him a kiss and closed the door so he could rest.

26

Thanksgiving

The observance of Thanksgiving on 17 November 1791, was a time of reflection, gratitude, and joy. But this holiday was tinged with sadness, for it had been a tragic year. Sarah knew her mother still mourned the loss of her husband, Myles, and James and Hannah still grieved for their beloved infant, Samuel. But there were new births expected soon, and Sarah was filled with hope and thankfulness for God's provision and blessings. After a few hours of singing and worshipping at the meetinghouse, the Thanksgiving morning service concluded.

Sarah paced herself going down the steps of the building. She could no longer see her shoes past her large belly, so she gripped the railing for support. Her baby was due the end of next month and walking anywhere was becoming more difficult.

"Let me help you, Sarah." Nathaniel cupped her elbow and she gave him a grateful glance.

"I never thought steps could be so difficult." She breathed a sigh of relief when she reached the ground. The baby began to kick and she grasped her belly. "I believe this little one enjoyed the adventure down the stairs."

Nathaniel's brows furrowed. "Do you want me to get the wagon to take you home?"

"No, I am fine, and the exercise is helpful for my birthing. That is what Mother says." Sarah had never been more thankful that her mother was a midwife. Since they shared the same home, Widow Eaton would be with her pregnant daughter at a moment's notice when the time came.

James and Hannah walked over toward them.

"We will be over soon for the feast. We need to pick up the breads and sundry foods that Hannah has prepared." James viewed Sarah with a jovial demeanor. "Now, I do not wish either of you ladies to interrupt our meal with a trivial excuse like, 'I believe my birth pains are starting.' At least wait until the feasting is over, I pray." He put his arms around his very pregnant wife and hugged her sideways.

Hannah and Sarah looked at each other and shook their heads. "Perhaps my husband would prefer to bear the child." Hannah grinned and poked James in his side.

He backed away. "No thank you. I shall leave the difficult work to you. God knew what he was doing by entrusting this to the fair sex. I am certain I would fare poorly under the circumstances. I salute you ladies in your accomplishment." He stood at attention and saluted Hannah and Sarah.

"Well said, James." Nathaniel put his arm around Sarah. "And we look forward to our Thanksgiving feast." He tipped his hat to the two and turned toward the Eaton farm. When they were out of earshot of James, Nathaniel spoke. "James is certainly jovial about the childbirth. I am terrified."

She looked up at him with sympathy. "I was unaware you felt that way." She squeezed his hand as he took hers and held it tight. "Do not fear, Nathaniel. All will be well." She smiled at him as they continued the walk home. "James has always been a jester. That is how he manages his own fears. I know Hannah's childbirth weighs on his heart as well."

They soon caught up with her mother, who had left the meetinghouse as soon as the service was over. There was much cooking to do and she was never one to dawdle. As they approached, the look of deep concentration on her parent's face told Sarah the meal was on her mother's mind.

"I must hasten to get the turkeys cooking over the fire. I hope they are safe in the pen we caught them in." The widow's brow furrowed.

"I am certain the rocks and wood I put over the opening will keep the wolves out, Mother Eaton. I'll slaughter them as soon as we arrive home."

"Thank you, Nathaniel. That will help me greatly." Her mother's steps became faster and she soon outdistanced the couple once again.

Sarah's face chilled from the cold and her steps grew slow and plodding. "I will be grateful to get home." She breathed hard but smiled at her husband. He pulled on her arm, causing her to stop.

"I love you, Sarah Stearns."

"And I love you, Nathaniel." He kissed her with moist lips and their embrace lingered. As he held her close, Sarah giggled at her unborn child who began kicking at his father.

"I say, little one, I can take a hint!" Nathaniel laughed and put his hand on Sarah's belly. The child continued to pummel his feet against Nathaniel's hand. "This is astonishing." He shook his head in wonder.

"'Tis a miracle, is it not? That our love can bring this new life?"

He wrapped his arms around Sarah and kissed her hair, which was falling out of her cap.

"Yes, 'tis a miracle," he whispered near her ear and she closed her eyes.

"Your kisses still melt my heart." She touched his cheeks and drew his lips to hers. Their kiss lasted only a moment as the baby kicked him again. Nathaniel grinned.

"I guess that is the order to halt! We'd best go celebrate Thanksgiving." They both smiled and returned home.

Arriving at the homestead, Sarah saw her mother chopping vegetables. "Sarah, can you begin the sweet cake?"

"Of course, Mother."

Nathaniel gave her hand one last squeeze before heading to the turkey pen. She watched him leave and once again admired his handsome ruggedness. She sighed. "I am so blessed."

Her mother stopped the chopping for a moment and stared at her daughter. "Yes you are, Sarah. And I am so thankful that you have such a loving consort. Not all husbands are this way. You are truly blessed."

Sarah fought back warm tears. "Thank you, Mother." She put on her apron and began to prepare the dessert.

In a few short hours, the smell of the roasting turkey began to fill the Eaton home. Sarah heard the voice of her sister, Mary, approaching outside. She was telling her children that Sunny needed to remain outdoors for the meal. Sarah smiled and went to the doorway.

"You can bring Sunny in. I've long wanted a dog." Her hand rested on her belly and the eyes of the Lowe children widened.

"Aunt Sarah! You are so large!" Sally stared at her in amazement.

"Sally!" Daniel scolded the girl.

"That is all right, Daniel. She merely speaks what the rest are thinking. Even you!" Sarah laughed.

"What?" Daniel's voice feigned surprise. "Far be it from my lips to ever speak such a thought."

"Well, you may not reveal it, but you are thinking as much. Welcome, everyone."

The mood was jovial and when James and Hannah arrived with their four children, the space was limited but the laughter abundant.

Danny and James sauntered over near the hearth. They leaned over the food their grandmother was preparing and sniffed in obvious pleasure. She gave them a stern look.

"Do not touch the food, young men. It will be ready forthwith." She smiled. "Go. Make yourselves useful. Set the tableboard for me."

Sarah handed the spoons, napkins, and wooden plates to the twins and they set them on the table.

"Thank you, gentleman." Sarah looked at Mary in astonishment. "They are almost men," she whispered to her sister.

Mary gave her a knowing nod. "They will be thirteen come spring. The other day, Danny's voice gave a crack." Mary kept her voice low.

"Where have the years gone?" Sarah shook her head in disbelief.

"Time to sup!"

The announcement from Sarah's mother was met with cheers.

Sarah's hunger stirred when she saw the fowl had roasted to perfection on the twisted twine in the hearth, and Nathaniel sliced a chunk of turkey for each person. Guests held out their plates to him, their lips moistened in anticipation.

Sarah handed each a sweet potato cooked in the ashes and her mother served each person the turnips, cabbage, and carrots from the large kettle. Mary sliced the bread she and Hannah had brought and Hannah placed dried pumpkin on each plate. The children sat on long benches that were high enough that a few of their short legs were left dangling.

All the adults and now Danny and James sat at the tableboard. Before anyone could indulge, they awaited the blessing for the meal. As the oldest male member of the clan, James Thomsen led the prayer.

"Our Almighty Father in heaven, Creator of the universe, we most humbly offer our sincerest gratitude for these abundant blessings You have bestowed on Your unworthy servants. You have truly caused the earth to yield its plentiful increase to our stores in order to supply us with our necessaries and comforts.

"Above all, we are grateful for the enjoyment of our civil rights and liberties, and, most especially, for the gospel of Jesus Christ. May we all bow to the scepter of Our Lord Jesus Christ and the whole earth be filled with His glory. Amen."

"Amen," everyone replied, looking up from the prayer.

"Let us sup, then." James picked up his spoon as a signal for all to begin. The family needed no further prompting.

Few words were spoken as everyone ate.

"Peter, eat with your mouth closed." James looked sternly at his seven-year-old. The red-haired boy giggled and covered his mouth.

"Mother, Alice is kicking me." Sally and Alice always seemed to be at odds.

"Alice, please keep your legs still." Mary gave a warning look to her youngest daughter.

"I did not kick, Mother. My legs don't hold still." Alice had a frustrated look on her face.

"It must be a burden to be so short, Alice. Fear not — your legs will grow and begin to stay still." Daniel smiled at her and Alice grinned with a mouthful of sweet potatoes showing.

Mary sighed. "'Tis a constant battle to teach manners."

"Lucky for you, James and I have always been so well mannered, right Mother?" Danny wore his false angelic look.

Daniel gave him a doubtful smile. "Is this so, Danny? Why, just the other day I remember —"

"All right, Father," Danny quickly interjected, his face turning red. "Perhaps not always so well mannered."

James jabbed his brother in the side. "Nice try, Danny."

Sarah laughed. "I was always the one getting into mischief, Danny, so I understand."

"And always saying the wrong thing." Her mother grinned at her.

Sarah blushed. "Yes, much to everyone's embarrassment."

Nathaniel looked amused. "Is this so? Pray, someone tell me a story." He put his arms around her shoulders.

Daniel grinned from ear to ear. "I remember a good one. And it was at my first Thanksgiving meal here."

Sarah covered her eyes in embarrassment. "I know what you are going to say, Daniel." Sarah turned even warmer with embarrassment.

Mary intervened. "Perhaps if I tell the shorter version, it will be easier on my sister." Thus Mary began to tell the tale of then six-year-old Sarah announcing that when the men returned from war on furlough, nine months later the wives were calling for the midwife. Sarah had no idea the implication of her words, but nineteen-year-old Mary was terribly embarrassed — especially in front of her new friend Daniel.

Daniel continued the story. "And then when her mother implied this was not proper conversation in front of a gentleman, Sarah apologized, saying that men did not understand this was the way of it. I thought I would choke on the cake!"

James Thomsen laughed so hard he almost spit out a piece of bread. "Sarah, you are a treasure."

Nathaniel's eyes crinkled with mirth. "Yes, she is a treasure." He kissed her and squeezed her shoulder.

James wiped tears of laughter from his eyes. "So, Sarah, have you come to understand the meaning of this story yet?"

She sighed and felt her cheeks turn warm. "Yes, dear brother." She placed her hand on her belly. "I believe that should be obvious." She smiled despite her self-consciousness.

Her older brother abruptly stopped laughing and gazed with fondness at his little sister. "I did miss a great deal of your childhood, did I not? So many years at war..." He stared into the distance with a sober expression.

Hannah took his hand. "We all missed you so, James. We knew why you needed to be gone. And we are so proud of you." She leaned over and kissed her husband.

He smiled, but the joy did not reach his sad eyes. "Thank you, Hannah, but those years with all of you are gone forever. That is what I regret the most." He took a sip of wine from his tankard and sighed.

Everyone was quiet for several moments. It was Widow Eaton who broke the silence. "Let us not dwell on the sad past, but on our joyous and bountiful future." She held up her tankard of wine. The others raised theirs as well.

"Hear, hear!" The chorus rang out from all.

Sarah looked at her husband. "To our joyous future with our new family," she whispered in his ear and nuzzled his ear lobe. Sarah heard his sharp intake of air as he grinned in pleasure.

"Hear, hear," he whispered back, before meeting her lips with his own.

27

Discovery

*S*arah's hands trembled as she read the letter, while her unborn child kicked at the parchment resting on her large belly.

He must sense my excitement! She placed one hand on the baby and stroked him. Staring with disbelieving eyes at the note delivered just moments before by a post rider, Sarah read the words again. Her head spun with excitement as she struggled to take in the full impact of the message:

2 December 1791

To Mr. Nathaniel Stearns, Esquire:

It is my sincere hope that this letter brings you some measure of comfort in the search for your father, a Sgt. Benjamin Stearns, formerly of the Continental forces that fought so bravely for the freedom of this nation.

I recently received your letter of summer last, after it had been through several hands. It was at first delivered to the captain of militia in Charlestown before wending its way through several readers. At last it has found its way to my desk. I hope I can be of assistance. I was the physician in charge at West Point when we received word of the terms of surrender, thus ending that long, bloody war. I do remember that his son — that would be you — was stationed at West Point as well, but I believe you had already returned to your home, honorably discharged.

An incident occurred during the celebration that followed the announcement of our victory. Several soldiers, with too much rum I daresay, carried on with amusement by discharging the last supplies of powder from their muskets. This folly, however, turned to near tragedy as one of the balls hit your father in the right shoulder. He barely survived the massive wound. It took him many months to recover. I personally transported him by wagon across the state to a physician in Boston who I deemed most suitable to aid in his recovery. And recover he did, but not without being crippled for life. He has lost complete use of his right arm and hand.

Though I regret to have to be the bearer of these sad tidings, I am happy to tell you that your father is alive.
I invited him to remain at my home and work for me but he said he would not be beholden any further. The last time I saw him he was indentured to another physician in Boston. His servitude was purchased at auction. I inquired of this physician when your father's year of bondage would be complete, and the doctor said that he had purchased him through the end of December. After that, I know not where his habitation will be.

I once inquired of him when he was under my care if he wanted to be returned to his home. He said that his family no longer wanted him. I took this to mean that you knew of his injuries and did not wish to bear the burden of supporting a cripple. Had I known you were searching for him, I would most certainly have made correspondence with you. Please forgive my lack of communication. I fear this has been a tremendous loss for you, as you wondered where your father had been these last eight years.

Since there is some concern on his part regarding your acceptance of his present condition, I will not inform him of your inquiry, lest he be frightened into hiding. Unfortunately, this is not an unusual response for our veterans dealing with injuries that have maimed them. However, after 31 December, I can no longer be certain of his whereabouts. Perhaps you can come to Boston and advise him yourself of your affections, should you be able to overcome the misery of his affliction. Please contact me upon your arrival, should you wish to come.

Your most humble servant,

Dr. Thomas Hardesty, retired captain, Army of the United States of America

Sarah put the letter on the table and stared out the window through the golden curtains. There was a smattering of snow outdoors on the ground, and the sun shone brightly today, the streams of light filtering through the linen.

He is alive. Sarah was stunned at the revelation. Her heart raced with joy, yet the news was fraught with turmoil. He had been seriously injured and was now crippled. Worst of all, he had assumed his family would not want him.

Tears stung at Sarah's eyes. All these years of her husband hoping his father would return, only to discover he was hiding from his family.

She heard Nathaniel approach from the barn. The squeaking of his shoes on the snow indicated how cold it was this morning. Pushing open the wooden door, he grinned as he saw his wife sitting near the table. His face was chapped and red from the cold.

"I had to blow on my hands many times to warm them up enough for Susie. Even then she complained. I think she was hoping your mother would appear." He set the bucket of milk on the table. "I heard the rider approach. News from your aunt?"

Sarah did not know where to begin.

"Please sit, Nathaniel."

Her husband's eyes narrowed. "Is all not well?"

"You must read this." She handed the parchment to her husband with trembling fingers. He hesitated and then took the paper from her. His eyes scrolled down a few sentences until he came to the part about his father being injured.

"No!" He stood up and walked toward the window for better light.

"Blasted rum! What fools!"

He kept reading, occasionally sniffing and wiping impatiently at his nose. He stopped and looked at her with disbelief.

"He is alive! I knew it." He burst into tears and Sarah rushed to his side. Wrapping her arms around him, she held him and stroked his face. When he was able to get control of his emotions, he put his hands on her face. "You were the only one who believed with me. Thank you, Sarah." Wiping the moisture from his cheeks, he kept his arm around her while he resumed reading the letter. His arms trembled and she could feel them grow tense with the rest of the news.

"We did not want him? What was he thinking? What is he thinking? How could he desert us like this?" He released his wife, his rage forcing him to put her at a distance from his anger. "And now he is a bond slave? When he could be home with us — with his family that loves him? How could he?"

Nathaniel paced in front of the hearth. Sarah saw the veins in his neck bulging and his face bright red. Finally, when the emotion of it all seemed to overwhelm him, he sat on the chair and hid his face in his hands. His muddled words were swollen with emotion.

"He is alive." Great sobs flowed from within, a reserve of grief that had built up for many years. At last, his belief that his father was alive had proven true.

Sarah ambled toward Nathaniel and rubbed his stooped shoulder. After a moment he looked up with reddened eyes.

"I must go to Boston."

"I know."

They sat in silence at dinner that evening. The only sounds were the spoons on the plates and Nathaniel's occasional gulps of cider. Her mother was away at a birthing, so Sarah took advantage of this opportunity to say what was on her mind. She took in a deep breath and ventured forth with the words she knew her husband would decry.

"Nathaniel. You must take me with you to Boston."

He stopped eating mid-bite and seemed unable to swallow the food still in his mouth.

"You cannot mean this, Sarah. That is not possible."

"But it is. I can ride Father Eaton's mare and you can ride the gelding. I can do this."

Nathaniel shook his head, wearing a wry smile.

"Sarah, have you taken leave of your senses? 'Tis one hundred miles from Springfield to Boston. We would have to cross the river. And you are with child and soon to birth. This is not something we can even discuss."

"Catherine Greene went to war with her husband when she was great with child." Sarah's lips thinned in determination.

"Who?"

"Caty Greene — the wife of General Nathanael Greene, hero of the Continental army during the Revolution. I read the account in the Boston newspaper. She traveled long distances — in the middle of the war — to be with her husband. If she can do it, then so can I!" Sarah folded her arms across her belly and gave her husband a self-satisfied nod.

"I am not Caty Greene's husband. I am yours, and you will stay home and be safe." His look was as determined as Sarah's.

Her mouth began to quiver. "I can do this. Our child will not come till the end of this month. I am strong, I can ride." Her voice rose in panic. "And you promised me!" Tears flowed down her cheeks as she envisiond being left alone, once again.

"I promised you?" He scratched his head.

"Yes!" She could barely get the words out. "You promised — when we first wed — that you would never leave me alone."

He shook his head and tried to grasp her meaning.

"But I am not leaving you alone... well, just for a few days... just until I can find Father and convince him that his family wants him. I shall hasten home forthwith. I shall return before the baby comes." He patted her shoulder as if his words would convince her.

Sarah snapped her shoulder away from him and stood up.

"You promised!" She could not continue, but waddled toward the bedroom to lay on the bed. She was inconsolable. When Nathaniel walked in after her, he appeared confused and anxious.

"Sarah." His voice was low and soothing. "How can I take you with me? 'Tis near winter. It would take several days and I know not what dangers might ensue. I cannot let anything happen to you." He touched her convulsing shoulder.

She turned to him, stricken with grief.

"And I cannot let you go without me. You cannot leave me alone." Her voice was high pitched and pained. He lifted her up and held her. After a long silence, he spoke.

"What will your mother say if I tell her I am taking you?" His voice was subdued and unsteady.

Sarah pulled away from him, a glimmer of hope and relief replacing her despair. "If you assure her I will be safe, she must relent. You are my husband. She must abide by your wishes." She touched his cheek. "I cannot let you leave me. I need you."

He held her close again and sighed deeply.

"Only God knows how we will do this. But I shall keep my promise."

28

Planning

Nathaniel felt the anger emanating from Widow Eaton as she sat beside him at the meetinghouse. The muscles in her arms were so rigid they felt like pieces of wood resting against his own. Her lips were frozen in a thin tight line, and her eyes narrowed and stared straight ahead at the minister in the pulpit. The tension was unbearable.

If anything happens to Sarah or the baby, she will never forgive me. Nathaniel took in a deep breath and slowly exhaled. Sitting on his opposite side, Sarah responded to his sigh by smiling and squeezing his hand. He tried to appear confident, but in truth he was terrified. He attempted a brave smile and squeezed her hand in return. *God help me.*

It seemed as if Sabbath service would never end, yet it finally dismissed for the noon meal. Widow Eaton stood up from the pew and, with a stern countenance, turned away from Nathaniel and Sarah without speaking. His mother-in-law found someone else to chat with while Nathaniel escorted Sarah out the door. Since the weather had gotten colder, the churchgoers were invited to the Beal home for food and rest in between services. While he was grateful for the warm location to eat, the last person Nathaniel wished to see today was Richard Beal.

Won't he think I am a fine husband, taking my wife who is with child on such a long journey. Maybe I am a fool.

Still, Sarah's words had sunk like an anchor around his heart. He had indeed promised her he would not leave her alone, were it in his power. Yet there he was, planning a journey of one hundred miles, ready to leave her behind. The look of hurt and betrayal in her eyes still stung. Sarah clung to his arm as if her life depended on it. It was as if she were afraid if she let go, he might leave without her. He covered her hand with his and squeezed her fingers.

"Let me help you down the stairs, love." He guided her awkward steps as she managed to descend without incident. He heard someone from behind and turned to see Daniel and Mary approaching. Their faces seemed tight with worry.

"Sarah, surely our mother misunderstands your intent." Mary's eyes narrowed. "You cannot mean that you intend to accompany Nathaniel to Boston. That is impossible."

Daniel was silent, but his eyes were dark and serious.

Sarah drew her mouth into a determined line. "'Tis quite possible, Mary. I intend to leave with him early tomorrow. I shall be back before our child is born."

"But Sarah, this is dangerous. And should the child come early, what will you do? Mother cannot go with you because Hannah's birthing is near." Mary looked helplessly at Daniel.

Without speaking, Daniel took Nathaniel's arm and drew him away from the group. When they were alone, he glared at Nathaniel.

"Why are you doing this? You know the dangers of travel, especially in winter. Why risk losing both Sarah and your child? You could return here faster if you went alone."

Nathaniel's eyes bore into his brother-in-law's and he spoke with measured words.

"Have you ever made a promise to your wife?" The question appeared to take Daniel by surprise. Nathaniel put his hands on both hips and locked eyes with him.

Daniel folded his arms across his chest. "Yes. Yes, I have. What does this have to do with it?"

"Then you must know how important it is to keep that promise." Nathaniel took a deep breath. "I never imagined that this situation would occur — a trip to Boston in winter, Sarah ready to birth — yet I promised her I would never leave her alone were it in my power. As complicated as this is, it is in my power to take her. I fear, should I leave her home, she will fare far worse for my betrayal." He swallowed with difficulty. "I do not know if she could ever forgive me." Tears welled in his eyes, and he wiped them away just as fast as they appeared. "And should anything happen to Sarah or our child, I will never be able to forgive myself."

Daniel's eyes softened. "I see." He paused in thought and rubbed his forehead, one hand on his hip. "So what is your plan then?"

Nathaniel took in a deep breath. "Sarah will ride the mare and I the gelding. There are taverns and ordinaries on the road where we can obtain victuals and lodge at night. I have a little money saved up — not a great deal, but it should suffice. It will take a few days, but we can do this." He looked at Daniel with fear in his eyes. "And should the child come early, we shall have to find a midwife." Despite the cold, sweat formed on his forehead.

Daniel patted Nathaniel's upper arm. "We shall pray that does not occur." The two men turned and returned to the family group. Nathaniel glanced at his mother-in-law, but she quickly averted her eyes. She had not spoken to him since they made the announcement about the trip the day before.

They all walked in silence toward the Beal home. On any other cold Sabbath day, Nathaniel's appetite would be hearty. Today, the ache in his stomach made him feel ill.

Approaching the large Beal cabin, Nathaniel looked up and saw Richard staring at him and Sarah. He could not read the look in Richard's eyes. Was it hatred? Jealousy?

Now he knows Sarah chose the wrong husband. Perhaps he's right.

Richard approached the couple, tipping his hat in greeting.

"Good day, Nathaniel. Sarah." He paused for a moment before speaking again. "Nathaniel, may I speak alone with you for a bit?"

Sarah looked at her husband, her eyes widening. Nathaniel tried to read Richard's expression but remained perplexed.

"Sarah, go ahead inside. I shall be there forthwith."

Accompanied by Mary, she waddled toward the cabin, looking back once at Nathaniel before entering the front door.

The two men stood together awkwardly for a moment.

"Come to the barn with me." Richard strode with purpose toward the large wooden structure.

Still confused, Nathaniel followed Sarah's spurned suitor with caution. Walking into the barn, he was greeted by the familiar smells of cows and horses. Richard walked past several stalls before he stopped and turned around. He waited for Nathaniel.

"Here." Richard pointed into the stall. "My sleigh. It will get you to Boston in three days unless the snow gets heavy. Sarah will be safer in this and you will make better time."

Nathaniel would have been less surprised if Richard had set upon him with a weapon. He was speechless. When he found his voice, it was hesitant and suspicious. "So you mean to assist Sarah and I in our journey?" Nathaniel's eyes narrowed.

"I know what you think of me, and I hold no affection for you either, but I am concerned about Sarah — and her baby." Richard mumbled the last words with difficulty. "Sarah has been my friend since we were children. Her decision to marry you does not change that. I do not wish any harm to befall her."

Nathaniel stared at Richard. For the first time, he noticed the pained expression in the man's eyes. He felt a pang of sympathy for him.

"I am grateful, but I've never driven a sleigh before."

"Then I shall teach you. When Sabbath is over at dusk, I shall train you in guiding the reins. My mare was shod with calks at the smithy not three days ago. The shoes will grip the ice to lessen the danger of her falling." When Nathaniel did not answer, Richard shifted his feet and seemed impatient. "Well, man, what say you? Shall we freeze out here whilst you decide?"

A slight grin of relief drew up the corners of Nathaniel's mouth.

"I say, yes. And gratefully so, sir."

"Good. Let us sup before the victuals are cold."

The two men walked side by side toward the cabin where the woman they both cared about awaited their return.

29

Journey

*D*awn was still an hour away, but Nathaniel's eyes were wide open. He had slept little the night before.

He turned to look at Sarah, who slept soundly beside him. She lay on her side, her mouth occasionally twitching into a slight smile, her long blonde hair draped across her shoulders like a silken shawl threatening to slip off at the slightest movement. She looked so calm — strikingly dissimilar to the turmoil in his own mind.

Her eyes fluttered open as if sensing his gaze. As she focused on him she smiled and reached out to touch his face. He took her hand and kissed her fingers.

"Good morning, love." He held her fingers close to his face.

She drew closer to him with difficulty, her belly catching on her shift that tightened across their unborn child. Sarah snuggled into his arms and he wrapped himself around her, kissing her hair. "I am the luckiest wife in the world." She yawned.

"And why say you that?"

"Because," she said, "my husband loves me so. So much that he keeps his promises to me."

A pang of guilt crossed Nathaniel's thoughts.

And what if my promise comes to a dreadful end?

As if reading his thoughts, Sarah looked up at him, still surrounded by his arms. "I shall be fine, Nathaniel. God will watch over us."

He kissed her hair again, pushing the worry to the back of his mind.

"Yes. Yes He will." He hugged her once more before moving away from her and sitting up under the quilts. He rubbed the sleep from his eyes.

"I must feed the livestock once more before we leave. Your brother will take care of them after that." Slipping out from under the warm covers, he donned his breeches and smoothed his dark blond hair back with his fingers before tying the strands back with a ribbon.

"You are so handsome, Mr. Stearns." She cast a flirtatious grin his way. His cheeks grew warm, as they always did when she admired his appearance.

Leaning over, he planted a warm moist kiss on her lips and stroked her cheek. "Stop flirting with me, Missus Stearns. I am a married man." With a mischievous wink, he headed out their bedroom door.

Mother Eaton stood stirring the gruel over the hearth. She wiped a fresh tear from her cheek and sniffed. Seeing Nathaniel, she paused in her cooking and looked squarely at her son-in-law. "You will not reconsider?"

Nathaniel walked with hesitation toward his mother-in-law.

"Mother Eaton, you know this is not an easy decision. But my word is my bond — as much as my vows to honor and keep her on our wedding day were. I cannot betray her trust. Believe me, I wish she would agree to stay here with you, but you know that once her mind is made up, she will not relent." He paused for a moment. "I love your daughter, Mother Eaton. I will make certain that she is safe under my care." The resolve in his own voice surprised him.

Mother Eaton was silent for a moment. "Then you must promise me something. Should this child decide to be born early, you will find her a proper midwife." Her eyes were wide with pain and fear.

"Yes, Mother Eaton. I promise."

She wiped the rest of the tears from her eyes. "You and Sarah must eat a hearty meal before you leave. I will have it ready when you return from the barn. And here." She took a small pouch from her pocket and handed it to him. "This is for you and Sarah."

He took the leather satchel and looked inside. "Mother Eaton! Coins... there must be several dollars here. Where —"

"My women in Williamston often pay this way. Their husbands are quite generous. You must take this to provide for Sarah's needs... and yours."

"I don't know how to thank you, Mother Eaton."

She gave him a pointed look. "I know how headstrong my Sarah is. I have known her since birth." She turned back to serve up the gruel.

"I shall see to all the needs of your daughter. I promise." He walked over to the woman, put his arm around her shoulder, and kissed her cheek.

His unusual display of affection toward his mother-in-law appeared to fluster her. Waving the wooden spoon, she pointed it toward the door.

"Go on then. Finish your chores before the cows die of hunger."

He smiled, put on his coat, and left for the barn.

Sarah groaned at the numerous blankets her mother spread over her as she sat in the sleigh.

"Are you sure you do not want another quilt?" Her mother tucked yet one more cover over Sarah's large belly.

"If you add one more quilt, I fear you shall encourage this child to be born from the sheer weight. I am quite warm enough. Thank you." Sarah pulled one hand out from the pile of blankets to squeeze her mother's frenzied fingers. Ruth Eaton gripped her daughter's hands and held tightly.

"I do not wish to let you go, Sarah." Tears welled in her mother's eyes.

"We shall return, Mother. Please do not fear." Sarah kissed her mother's hand and released her grip.

"Fare thee well, my daughter. Watch out for her, Nathaniel."

"I shall, Mother Eaton." He waved at her and Sarah's brother, James. He and Hannah and their children would be staying with the widow during their absence.

"Godspeed, Nathaniel. Take care of my sister." James tipped his hat at the couple. Nathaniel tipped his hat in return, then tapped the reins to start the sturdy mare on her way. She jerked and tugged till the sliders found their bearings over the snowy terrain. Then they were off. Their journey to find Benjamin Stearns had begun. The air was cold but the skies only slightly overcast. The clouds kept the sun from shining in their eyes, making the navigating that much easier.

"I'm grateful we are not blinded by the sun on the snow." Nathaniel felt inside his jacket and his eyes showed relief. "Wanted to be sure I had the letter from the doctor."

Sarah's cheeks chilled from the cold so she huddled farther down under the covers. "What an adventure. My first sleigh ride."

"Mine as well. Although I must say that guiding a horse pulling a sleigh is a far sight easier than being wagoner. I did enough wagon hauls in the war to sour me on them. Holes in the road, broken wheels — not a pleasant ride." He glanced at Sarah. "What are you grinning at, Missus Stearns?"

"You. You look like you are on a mission to battle. Jaw set, eyes determined, strong arms at the ready. Even your musket is standing sharp, ready to defend our cause."

Nathaniel reached over and stroked her cheek.

"In a way it is a mission. And hopefully it will be my last in this lingering battle to discover my father. I would love to put this war behind us… once and for all."

Sarah's eyes grew moist. "I love you, Nathaniel Stearns."

He cleared his throat loudly. "Miss, no pronouncements of affection are allowed on this battlefield. Understood?" He spoke with mock gruffness.

"Yes, sir." Her hand covered the grin that threatened to emerge. She reached under the blankets to squeeze his leg.

He jumped and laughed. "Now, miss, I have warned you, no fraternizing with the soldiers."

She blinked her eyes and gave an innocent look. "Why whatever do you mean, sir? I was merely sitting here minding my own concerns."

Nathaniel glanced at her belly and grinned. "Looks as if you've been minding someone's concerns."

Her mouth dropped open and her cheeks burned. "Why Nathaniel Stearns, you are embarrassing me."

His mouth turned upward in a playful manner. Leaning toward her, he drew her head toward him with one hand and kissed her long and deeply. When he pulled slowly away, his mouth was moist from the prolonged kiss. "I am glad you mind my concerns. I'm glad you are my wife."

Releasing his hand from her head, he cleared his throat. "I'd best pay attention to the road."

Sarah smiled at him.

Nathaniel's shoulders leaned forward in determination. She pulled one hand out from under the covers.

"Let me rub your shoulders a bit. They feel so tight." Sarah massaged his muscles but stopped after a few moments. She yawned and her eyes grew heavy.

"Best you rest a bit, Sarah. We've a long journey ahead. But we'll be at the ferry crossing in an hour or so."

He did not need to tell her twice as she gave in to the sleepiness that overwhelmed her.

The change in temperature told Nathaniel they were near the Connecticut River. As they neared the crossing, he craned his neck to find the landing point. Following the men's voices loading up cargo made the job easier. As he guided the horse down the gradual incline, Sarah awoke from the jerking motion. Looking around, she rubbed at her eyes.

"The ferry?"

"Yes. And I'm glad it's not snowing." He looked with trepidation at the expanse of black, churning water in the river. He swallowed with difficulty and leaned toward the man running the ferry.

"Sir, what is the distance across here?"

The burly man with the balding head and gray ponytail turned halfway around to look at the horse-drawn sleigh and its riders. His eyes played up and down, taking in the sight of the young couple, especially the very pregnant woman. He chewed his tobacco wad a little faster and spit a huge squirt out on the ground. Glancing upward he put his meaty hands on his hips.

"Near a hundred rods." He spit another wet ball on the snow. It melted the spot as soon as it landed, leaving one more in a series of pock marks on the white terrain. "So, yer crossin' today, are ya?"

"Yes sir." Nathaniel waited for the man to pull the mare in position but he stood stock still.

Finally the large man grew impatient.

"Well are ya gettin' out of that sleigh, or not? Unless o' course yer figurin' on takin' a swim in the freezin' deep?"

Nathaniel's eyes widened.

"Of course, sir." He stood up without delay and jumped out. Walking around to the other side of the sleigh, he helped Sarah step down. He wrapped two quilts around her shoulders to keep out the cold air. The ferryman glanced at Sarah's belly and shook his head.

"Hope she don't sink 'er," he mumbled. Speaking louder, he began directing. "You, mister, hold on to your lady friend there and lean on the rail whilst we cross. I'll watch your mare, there."

"She is not my lady friend, sir. She is my wife." He placed his arm protectively around Sarah.

"Oh, I see." He spit on the ground and turned to one of the ferry workers. "That's what they all say," he mumbled under his breath. Nathaniel heard the rude remark but swallowed his anger.

Holding onto the side rail for support, he and Sarah stepped onto the wooden ferry. The wood rail was cold and splintered and Nathaniel gripped it with one hand despite the discomfort. His other arm wrapped around Sarah to hold her steady. She clung to his waist and held on.

"My fingers are numb from the cold."

"Just hang on a bit, Sarah. We'll be across before you know it."

The ferryman led the mare onto the wooden slats. The horse started to balk at the sensation of the water underneath, rocking the ferry to and fro. It was obvious the man was used to this task, as his calm manner with the horse belied his gruffness with his human passengers.

"Perhaps if we were horses he would be more friendly to us." Sarah scowled at the man as she clung to Nathaniel's torso.

"Good you have calks on her shoes." The man pointed down to the mare's shod feet. "They'll grip the wood fer sure."

The man on shore gave the signal and the ferry began its slow, deliberate crossing, guided by a rope strung the five hundred yards across the river. Sarah gasped at the sensation of the water. The farther they went toward the deeper part of the river, the faster the current seemed to propel them.

Nathaniel forced himself to stay calm for Sarah's sake, but he could feel his heart pounding. He clung to his wife, ignoring the freezing wind against his face, which stung like pellets of ice spraying against his bare skin. He held the quilt over Sarah to protect her from the onslaught of frigid air.

Terror seized him when the mare started to panic midstream. Her actions made the ferry even more unsteady and the rocking motion became more nauseating. The burly ferry worker held tight to the mare's reins. Speaking softly, he calmed the terrified creature.

"Now there's a babe." He stroked the horse between her ears and cooed affectionately. "We're almost there, sweet babe."

Nathaniel watched in amazement as the horse responded to the man's voice and touch. The ferry resumed a more steady rocking sensation that seemed to lull everyone to tranquility. In a few short minutes, the ferry reached the opposite shore.

Thank you, God. He uncovered Sarah's face from the quilt. Her eyes were wide and unblinking.

"Are you well?" He stroked her face with his hands that bled from the splinters in the railing.

"Yes." She held his hands and inspected them. "I need to remove these pieces of wood lest they cause you infection."

"Later. Let us get off this ferry and you back in the sleigh."

The ferry lurched a bit as it bumped against the snow-covered shore. Nathaniel helped Sarah up the incline. Turning around, he saw the burly man leading the mare up the shore toward the road.

"Thank you, sir. Here is your fare." He handed the man a coin and scratched his head. "You have quite a way with horses, do you not?"

The ferryman glared at Nathaniel and spit a juicy wad sideways into the snow. Not saying another word, he walked away. Nathaniel and Sarah stared after him with open mouths. Nathaniel finally broke the silence.

"Well, at least we know now what to call the mare." He grinned at Sarah. "We shall call her Babe."

30

Lodging

$\mathcal{S}$arah was lost in a dream when a jerking motion of the sleigh interrupted her sleep. Opening her eyes, she blinked from the sharp sensation of the cold air.

Nathaniel noticed she was awake. His reddened hands gripped the reins as he guided Babe.

"Rocks in the road. Sorry they woke you."

Sarah sat up but clung to the quilts surrounding her shoulders.

"Your hands are bleeding. We must stop so I can tend them."

"We shall be pulling over soon. It's time we found an ordinary to sup in. You must be starving."

"Just a little. Mostly just numb from the cold." As she looked around, the beauty of the landscape caught her eye. "'Tis truly lovely here, despite the cold."

"It's all starting to look the same to me. One snow-covered tree after another. A few houses here and there but not many. I did see a sign back a bit for some victuals up ahead."

"I guess I am rather hungry."

"You are eating for two, after all." He smiled at her, but there were circles under his eyes.

"You did not sleep much last night."

"No, but sleep will find me a willing partner tonight." He glanced ahead and saw the sign he'd been looking for. "Victuals — at last."

He slowed down the trotting mare and brought her to a standstill at the side of the house. It was a simple cabin much like any other, but it offered a noon meal to travelers along the road. Nathaniel stood up and stretched his stiff limbs before jumping off the sleigh. After tying Babe to a post, he went around and helped Sarah down from her seat.

"We shall stay just long enough to eat and warm up a bit. The sooner we are back on the road, the sooner we can find lodging to rest for the night."

Sarah leaned against Nathaniel and walked to the door. Their gentle knock was met by a shout.

"Come in speedily and leave the cold out." The woman's voice boomed through the closed door.

"I suggest we hasten inside." Nathaniel grinned as they hurried through the door and shut it. The room was dark and it took their eyes a few moments to adjust.

A voice spoke in the dimness. "Well now, what brings you to travel on such a day? And your lady friend with child!"

Nathaniel rolled his eyes. "She is not my lady friend. She is my wife. And we wish to purchase a meal and warm ourselves before hastening on our way again."

Sarah put her hand on his arm. "We appreciate your hospitality, madam."

The woman lit a candle and they were able to see her face more clearly. Dark hair pulled back in a linen cap framed a face with features that were less than delicate. Her booming voice did little to soften her demeanor.

"Well then, have a seat by the fire. I'll bring you over some rabbit stew. My husband is out looking for deer. No luck so far." Dipping a large ladle into the kettle, she scooped a hefty portion into two wooden bowls and handed them to the couple. She sniffed and wiped her nose on the sleeve of her gown. Her arms looked muscular and efficient. "I'll go chop some more wood for the fire." Throwing her cape around her shoulders, she went outdoors and slammed the door shut.

Sarah and Nathaniel stared after the woman, their eyes crinkling in amusement.

"So do we not look like we are married, Nathaniel? Or do I just appear to be a wanton woman?"

"I think that most husbands would likely keep their wives home when they are in such a condition. I suppose they imagine we are not married, since we are journeying and you are… quite close to birthing." Nathaniel stirred his stew and looked somber. "They probably do not think me much of a husband for putting you in danger."

Sarah was quiet as she swirled the spoon around in the tasty looking meal. She thought for a moment before speaking.

"I'm sorry if I am cause for embarrassing you, Nathaniel. I never meant to —" Before she could finish speaking, he set his bowl on the floor and grabbed her hands.

"You would never embarrass me by your presence. I just tire of those who assume you to be without honor." He paused for a moment. "And I am concerned about you and our child. Perhaps I should have awaited this journey until after the little one was birthed."

"We are both strong, Nathaniel — this child and I — and we could not risk the chance of losing your father once again. This is too important."

He touched her hands to his lips and kissed her fingers.

"Thank you, Sarah." He attempted a smile.

"You are most welcome." She touched the side of his chapped face with her fingers that were moist from his kiss.

"Let us eat these victuals and hasten on our way. Somewhere, a warm bed awaits us tonight." He squeezed her hands and resumed eating the rabbit stew.

The keeper of the ordinary returned with an armload of chopped wood. She carried the load to the hearth with little effort and dropped it onto the floor.

"There. That should do for a bit. Does the stew suit your taste?"

"'Tis quite good, Missus…?"

"Smythe. And you are?"

"Nathaniel Stearns. And this is my wife, Missus Nathaniel Stearns."

Missus Smythe stared at the couple, her thick hands on her generous hips. She stared at the young woman with the large belly and squinted.

"Right… Missus Stearns, is it?" Shaking her head she walked away mumbling under her breath. "That's what they all say."

Sarah and Nathaniel stared at each other and burst out laughing.

The afternoon sleigh ride seemed endless. Mile after mile, forests of chestnuts, oaks, and maples lined the roadway. Occasionally an open field widened the landscape and a few deer in the meadows would scurry away at the sound of their sleigh. Dusk was nearing, and Nathaniel prodded Babe to canter a little faster. They had already traveled a total of thirty miles or more and were trying to reach a town called Brookfield before dark. At last Nathaniel caught sight of a two-story house with a sign in front.

"There! There's the tavern, Sarah."

Exhausted, Sarah peaked out from beneath the quilts.

"It could not have come any too soon." Sarah sat up, her face twisting in pain. "I feel so stiff and sore."

They both read the wooden sign out front:

Drink for the thirsty
Food for the hungry
Lodging for the weary
And good keeping for horses

Nathaniel grinned at Sarah.

"I'm certain Babe will be relieved at the keeping for horses.'" He jumped out of the sleigh, the prospect of warmth and rest invigorating his limbs. "Let us get you inside first." He carefully helped her out of the sleigh and hurried her inside out of the cold. A blast of warmth and pulsating light from the large hearth inside greeted them.

The tavern keeper was pouring ale for a customer. When he looked up and saw the couple a look of concern swept across his face.

"Needin' a midwife, are ye?"

"No sir... not yet. But we do need lodging for the night."

"That I can provide. But birthin'? Not part of my hospitality, sir."

Nathaniel led Sarah to the fire and helped her sit on a chair. He rubbed her cold legs and held them near the warmth. It suddenly became quiet. He looked up and noticed the men in the tavern gawking at Sarah's legs, which were unexpectedly revealed. Nathaniel covered them up with the quilt and glared at the men. They turned away and looked downward. No one spoke a word.

Nathaniel shot the tavern keeper a warning look.

"I shall return forthwith. I must tend to my horse in the barn. My wife is in a delicate condition and must not be disturbed. Is that clear?" He held up his musket for all to see.

"Aye. No one here will raise yer husbandly ire, sir."

"Good." He turned back to his wife and softened his voice. "Sarah, I shall hasten to take care of Babe and then return. I'll have the tavern keeper serve you some victuals." He touched her cold cheek. Her lips turned upward in an effort to smile. He kissed her and glared at the men one last time.

"Bring her some warm food, sir."

Hurrying out the door, he pulled Babe's reins with hands too numb to get a strong grip. Fortunately, the horse readily complied with his less-than-sturdy guidance. The smell of fresh hay in the barn seemed sufficient to draw her attention. Nathaniel unhooked the mare's reins from the sleigh and set her in one of the stalls with an armload of dry hay and some water. He secured her with a rope attached to her bridle and hurried back to the tavern. Walking inside, he relaxed at the sight of Sarah enjoying a warm meal by the fire. Looking at him, she grinned.

"Do come eat, Nathaniel. This stew is fine."

"Fresh venison." The tavern keeper stood taller and smiled. "Shot him myself."

Nathaniel still had a guarded edge to his voice.

"Thank you, sir. My name is Stearns and this is my wife." He said the last word with emphasis.

"Welcome, Mr. Stearns. Missus Stearns. My name's Martin. Ezekiel Martin. What brings ye on a journey in this cold winter?"

Nathaniel took a sip of the warm cider Martin had handed to him and set the tankard down on the wooden bar.

"Lookin' for my father." He drank another swig that sent warmth throughout his insides. Walking over toward the fire, he touched Sarah's hair for a moment before sitting in the chair next to her. He exhaled a long, labored breath. The landlord brought a bowl of steaming stew from the opposite end of the hearth to the weary Nathaniel.

"Some victuals for ye hearty appetite, sir." Martin stood looking at the couple with his hands on his hips. "Father lost, is he?"

"Yes. Since the war." Nathaniel pulled a spoonful of steaming meat near his lips and blew on it.

"Bloody war." The voice came from the man sitting by himself at the bar.

Nathaniel glanced at the poorly shaven face almost resting on the tip of his tankard. "Yes. Yes it was." Nathaniel took a bite of the stew and closed his eyes and moaned in pleasure. "Fine stew, sir."

The man at the bar was not finished with his sad laments.

"Fought eight years for this ungrateful country. Came home to my farm and lost it to bloody Bowdoin. Governor indeed. Calls out the militia to shoot at decent citizens trying to spare their farm!" The man's voice grew louder the angrier he got.

"Settle down, Mr. Stone. You know the law keeps me from suffering drunkards in my tavern. Persist and I shall receive a penalty. Then where'll ye drink your ale? Not here again, I assure ye."

Stone quieted down. Then he spoke in a more tempered but slurred tone.

"Well at least allow me, Mr. Martin, to drink a toast. To Mr. Benjamin Franklin. As he was wont to say — when the dear fellow was yet alive — 'Beer is proof that God loves us and wants us to be happy.' May God rest that fine American's soul." Tears began to roll into Stone's ale as he drank a hearty gulp.

Martin rolled his eyes.

"That'll be yer last pint, Mr. Stone. And if ye have nowhere to go, there's plenty of room in the barn where the animals'll keep ye warm."

Stone quieted down, staring into his tankard.

Nathaniel and Sarah were silent, eating the stew.

"You do not seem very hungry, love." His eyes narrowed in concern.

"No. I am more tired than hungry, I fear. Perhaps I can go to bed?"

"Of course." Nathaniel set his empty bowl onto the floor and hurried to remove hers from her lap. Her arms were limp as he helped her stand.

"Mr. Martin, can you show us to our room?"

"Of course, lad. Ye may need to help your missus up the steps. There's plenty o' clean quilts on the bed in the first room at top of stairs. Let me know if ye'll need more."

"I will, sir. Thank you." Nathaniel supported her as she walked toward the staircase. "It's just ten steps, Sarah. I'll help you."

Sarah's eyes widened at the impending climb.

"It looks like a steep cliff." They slowly ascended. By the time they reached the landing, Sarah was half asleep. "Come with me, Sarah." Setting his musket against the wall, he half carried his wife through the door into the small room. It was sparsely furnished but clean. Sitting Sarah on the edge of the bed, he removed her shoes. She fell back onto the straw-filled mattress and nuzzled into the feather pillow. Covering her with the quilt, he went out to the hallway to retrieve his musket. He leaned a small chair against the door in case someone attempted to enter. He also kept the musket beside the bed, just in case the need arose. Nathaniel undressed and crawled under the quilts, snuggling next to his wife for warmth. He kissed Sarah's hair before falling into a deep slumber.

31

Danger

*S*arah dreaded resuming the sleigh ride the next morning but she hid her displeasure from Nathaniel. Her sleep had been uninterrupted but seemed far too short.

She climbed into the seat once again, making an effort to avoid complaining about the cold. After all, she was the one who had insisted on coming and she did not want to exasperate her weary husband. Sarah knew that, had she allowed him to go alone, his timing would have been faster and she would not have become such a burden. A tinge of regret filled her thoughts.

"Well here we are again." Nathaniel's voice interrupted her musings. "Are you ready for your carriage ride, milady?" He gave her a teasing grin. She could not help but be warmed by her husband's attempt at joviality.

"Why, yes, sir, I am most anxious to be taken to the palace." She touched his face with her chapped hand. "So long as my lord will be there, I shall be joyful, indeed."

"Well then, fair lady. Let us be off." He clucked his tongue to encourage Babe to begin this second day of travel. She hesitated but then gradually moved at a faster clip.

"Looks like we could see some snow today." Nathaniel glanced upward and pulled his woolen scarf closer around his neck. "Those clouds look heavy." As he spoke a few flurries began to land on his tricorne hat.

Sarah looked at the sky and scrunched her nose as a few flakes landed on it. "I pray it does not turn to a blizzard." Her eyes begged

Nathaniel for reassurance.

"I think not. Not much wind." He smiled, but Sarah could see the worried set to his mouth. She had come to recognize it well.

"Was speaking with Mr. Martin."

"Yes?" She knew he was trying to keep her mind off the weather.

"He tells me this road is the very same one used by Henry Knox when he transported the cannons from Ticonderoga."

"Is this so?" Sarah smiled in surprise. "So Babe is trodding on the same ruts that the oxen did. Perhaps that will inspire her to get us to Boston just like the oxen managed to do."

"We will be sure to inform her that she is on a distinguished highway." His smile crinkled small lines around his face.

"Your eyes. Even without the sunlight, they dazzle with warmth." She stared in admiration at this man she loved — this man whose child she carried. "I pray our little one has your splendid sapphire eyes."

Her husband's face reddened. He reached with one hand to touch her cheek. "If 'tis a lass, I pray she favors you with your fawn eyes." He grinned at his wife. Sarah took his hand and kissed the snowflakes from his fingers.

The snow drifted down like feathers. The motion of the sleigh lulled Sarah into sleepiness but she fought the urge to close her eyes.

"Sarah, do not resist. Rest your eyes — you need sleep." Her husband stared at her, concern in his demeanor.

"Perhaps just for a moment…"

She dreamt of a fairy tale swirl of snow. The flakes danced before her eyes, tumbling to and fro in an enchanting pattern that decorated the landscape and naked trees. Soon deer appeared, prancing across the meadow, keeping time with the winsome wintry ballet.

But a loud whinny from Babe awoke her from her sleepy reverie. Somewhere between a dream and reality, the vision of graceful deer morphed into the frightening truth of the animals running at a distance parallel to the sleigh. A pack of wolves raced alongside, keeping pace with a frantic Babe.

Sarah gasped and sat up. Heart racing, she grabbed Nathaniel's arm and gripped tightly.

He did not move but leaned forward, his eyes glancing nervously back and forth from right to left. He struggled to maintain control of the reins attached to the terrified mare.

"Sarah. Load the musket for me."

It was not a task she did often, but she had observed it for many years. He reached underneath his coat and pulled out the bag containing the lead balls and the cow horn filled with gunpowder. Grabbing the firearm, she began to insert a lead round into the barrel but dropped a few as she struggled. Between the movement of the sleigh and her trembling hands, she fumbled as she loaded the gun.

"I can do this." Her throat was dry and her breathing far too fast. Nathaniel glanced at her, making sure the loading was accomplished.

"You're doing well, Sarah. Plunge the rod down the barrel now." He coached her through the steps until it was ready to fire. "Well done."

The wolves — at least eight of them — stayed at a distance from the sleigh, but Sarah and Nathaniel both knew it was only a matter of time. Once the horse was exhausted from the faster pace, they would make their move. Nathaniel licked his tongue across his dry lips. Sweat appeared on his forehead. Sarah was too terrified to speak. She felt her baby kick several times and she grasped at her belly. The reminder of this new life waiting to be born added to her terror.

What if he is torn from my womb without a chance to live? Tears brimmed her eyelids. *Dear Lord, please save us!*

Nathaniel glanced at her with concern. Often he masked his emotions from her, but at this moment the look of fear in his eyes was as vivid as the starkness of the landscape. He managed to find his voice.

"Sarah, if they come any closer, I must fire the musket. Do you think you can handle the reins?" His eyes implored her to say she could.

"Yes. I know I can." She spoke with firm resolve. She would do what she needed to do for the ones she loved. She would not allow this danger to threaten her child, no matter how fearful she was. With God's help, she would be strong.

"All right then. When I say the word, you grab the reins and hold as tight as you can. Understand?" His voice shook.

"Yes." She gripped the musket, ready to release it to her husband the moment he spoke the word. Her heart raced and the baby kicked. Tears threatened to melt her countenance, but she held them back.

Gradually, the wolves seemed to sense that Babe was tiring. Almost imperceptibly, their path moved closer to the sleigh. Following what appeared to be their leader, each animal came a little closer, their features becoming more detailed. Their determined eyes focused straight ahead, only glancing now and then toward the mare. Their deadly intent was apparent as the sharp points of their fangs appeared, preparing for the inevitable attack.

Dizziness and nausea threatened to overpower her.

Dear God, please help us.

As the animals moved a few paces closer, they began to lurch one by one at the legs of Babe, their eager jaws drooling and snapping.

"Sarah, now!" He handed her the reins and grabbed the musket. "Hold her tight."

She gripped the jerking reins that threatened to lift her off the seat. Setting his sights on one wolf, Nathaniel fired and hit his target. The rest of the wolves moved away temporarily while Nathaniel reloaded his firearm.

The sound of the gun so close to Babe sent her into a frenzy. She bolted, nearly lifting a screaming Sarah upright. Nathaniel set the musket down and grabbed the straps of leather to control the terrified mare. Sarah fell back onto the sleigh and grabbed her unborn child. She winced in pain.

Lord, protect my baby!

The remaining wolves were just honing in on the mare again when they were suddenly alarmed by musket fire in the distance. Nathaniel glanced toward the source. Babe was alarmed by the sound and ran even faster, despite her already heaving breaths.

Sarah saw one of the wolves drop dead in its stride. Then another. Just as quickly as the nightmare had materialized, the wolves dispersed, followed by several men on horseback.

Nathaniel pulled Babe to a halt. He grabbed Sarah and held her tight. Finally allowing the fear to be felt, she sobbed and buried her face in his jacket.

"We're safe, Sarah." His voice still shook but she heard his relief.

One of the riders who had rescued them approached the sleigh.

"Lucky we were out tracking this pack. Where you headin'?"

"Marlborough. I think we're still a ways from there."

"Your missus all right?"

Sarah drew away from Nathaniel's embrace and wiped the tears from her face.

"I am well. Thank you, sir." She clasped her belly and smoothed her hand over the unborn child.

The hunter glanced at Sarah.

"Best be getting you somewhere safe and warm, ma'am. How about I ride with you to Marlborough, in case there's any more trouble?"

Nathaniel exhaled. "I'd be beholden to you, sir. Thank you."

"Got young'uns of my own. Don't want no trouble for ya." He tipped his hat at Sarah. "Ma'am."

Sarah clung to Nathaniel the rest of the ride to the inn. They had covered several extra miles during the wolf chase, so they arrived in Marlborough earlier than expected. They had not eaten since breakfast at the Brookfield tavern and Sarah grew weak. Arriving at the inn, Nathaniel assisted her out of the sleigh.

The rider that accompanied the couple bid them farewell.

"I cannot thank you enough, sir." Nathaniel held Sarah next to him as he spoke. "I am certain we owe our lives to you."

"Thought I was just saving two lives when we first saw ya. Looks like it'll be three lives soon enough." He smiled at them and unexpectedly dismounted. "How about I set your mare up in a stall. Looks like she could use some food and rest."

"I'd be grateful to you, sir. Again, you have my thanks."

The stranger smiled and then led the exhausted Babe to the barn.

"Come, Sarah. I know you are in need of victuals." Walking toward the inn, Nathaniel put his arm around her and guided her indoors. The smell of cooked vegetables and fowl greeted her nostrils. Her husband took her straight toward the hearth and found her a chair.

"I can barely feel my feet." Sarah stretched out her legs in front of the flames. "Can you help me take my shoes off." Her voice sounded weary and small.

Nathaniel started to remove her shoes but stopped abruptly.

"Sarah." His voice was filled with concern.

"What is it?"

"Your shoes. I can barely remove them." His eyes opened wide.

Sarah was bewildered. "Why not?"

"Your feet… they are swelled."

"What?" Sarah struggled to see around her large belly. She caught a glimpse of her lower limbs and breathed in sharply. "They do not look like my feet!" She tried not to panic. "Perhaps I should go lie down."

Nathaniel visibly swallowed. "I shall bring you some victuals in bed."

She attempted a brave smile. "Yes. That would be perfect."

"Let me speak to the landlord so I can arrange a room."

"Thank you, my love." She squeezed his moist hand.

He leaned toward her and gave her a kiss with trembling lips. "I shall hasten and return forthwith."

He spoke earnestly to the tavern keeper and before long Sarah was again faced with a steep flight of stairs. She did not think she could ascend them, as fatigued as she was, but with Nathaniel's strong arms and encouraging words, she soon found herself back in a warm bed covered by a multitude of quilts. It was a comforting end to a harrowing day.

She managed to swallow a few morsels of food before sleep overtook her once again. This time, instead of dreaming about animals and snow, she dreamt about a baby with sapphire blue eyes.

32

Desperation

Back in the sleigh for the last leg of their journey, Nathaniel was more than ready to be at their destination. He knew they were nearing Cambridge by the increasing numbers of houses along the road. After Cambridge came the ferry ride to Boston.

Although he was relieved the journey was drawing to a close, something seemed wrong.

Sarah's so quiet. "How do you fare, Sarah?" He reached over and squeezed her hand hidden under the quilts.

She tried to smile. "Well enough." She would not meet his eyes, but stared at the trees in the distance.

"Sarah, look at me." She instead looked at his hand holding hers. Her lips were starting to tremble. Reaching her chin with his fingers, he turned her face to look at his. "Please tell me what's wrong."

She tried to speak but the words seemed to choke in her throat. Taking in a shuddering breath, she tried again.

"I fear... I fear our child will be birthed soon."

Nathaniel's jaw tightened and his breathing quickened.

"Soon? What does that mean exactly?" He tried to slow his rapid breathing and keep his tone level. "Soon, like now? Or soon like... sometime tomorrow?"

Her face contorted and became red. She grabbed at her swollen belly and tried to breathe. Instead gasps of small breaths ensued. After a moment she relaxed, but then burst into tears.

"Soon like… today."

Nathaniel fought an overwhelming fear.

I dare not let her see my terror. Calm yourself, man.

"Today." He sucked in a deep breath. "Do we need to stop very soon?"

"Soon enough." Sarah sat up as well as she could and stretched her neck to look ahead. "I see the river in the distance. Let us cross on the ferry first and then we can stop."

Nathaniel's heart raced. He swallowed, but there was little saliva in his mouth. He licked his dry lips.

"How long… have you known?"

Her eyes glanced downward before they met his.

"This morning, I thought something was amiss. Then… as the day went on, it became more difficult to bear the ride. Now, it feels more urgent." When she finished speaking, her face again turned red and she grabbed her unborn child. It was a moment before she breathed with ease again.

After glancing at her distress, he wiped his sleeve across his forehead. "Come on, Babe." He urged the mare to increase her pace. She seemed to sense the driver's desperation as she picked up her speed to a faster trot without any hesitation.

Dear Lord, do not let this child be born on the streets. The thought of Sarah delivering their baby before arriving at the home of a midwife filled him with terror.

The drive through Cambridge was fraught with frustration. The streets were busy and it was difficult to wend their way through the people and the pigs wandering everywhere.

"I say, unless you are a midwife, remove yourselves!" Nathaniel's voice was loud and angry as he shouted at slow passersby. Sarah was quiet, but he saw her gripping her belly every few minutes and wincing. He could hear the blood flowing in his ears, even amidst the street sounds.

When they reached the line for the river ferry, Nathaniel craned his neck to see how far back they were. Cartloads of wood hauled by oxen awaited the ferry transport and the stench of the Boston tanneries filled the air even across the Charles River. Nathaniel fought back the sick feeling welling in his own stomach. He felt a hand on his shoulder.

"Say there, lad. You needin' transport quick like?" The man with the greasy hands and face glanced at Sarah holding her belly.

Nathaniel swallowed to keep from vomiting. "Yes, sir. My wife is in need."

"I can see that. Come with me." He grabbed the lead rein on Babe and deftly made his way through the crowd of carts awaiting the ferry. "Back you beasts," he yelled at a pair of oxen that refused to wedge to the side. "Make way for the lady."

All obstacles in the sleigh's path seemed to disappear with the skilled maneuvering of the city worker through the thick crowd. Suddenly, they were first in line.

Nathaniel swallowed.

"Thank you, sir."

The greasy man tipped his filthy hat and returned to his own cart.

Glancing at Sarah, Nathaniel gripped her hand.

"We will cross soon. Then we will find you a midwife." He barely recognized his own strangled voice.

Sarah gave a weak smile. "We will be fine." For a moment, he believed her, but then another contraction gripped her belly and she leaned back and moaned.

Dear God. He did not even know how to pray. He remembered when his mother looked like this when she went into labor with his youngest sister. He envisioned that day, running as fast as his lanky thirteen-year-old legs could carry him. Pounding on the door, begging for the midwife, looking up at his future sister-in-law Mary. And inside that very house, sick and fevered, lay his future wife.

Sarah.

Glancing at his wife struggling to bring his child into the world, he was strangely warmed by the memory.

Sarah will be fine. Just as my mother was.

Still awaiting the ferry transport, Nathaniel reached over and smoothed her hair, which had fallen loose from her cap.

"Sarah. I will care for you and see that no harm occurs."

She gripped his fingers and kissed them. "I know you will."

The ferry finally docked. The large hands of the ferryman held

Babe's bridle and waited for the couple to get out of the sleigh.

Nathaniel climbed out and reassured Sarah.

"I will hold onto you and will not let go." Helping her out, he placed the quilts over her shoulders once again. Leaning on the sturdy side rail, he put both arms around his wife. When another contraction occurred every few minutes, he could feel her legs buckling. He held onto her and whispered calmly into her ear.

"I love you, Sarah. Know that I love you."

Tears poured down her cheeks as she nodded. "I know." She whispered in between her sobs.

Suddenly a wail of distress burst from deep in Sarah's throat. She gripped her tight belly and screamed so loudly, the other passengers on the ferry gawked at her.

This was a mistake. We should have stayed in Cambridge.

When the contraction ebbed, Sarah moaned in Nathaniel's arms. "I'm sorry." Her voice trembled.

"You've nothing to apologize for, Sarah. I am the one who needs to repent for bringing you on this journey." Sweat trickled down his neck, despite the cold air.

Loaded and ready to move, the ferry began the ride across the Charles River. For Nathaniel it seemed to be the longest journey of his life. He had to be strong for Sarah, but his emotions were weak. Holding onto Sarah in her discomfort was the easy part. Holding back his tears was much more difficult.

Lord, I beg of you to spare my wife and this child she struggles to birth. Please, O God, provide a safe place for us to go. Please, Lord.

Trying to distract her from her pain, Nathaniel pointed toward the wooden and brick structures, each several stories high, that were framed against the blue sky.

"Look, Sarah. Boston. That is where our baby will be born." He nuzzled her dampened hair and held her close. She clung to him as well as she could, but he could sense her hands were growing tired. He held onto her with a sure grip.

Nathaniel glanced over at the ferryman holding Babe's reins. The mare was calm in the man's steady grasp. Once again Sarah was seized with a powerful pain. They seemed to be coming closer together, and each time her knees buckled even lower, driving her downward. It was all he could do to keep her from falling to the wooden floor. The intensity of her cries was increasing as well, attracting the concerned glances of everyone else on the ferry.

They reached the other side of the river, none too soon for Nathaniel. As the ferryman led Babe and the sleigh up onto the bank, he held the horse steady while Nathaniel picked Sarah up in his arms and carried her to the seat. As she went to sit down, another strong pain grabbed her belly. She screamed uncontrollably.

The ferryman frowned. "There's a tavern up on the hill. May want to take yer missus there." He pointed to a wood frame building several yards up the street. "I believe they have a birthin' room."

"A birthing room? Thank you. I am much obliged."

Nathaniel hurried to climb in the seat and drove Babe up the cobbled street. The runners of the sleigh easily slid across the snow-covered lane.

A stable stood next to the tavern and Nathaniel drove the sleigh into it. The lurching of the runners on the wooden floor made Sarah gasp and cry out.

"Every time we hit a bump, I get another pain." Sarah's face was red and covered with sweat. She appeared on the verge of vomiting.

"Here." He handed the reins to the liveryman. "Please see to my horse. My wife needs help."

The attendant took a coin from Nathaniel and looked at Sarah.

"Hope she makes it inside in time," the stable worker mumbled.

Nathaniel ignored the man's mumblings and lifted Sarah in his strong arms. Carrying her toward the door of the tavern, he kicked it open with one foot. The taverner looked up in surprise but then looked at the woman in his arms. He pointed toward the back of the hallway.

"Birthin' room's back there. Last door." The aloof middle-aged man calmly resumed drying a tankard he had cleaned.

Nathaniel walked with awkward steps down the hall trying not to jostle Sarah. He kicked open this last door and set her down to a standing position so he could get the bed ready.

Upon drawing the quilts back, both Nathaniel and Sarah gasped.

"Dirty bedding! And bed bugs! Nathaniel…" Sarah sobbed.

"We shall not stay here." Anger coursed through his veins. He picked up Sarah again, fighting back rage.

As he approached the tavern keeper, he tried to control his outrage for Sarah's sake.

"Don't suppose you'd think about cleaning the bed after a birthing!" He glared at the landlord who did not say a word but kept drying a tankard with a filthy towel.

Nathaniel kicked the door open and carried Sarah out to the street. The sun glared. He shielded his squinting eyes, desperately looking around.

"Please put me down, Nathaniel." Her voice strained. He did as he was asked and set her beside him. "Perhaps I could just sit here on the street for a bit." Her pale face and weak voice alarmed him.

"No, Sarah, do not sit on this foul ground." He stared with horror at the piles of pig and dog manure that seemed to be everywhere.

"I am so tired…"

Dear God, please help her.

Suddenly a woman appeared in front of them. The sun was so bright, she looked dark against the glare.

"Please, may I assist you both somehow?" The voice was kind and earnest. The woman moved a bit so her features were more visible. "I am Missus Joseph Bainbridge. I see that you are in need. Are you far from home?"

"Yes, very far. " Nathaniel's hands shook and beads of sweat grew on his forehead. "We went inside here, but the place is filthy."

"Please, come with me."

Nathaniel picked Sarah up again and carried her over toward a carriage unlike any he had seen before. There were two cushioned bench seats, one behind the other, and two horses pulled the wagon.

"Put your wife in the back here and hold her steady. We shall hasten to my home." The woman climbed into the front seat next to the driver.

Nathaniel began to think he was dreaming. The woman's finely woven wool cape surrounded a dress of equally fine material. Her dark hair, tinged with gray, was piled high on her head and topped with a fur cap. He had never seen such clothing in Deer Run — nor anywhere else.

Sarah's constant moans were becoming louder and it seemed that each pain lasted longer with a gut-wrenching crescendo.

The woman turned to look at Sarah. Concern was written across the stranger's face. "My driver will get us home soon."

Nathaniel found his voice. "Madam, we must find a midwife. And very soon!"

"Here, we are at my home."

Nathaniel had not even noticed that they had come to a different neighborhood. It was a far cry from where the tavern was. Stately homes towered toward the sky with large portals making even a frightened stranger feel welcome.

It looks like the gates of heaven.

Despite the tension, he was awestruck. Reality hit him soon enough, as Sarah began to cry out. He jumped out of the carriage and helped her down from the seat.

"Nathaniel!" Her face turned redder than he had seen it before and he thought she was going to fall on the ground.

The Good Samaritan turned pale when she looked at Sarah.

"Please, bring her inside — hasten!" She directed a woman servant to show Nathaniel where to bring Sarah.

And then he heard the woman whisper words that sent chills down his spine. "Send for Dr. Sheffield."

33

Delivery

*G*et out!" Sarah's eyes widened and her heart raced even faster. "I want a midwife." She fell back onto the huge pillow in anguish.

Nathaniel rubbed his hand nervously through the hair that had come undone from his ribbon.

"Sarah, there is no midwife." His voice was shaky and low.

"Then I shall deliver myself."

Nathaniel looked at the ceiling with his eyes closed and rubbed the back of his neck.

Dr. Sheffield's eyes grew wide. "I have never seen such a reaction in all my years of practice." He tossed his head back and stiffened his shoulders.

Sarah heard Nathaniel trying to mollify the doctor. "Her mother is midwife in our village. None of the women there would think of allowing a man to deliver their child."

The doctor did not seem appeased. "Well, there is no choice now is there?" The slightly built man meticulously removed his fine black coat and ran his fingers through his graying hair. "Besides, I have studied under the finest doctors in England."

Sarah glared at the stranger. "I do not care. Stay away from me!" She writhed on the bed as another contraction gripped her belly.

The doctor ignored her and proceeded to open his bag to remove something. When he turned around, he was holding up a forceps. "Just in case things do not proceed as expected." He gave Mrs. Bainbridge a quick smile.

Mrs. Bainbridge silently stood to the side, her brow furrowed.

The doctor directed the maid to bring more hot water and towels. She curtsied and scurried out the door.

As Dr. Sheffield approached the bed, Sarah screamed. "No! Nathaniel, stop him."

The doctor ignored her plea and started to remove the covers. Nathaniel gripped the thin arm of the physician.

"Stop. Let me speak to her." Nathaniel leaned over his wife. "Sarah, we have no choice." His voice trembled. "I do not know what to do. Please allow the man to do this." Tears welled on the rim of his eyes.

"Nathaniel, no! I will not let him touch me. Please…" Her words became lost in great sobs.

The doctor stiffened his shoulders and his lips drew into a thin line.

"Missus Stearns, you must calm yourself."

Rage energized Sarah as she pushed up onto her elbows.

"You calm yourself!" Her eyes glared at him in fury.

"Really, Missus Bainbridge, I feel I must give her laudanum."

At these words, Sarah became hysterical. Nathaniel stepped in between the doctor and Sarah and gripped the man's arms.

"You will speak to me, sir. I am her husband." His words were sharpened daggers.

The doctor paused, staring calmly at Nathaniel's large hand gripping his arm. Nathaniel released his hold. Dr. Sheffield straightened out his waistcoat and cleared his throat.

"Very well, then. I still think your wife needs some laudanum."

Missus Bainbridge interrupted.

"I feel that we might try a different approach, gentleman. Missus Stearns is obviously distraught. While I am no midwife, I believe perhaps the three of us could devise a way to help this child be born sooner rather than later. I have seen it done this way some twenty years ago when my sister gave birth. Are you all willing to try?"

"Yes, anything to help Sarah." Nathaniel paced.

The doctor appeared unimpressed. "Really, Missus Bainbridge…"

"We try it her way." Nathaniel glowered at the man. Dr. Sheffield tossed the forceps onto the chair and threw his hands in the air. He sat down on the metal instrument by mistake, and jumped up to remove it. Sitting down, he had a look of disapproving disgust on his face. Missus Bainbridge took charge.

"Very well then, Mr. Stearns, climb onto the bed and sit behind your wife. We will place her on the edge of the bed."

Nathaniel did as he was told and scooted Sarah over toward the edge of the bed.

"Wrap your arms around her and hold her up. There. Now, Missus Stearns, I'm going to put some sheets down below you here. We shall allow the good Lord's plan here to unfold. I will merely guide you." She glanced back at the doctor. "With the advice of Dr. Sheffield, of course." She gave a placating smile.

He grinned, but it was only from his mouth. His eyes remained pointed and glaring.

Sarah sobbed and gripped Nathaniel's legs.

Missus Bainbridge touched Sarah's arm. "Missus Stearns, try to ease your mind. Think about this baby. How beautiful he or she will be." Sarah glanced at Missus Bainbridge and thought she noticed the woman's eyes moisten. Sarah's heart raced and her breathing was jagged and out of control.

Suddenly she felt Nathaniel's rough cheek rub against her own. His voice was calm and soothing, yet filled with passion.

"Sarah, remember our first dance?" She did not answer. "Remember?" His voice was a whisper.

"Yes." Her breathing came in spurts from all the crying.

"Sarah, you were the most beautiful woman I had ever seen. When I saw you standing there in your blue gown, I thought, now there is a woman who would never marry me. She is too beautiful for me. Then I saw you look over and you smiled." Nathaniel gulped back tears. "And I thought, I could look at that smile the rest of my life and be a joyous man. And then, when we danced, I felt as though I had wings and could have flown away with you and not regretted leaving everyone else behind." He pulled up one hand and wiped tears from his face. "Then when we kissed, I knew I had found the love I had long hoped for — a love I had never known before — in you." He kissed her cheek with moist lips. "You are truly my treasure."

Sarah could feel his blood coursing through the pulses in his hands as he held her up. Her breathing quieted as did her terrified heartbeat. That hidden place in her heart that had longed to be filled by his love was now overflowing. She smiled and touched his cheek with her hand, smoothing away his tears.

"I love you, Nathaniel."

"I have never loved another as I do you." He kissed her cheek and continued to hold her from behind.

Suddenly Sarah felt a strange sensation. An urge to push unlike anything she had ever felt before. She began to groan a deep instinctive sound as she tensed up and began to expel her baby.

Nathaniel's breathing was uneven but he continued to hold her with a sure grip. Dr. Sheffield was by now sitting up straight and ready to leap into the birth, but Missus Bainbridge held him back with a motion of her hand. He sat back down, his mouth gaping.

"Well done, Sarah. Good push."

Sarah paused from her efforts and gasped for breath. The maid came in and scurried over with the hot water.

Missus Bainbridge grabbed some towels and moistened them before applying them to Sarah. After a moment, Sarah felt another urge to push, followed by another few moments of gasping.

Nathaniel kissed her cheek. "Well done, my love." Sarah could feel his tears dripping down her neck.

She gripped her husband's legs and concentrated on birthing this child. She pushed and groaned with all her might.

"The child is coming!" Missus Bainbridge cried and smiled all at once. "I think perhaps once more, Missus Stearns."

"I am so tired." Sarah leaned back against Nathaniel. Her gown clung to her body and her dampened hair was completely disheveled.

"Hang on, Sarah. You can do this." His words were the encouragement she needed to push once more. Slowly the child's head emerged, and with one more effort, the baby slipped into the hands of Missus Bainbridge.

"It's a boy!" Missus Bainbridge melted into tears.

"Let me help you." Dr. Sheffield sprang into action, grabbing the child and drying him with a cloth.

Sarah and Nathaniel wept with relief. "Let me hold my son." Sarah reached out toward her baby.

"I would like to examine the child first."

Nathaniel glared at the man. "Give my son to his mother."

The doctor handed the squirming infant to Sarah. She pulled her gown down and put him to her breast. The chubby boy latched on to his mother, ready for his first meal.

Missus Bainbridge stared at the sight of the family and fresh tears flowed down her cheeks.

After a few moments, Nathaniel took the infant from Sarah's arms. The afterbirth was delivered, and the maids helped Sarah clean up. Missus Bainbridge and one of the maids pulled Sarah back up onto the pillows.

"Well then." Dr. Sheffield put his forceps into his bag. "Perhaps I am finished here."

"Thank you for coming, Matthias." She touched his arm. "I am beholden to you."

He shook his head. "I did nothing. She did all the work. And you." He put his coat back on. "Good day, everyone."

He left the room, and Missus Bainbridge turned to speak to Sarah and Nathaniel.

"I shall have my maids serve up some supper for you both. I'll return shortly." She left the room smiling.

Nathaniel kissed Sarah's cheek and handed the infant back to her. Since the baby had been rooting around with an open mouth, she placed him on her other breast so he could continue eating.

"I have never seen a newborn who looked so much like his father before." She smiled at her husband.

"Perhaps 'tis the wrinkles." His eyes crinkled as he smiled.

"He is so handsome, just like you."

Nathaniel leaned over and kissed his wife and then his newborn.

"Thank you, Sarah." Tears brimmed his lids. "You have been my most unexpected joy." He kissed her and lay beside her in the bed.

As Nathaniel wrapped his arms around her, Sarah felt him relax and fall asleep while their baby eagerly nursed. Nathaniel's arms encompassed his new family and Sarah sighed with contentment as she felt her husband's embrace surround the family he had long hoped for.

34

History

A re you well, Missus Stearns?"

The voice of the maid startled Sarah awake. It took her a moment to remember where she was.

"Yes, quite well. Thank you." Sarah glanced at her sleeping infant. Smoothing her tired fingers across his round cheek, the child moved his mouth as if suckling in a dream.

Nathaniel stirred from sleep and sat up abruptly. He glanced down at his clothing, still unchanged from the previous evening. Rubbing his hands through his unkempt hair, he looked at Sarah and their sleeping infant. A small smile crept across his face.

"Good morning, love."

"Good morning." Sarah tried to sit higher on the pillow while still holding their infant. Nathaniel took the sleeping child from her arms while she repositioned herself. The movement awoke the boy and he started turning his head looking for his breakfast. Sarah put the infant to breast and closed her eyes.

"I am so tired, Nathaniel." Weariness filled her voice.

"Here's a tray of food for you both." The maid had a friendly countenance. "I've set some towels and fresh water in a basin for you here." She curtsied and then left the room.

"She must think we are upper class." Nathaniel shook his head. "Does she not realize we are poor farmers?"

"I am certain she does." Sarah looked around the room. Fine, thin curtains draped over the windows clear to the floor, allowing a muted glow of sunlight to shine through. For the first time, Sarah took note of feather-filled quilts with lace edging that begged her to touch the intricate pattern. "Such beautiful furnishings. I've never seen such material before."

Nathaniel cleared his throat and appeared self-conscious.

"You will never be content with our simple home after such a splendid display here." He tried to smile, but his eyes were filled with worry.

"I shall never want for more than we have, Nathaniel. You and our little one are worth far more to me than finery."

He kissed her fingers. "Thank you, Sarah." He leaned over his son and kissed the infant who nursed with vigor. "Good morning, my son."

"Nathaniel, we've not chosen a name for him yet."

"No, we have not. And we must choose one soon. Every time I think of a name, it somehow does not seem fitting."

"I'm certain we will know it when we hear it." She pulled his face to her own and kissed him warmly. "I'm starving!"

"For food… or for kisses, Missus Stearns? For I can accommodate either." His grin was mischievous.

"Let us start with the food, sir." Her eyes teased him.

"All right then." He exhaled in an exaggerated show of disappointment. "I shall just have to put off the kisses until later."

"Much later." Her heart soared as she grinned.

Bringing her the tray of food, he uncovered a bowl of golden, steaming gruel. Sarah's eyes widened.

"Gruel has never looked so enticing." She licked her lips.

"Here let me help you." Nathaniel held the bowl in front of her so she could eat with a spoon in one hand while holding their infant in the other. She devoured the hot cereal and Nathaniel uncovered another bowl filled with cooked eggs. These were consumed with equal enthusiasm.

"It's a good thing she sent more food." He looked at the empty bowls in mock surprise.

Sarah's face burned with embarrassment.

"I'm sorry, Nathaniel. I've never been so hungry. Is there enough for you?"

"Of course. I'm merely teasing. Missus Bainbridge has sent up an abundance of food for us both." His brows furrowed as he stood up from the edge of the bed and walked over to the tray. "I still do not know why we are here. Or why she has helped us." He shook his head and ate a few bites of the sausage from one of the plates.

Sarah leaned over to kiss the top of the baby's soft head.

"God sent her to us."

"I know this. But who is she?"

As if in answer to his question, there was a knock on the door.

"May I come in?" Missus Bainbridge called from the hallway.

Nathaniel rushed to the door and opened it.

"Of course, Missus Bainbridge. This is your home." He rubbed his hair back and swallowed with difficulty.

The friendly woman smiled. "Please, feel at home. You are my guests." Glancing over at Sarah, her face beamed with delight. "May I come see the baby?"

"Of course." Sarah pulled her gown up and her eyes met the woman. Sarah tried not to appear startled at the woman's fine clothing.

The older woman's hair was piled high on her head and covered with a fine cap of gauzy linen, held snugly with a silken bow that kept it in place across the width of her head. Her finely woven linen gown was dyed a pale blue and enhanced at the neckline by a wide drape of gauze that matched the material on her bonnet. The middle-aged woman's waist was still slender and delicate in appearance.

Sarah self-consciously pulled the quilt higher over her simple homespun shift.

Missus Bainbridge walked over to the bedside and looked with large brown eyes at the sleeping infant. "Oh my." She touched his silken face. "So soft…" Her words faded away. Sarah noticed tears well in the woman's eyes.

"Would you like to hold him, Missus Bainbridge?"

"May I?" Her eyes sparkled.

"Of course." Sarah handed the sleepy bundle wrapped in a woolen blanket to the delighted woman.

Missus Bainbridge could not take her eyes from the baby for several moments and spoke not a word. Finally she looked up, seeming to remember there were others in the room.

"He is beautiful. So much like…" Her words stopped again. She handed the baby back to his mother. "He favors his father, does he not?" She wiped the tears from her eyes.

"Yes. I have told Nathaniel the very same." Sarah smiled at the woman, then paused, not certain if she should inquire, but her curiosity was too great to maintain silence.

"Do you have any children of your own, Missus Bainbridge?"

The woman looked down at her hands and then back at the new mother.

"No, Missus Stearns. I am afraid my one child died at birth. That happened when my husband was away fighting the Redcoats." She started to say more but stopped.

Sarah's eyes welled with tears. "I'm so very sorry." Her voice choked but she forced her way past the emotion. "And your husband?"

"I am afraid he never returned from the war." She looked out of the window, her thoughts seeming to drift to another time. "Joseph was a brave man — a captain in the militia. After he left to fight, my household and I were forced to flee Boston. I was with child at the time and we barely escaped to the countryside. The strain of our flight and our difficult circumstances brought on my travail too early." She sniffed and took out a handkerchief. "My son was birthed too soon — and he did not survive." She looked down at her hands and took a deep breath. "After the war, my husband's men found me at my cousin's home. As he lay dying, he had given them instructions to help his wife return to our home in Boston after the war. His men loved him so much, they brought me home before they ever returned to theirs." Her lips quivered. "Even as he died, he thought of me."

Sarah's cheeks were covered with tears and she could hear Nathaniel sniffing across the room.

"I'm so sad for you, Missus Bainbridge."

The older woman seemed to recover herself. "Well then, that was long ago." She straightened out the folds on her blue gown. "And now, you have been blessed with a lovely son. Born in this very home that I shared with my husband." Her moist eyes crinkled into a smile. "Such a joy!"

"We are so very beholden to you, Missus Bainbridge." Nathaniel approached her, wiping off a few tears with his sleeve. "I fear that, had you not rescued us, my Sarah may have delivered our child on the filthy street. I cannot thank you enough." His voice was low and shaking.

"I thank God that I happened to be in that part of town yesterday. One of my maids was ill and I was delivering her some food. That's when I looked over and saw you both — in obvious need, I might add." Smiling, she touched his arm for a brief moment and then continued.

"And it is I who am grateful to you. Your son being birthed in my home has been a gift to me. Especially at this time of year." She took a deep breath. "You see, my husband was from England and he was of a church that celebrated Christmas — the birth of Jesus. Every year at this time, I light a candle in memory of his December celebration. How happy it would have made him to know that I was able to provide lodging for a couple about to birth their son — strangers far from home. Much like Mary and Joseph in the account in Luke." Her eyes were filled with warm emotion. "So I thank you, Mr. and Missus Stearns, for allowing me to partake in a very precious Christmas. My Joseph would have been filled with joy."

Sarah's face was a river of tears. "Thank you, Missus Bainbridge."

"Well then." The woman clasped her hands together. "What else may I get for you both? I am uncertain as to why you were traveling here to Boston." Her eyebrows lifted as she awaited an answer.

Nathaniel spoke up.

"The reason we are here in Boston, Missus Bainbridge, is to find my father. He has been missing from his family since the war. I recently discovered that he is here in Boston — working as a servant in a physician's household. I found out that my father was wounded seriously in the war." Nathaniel struggled to continue. "His injuries caused him to believe that he was not wanted by his family." He pulled the letter out of his coat pocket and opened it. "This letter states he will only be with this doctor through December. Had I waited any longer, I might have lost him again — forever." Nathaniel lowered his head.

Missus Bainbridge inhaled sharply. "Oh my. The war continues to cause so many to suffer." Her mouth drew tightly in determination. "May I see the letter?"

"Of course." He handed the parchment to her.

"I will see if I can locate this physician for you." She turned to leave and then spun around. "This is a needless separation for your family. I would have taken my husband home in any condition." Her eyes softened. "I know that you feel the same." She left the room.

Nathaniel had circles under his eyes as he turned toward Sarah and the baby. Walking over to his new family, he sat on the edge of the bed.

"Sarah. I'm so grateful you and the baby are well." He stroked her hair back from her face. His blue eyes were moist as he cradled her chin in his hand and leaned over to kiss her.

"Thank you for taking care of us, Nathaniel." Her eyes welled once again.

"I did my part. But God provided this refuge for us. I love you so much, Sarah."

"And I, you." She grasped his hand in hers. "Nathaniel, I think I know what we should name our son."

"Yes, I know." Nathaniel kissed her hand then looked at his sleeping son. "We will call him Joseph."

35

Fathers

The carriage ride on cobblestone streets was bumpy, but even the discomfort to his body could not compare to the jarring emotions filling Nathaniel's mind.

What shall I say? What will he do? Will he recognize me?

But even more disturbing came the realization that his father had made the decision to stay away from his family — to hide his injury from them. Anger roiled in Nathaniel's spirit.

"We're nearly there, sir." The coachman slowed the team of horses and drew the reins to guide them to the side of the road. "Here 'tis, sir. The home of Dr. and Missus Phillip Wilkins."

"Thank you, Mr. Cross."

Nathaniel looked up at the three-story structure, its brick façade interspersed with rows of shuttered windows, each enhanced by a crown of decorative stone. Missus Bainbridge had explained to him and Sarah that most of the fine houses on the north end of Boston had been spared from ravages of the British during the war.

At least something survived unscarred.

Walking up to the iron entry gate, he unhooked the latch and pushed his way through. The hinges groaned as he swung the gate shut. The sound of children's voices floated down from the upper rooms as well as female voices scolding the apparent antics of the Wilkins' children. Nathaniel smiled at the sound.

He slowly walked toward the front door. Glancing down at the unfamiliar breeches — formerly a part of Joseph Bainbridge's wardrobe — and adjusting the woolen waistcoat and overcoat that Missus Bainbridge had so generously provided him, he realized his hands trembled.

As he knocked on the door, he had the urge to run away. His desire to escape was thwarted when the door opened.

"May I help you, sir?"

The smile of the maidservant renewed his courage. "Yes, miss, I am looking for a Mr. Benjamin Stearns. I understand that he is in the employ of Dr. Wilkins." Nathaniel could feel his face turning warm.

Your voice is weak. Take courage, man.

He stood taller and tried to ignore the pounding of blood in his ears. The maid's smile faded. "I am sorry, sir. He is not here."

Nathaniel's heart lurched. He tried to swallow but there was no moisture in his mouth. "Not here?" He labored to get the words out.

"No, sir." She smiled sweetly. "He will be back in a bit, though. He has gone to the Common off Tremont Street. Old Mr. Stearns." She shook her head and giggled pleasantly. "He does love to make his 'journey to Deer Run' as he calls it. Says the trees and meadows remind him of home — wherever that is."

Nathaniel's heart raced. "This Common you speak of, pray, where is it?" He nervously twisted his hat with moist hands.

She pointed up the street. "Not far. Follow this road to the end and take a left. You cannot miss the sheep grazing." She paused. "Should I tell him who has called for him, just in case you do not find him?"

Nathaniel put his hat back on. "No. I shall find him. Thank you, miss."

He spun around and ran toward the carriage.

"Mr. Cross, I must run to the Common. You may wait here." Nathaniel ran up the cobblestone street as fast as his legs could carry him. The cold air bit against his bare face, but he ignored the discomfort. He was so focused on his destination that he almost ran into a cartload of firewood being hauled by a merchant.

"Sorry." He tipped his hat at the merchant and kept running.

He heard the bleating of sheep and knew he was close. He was not sure if his racing heart was due to his frantic run or the realization that he might see his father at last. He passed by the wooden fence that outlined part of the common area and went around numerous elm trees.

At first, Nathaniel did not see him. Scanning across the expanse of meadow, he wiped the sweat from his brow and squinted in the bright sun. His heavy breathing was visible in clouds of exhalation because of the cold air.

Then he saw him — a stooped figure of a man, covered in a simple woolen coat, staring off at the ships in the distant bay. Nathaniel stopped and stared, taking in the sight of the man he had awaited for eight long years. Eight years of waiting, hoping, despairing, grieving — the same number of years the war had lasted. It had been a battle all its own.

As he slowly approached the old man, Nathaniel fought the urge to scream at him. To ask him where he had been all this time while their village had despaired of his return and its people had thought his son a fool for believing him still alive. Why? He wanted to shake him and make him answer. But the closer he got to Benjamin Stearns, the sadder he became. The man was obviously crippled. His right shoulder and arm were thrust forward in a grotesque manner. His movements were awkward, as he had to carry his body by balancing with only a single upper extremity. Compassion filled Nathaniel's heart as he approached the man from behind and stopped just a few feet away.

"Father?" His mouth twisted as he fought back tears.

The crippled man turned around abruptly and narrowed his eyes. Nathaniel noticed the deep lines the years had furrowed into his father's face. And even more painful to the son was the look of utter despair in the father's eyes. Nathaniel inhaled deeply.

Benjamin Stearns stared at Nathaniel for several moments, his eyes reddened from the cold and pain. He seemed to be struggling to remember, to sort out the appearance of this unexpected stranger. But soon, a small light of recognition flickered in the man's eyes.

"Nathaniel?"

"Yes, Father. 'Tis I."

They both stood unmoving. Benjamin pulled his coat up over his right shoulder a little higher with his gloved, trembling left hand.

"Why are you here?"

"Why am I here?" Nathaniel's face grew hot and his heart continued its frantic pace. "Why am I here? I might ask you, Father, why are you here? Why did you not send for us? Why did you not come home to us?" Rage seethed in his voice.

Benjamin turned and started to walk away. Nathaniel trekked with determined steps to block his escape.

"Oh no. You may not escape my inquiries so easily. I want to know! Why?" Nathaniel was so distraught, he felt lightheaded.

Benjamin would not meet his intent gaze but looked at the ground.

"It should be obvious, Nathaniel. I do not wish to be a burden to my family." The man's lips trembled.

"You did not even give us a chance, Father. You never even sent word that you were alive." Nathaniel was crying now. "Everyone thought you were dead, but I believed in my heart that you were not. All of Deer Run thought I had taken leave of my senses." He paused and then spoke more softly. "All, that is, except Sarah."

His father peered upward. "Sarah?" His blue eyes were moist and rimmed with red.

Nathaniel wiped the tears from his face.

"My wife. You would have known her as Sarah Thomsen."

Benjamin looked into the distance.

"Sarah Thomsen. James' youngest, born after he drowned in the river." He looked back at Nathaniel. "Little Sarah?"

Nathaniel managed to smile. "The very one. Only she is quite grown up now." His face grew serious again. "Why did you not write to us, Father? Please — I need to know."

His father looked down with sad eyes.

"I almost wrote to your mother once." He half turned away, but Nathaniel drew him back to face him.

"Almost…?"

Benjamin took in a deep breath. Tears rolled down his cheeks.

"A nurse came in when I requested help in writing a letter." He looked up and closed his eyes, the rivulets of tears flowing unhindered. They glistened on his face in the bright sun. "She said to me, 'Are you sure you want to write to your family? Are you certain they want a cripple to take care of? Perhaps, it would be better if they thought you dead.'" He was sobbing now. "I did not want to be a burden to you... to your mother. I felt worthless, like half a man."

Nathaniel's mouth quivered.

"You are not worthless, nor are you only half a man. We want you back, whatever your state. Our family needs you." He swallowed back a rising wave of tears. "Your grandson needs you."

Benjamin looked up slowly.

"My grandson?" A glimmer of joy infused his bleak countenance.

"Yes." Nathaniel reached out for the first time to grab his father's arm. "Yes, your grandson. Born not two days ago here in Boston." He reached out with his left hand and grabbed his father's crippled right arm. "Come home to us, Father. I beg you."

The two men embraced, lost in a grip of emotion.

At last, Benjamin Stearns had finally come home from war.

36

Curtains

Nathaniel watched his mother pace back and forth in front of the window. She fidgeted with her hair, pushing small strands back under her lace cap. She adjusted the folds on her gown, making sure it lay smoothly.

"What if I look old to him, Nathaniel?" Her words surprised him.

Standing up from his chair, he walked over to his mother and put his arm around her shoulders. "He will think you are the most beautiful sight." Nathaniel regarded her with reassurance. "I believe that he is the one concerned about your reaction — to his injury." His mother covered her mouth with trembling fingers.

"I still cannot believe you found him." Elizabeth Stearns' voice was strained with emotion. "To think, all this time he and I have been in the same city...."

"In a city of thousands, 'tis quite easy to live not a mile away and never meet." He pointed toward the leather-covered chair. "Why do you not sit, Mother, and wait for him?"

"I cannot." She walked over toward the front window and her eyes squinted at the light. Nathaniel accompanied her to the window and peered outside. A lone figure was shuffling toward the house, which belonged to his Aunt Abigail and her husband. His mother touched the golden curtains that she had brought with her from Deer Run and pulled them aside, then clasped her hands over her heart.

"He is here," she whispered.

Nathaniel hurried over to the door and flung it open. His father's head hung low as he climbed the steps one at a time.

His mother came to the doorway, excitement and fear filling her face.

"Benjamin?" The name was almost inaudible from her throat.

Her husband looked up and his eyes took in the sight of the woman he had not seen for ten years. He reached the top step where she stood and he stared at her without speaking.

His wife put her arms around his upper arms.

"Welcome home, my husband."

He tried to speak but sobs filled his throat. At last he found his voice. "I cannot... I cannot embrace you, proper-like." The words were a desperate declaration.

His wife wrapped her arms around him and held him tight. "I am content in your caress, my husband."

He exhaled so loudly, it seemed to Nathaniel that his father's years of fear about her love and acceptance flew away on the wind. "I love you, Elizabeth. Please forgive me."

She pulled away slightly and touched one finger to his lips. They kissed so long that Nathaniel became embarrassed and left them in their embrace — an embrace that was partially crippled, yet whole in its warmth and love.

37

Grandchild

arah fidgeted with the lace trimming the bodice of her gown.
What will his parents think of me?
She watched baby Joseph, already a week old, resting in the crook of her arm.

If only I could be so relaxed. She sighed.

Nathaniel walked into the room provided by Missus Bainbridge.

"And how does my lovely wife fare?" He leaned over to kiss her. "I cannot wait for my parents to meet you and Joseph." Sarah sat silently. Nathaniel cocked his head sideways and reached for her hand. "Are you well?" His eyes narrowed with concern.

Sarah attempted to smile. "I am well... just nervous. I know that your mother remembers me in the stocks as a child..." She breathed in and felt her face flush.

"You were just a child... who wished to go to school. Besides, she has written of how delighted she is that we married. And now that you have given us a son... well, she is beside herself with joy." He kissed her again. "You fret too much, my love."

"I suppose so." She looked up sharply when she heard a knock at their door. "They are here!" She sat upright in the chair. Nathaniel hurried to the door and welcomed his mother and father into their room.

Sarah smiled shyly. "Good day, Mother Stearns. Father Stearns. Forgive me for not getting up."

"Nonsense, my dear, you must stay sitting." Her mother-in-law hurried over and gave Sarah a kiss on the cheek. Her eyes were drawn to the sleeping child and she drew in a quick breath. "Oh my." She glanced at her husband. "Benjamin, come meet your grandson. He looks just like Nathaniel as a babe!"

Benjamin Stearns shuffled over toward his daughter-in-law.

"Sarah Thomsen. I never imagined that bit of a child would one day be married to my son. And bear us a grandson." He touched Sarah's cheek. "Thank you, my dear."

Sarah smiled at their warm greetings.

"It is I who must thank you — for bringing my husband into the world. He has made my world complete."

Elizabeth and Benjamin looked at each other and grinned. Nathaniel turned red as he stood there.

"Well then, would you like to hold your grandson?" Nathaniel lifted the child from Sarah's arms and handed him to his grandmother.

The woman eagerly wrapped her arms around the sleepy infant enveloped in a warm blanket. She touched his cheeks and hands, and smoothed his downy, blond hair against his scalp.

"It is uncanny." She looked up at her son. "Nathaniel, this is just what you looked like as a newborn." She grinned with unabashed pride at her first grandchild.

"He certainly has his father's appetite." Sarah's eyes danced. "And his tenderness."

Nathaniel looked down at his feet and put his hands in his pockets. "She has brought out the tenderness in me."

"Well, someone had to, lad." His father patted him on the shoulder with his left hand and walked over toward Sarah. She noticed the way he tried to hide his right hand that was clawed and shriveled into a tight ball.

"Come, sit next to me, Father Stearns." He drew a chair next to hers. She reached over and purposely grasped his right hand in hers. At first he flinched but then relaxed as she smoothed her fingers over his stiff fist. "I am the luckiest wife in the world." She spoke in a whisper that was overcome with emotion. "I want to thank you for raising such a fine son. I love him with all my heart."

She could see her father-in-law fighting back tears, but he seemed to be losing the battle. "When last I saw Nathaniel, he was a lonely man. He had been hurt many times — not in his body but in his spirit." A few tears dripped onto his woolen coat. His mouth quivered. "I despaired that he would ever know joy." He looked at Sarah. "But I know now, I need not have despaired. For he has found you." He squeezed Sarah's hand with his left fingers. "And I can see the joy shining in his eyes."

Sarah leaned over and embraced him. "Thank you, Father Stearns." She kissed his cheek. "I am so happy I could give you your first grandchild."

"He is a fine lad." Benjamin touched her cheek and gave it a gentle pinch. "That is what your father used to do to your sister Mary. I am quite certain he would have loved you as well — and pinched your cheek, too." His worn face crinkled into a smile.

Sarah could not hold back the tears any longer. "My father?" The words caught in her throat as she touched her own cheek. "He would do that?"

"Aye. He would have been proud of you, lass."

Sarah could barely speak but managed to say a weak "Thank you." She had forgotten that Nathaniel's father would have been friends with her own.

Nathaniel approached the two sitting side by side. He was carrying a squirming Joseph and handed the hungry child to his mother.

"I fear Joseph is complaining that I am not making him happy. He says he wants his mother." He handed the fussing child to Sarah. She started to undo her gown and then realized that Nathaniel's parents were still there. She looked up with wide eyes.

"Time to let our grandson eat." Elizabeth walked over to her husband and coaxed him out of the chair. Benjamin kissed his daughter-in-law on the top of her head and touched his grandson.

"Be good for your mother, little one." He got up and accompanied his wife to the door. After the parents left, Sarah started to nurse Joseph.

Nathaniel sat in the chair vacated by his father and observed his son suckling. "I never thought…" He cleared his throat. "I never thought I could be this happy."

Sarah reached over to touch his face. He grasped her fingers and kissed her hand.

"Nor I." She smiled and her lips trembled. "We have found each other — and we have found our family."

He reached over and encompassed Sarah and the baby in his arms. It was the embrace that always made her feel safe in the promise of his love.

38

Homecoming

aby Joseph was a month old before Sarah was recovered enough to travel home. Although anxious to return to Deer Run, there were now many loved ones in Boston that she would miss. This made their departure joyous and painful all at the same time. They had promised to keep in touch with Missus Bainbridge and invited her to come see them in Deer Run.

"Do you suppose your parents will come visit us this summer?" Sarah shifted in the sleigh trying to get comfortable. It was almost the end of their journey and she was ready to be home.

"I hope so. Perhaps after my sister Sadie's wedding in June. They will be quite busy until then." He glanced at his sleeping son. "Joseph gets fatter every day, Sarah. What are you feeding the boy?" His voice teased.

"Oh just a few legs of mutton and fat fowl with his milk." She had an impish grin. "I told you. He has his father's appetite."

"Ah, well, 'tis fortunate Father Eaton left us so fine a stock of animals to meet his needs." He reached over and squeezed her hand. "We're almost there, love."

Sarah craned her neck ahead.

"I wonder if they know we are coming today?"

"Well, I sent them a post to give them an idea as to our arrival day. I am certain your mother cannot wait to see her grandson."

Sarah noticed someone in the distance, and as they drew near, she could see it was her nephew Asa. When he saw the sleigh approaching, he jumped up and down waving. Then he dashed off.

"Asa will spread the word quick enough." Sarah looked down at Joseph beginning to awaken. "You had best prepare yourself, young man. You are about to be besieged by thousands of kisses." Sarah held him up to her face and smooched his cheek.

"And here come the kissers now." Nathaniel slowed Babe down as numerous family members trudged through the snow to greet them.

"I say, travelers. I thought there were only two of you when you left Deer Run. I see now three members of the Stearns family arriving home." Daniel greeted them as he trudged through the snow, accompanied by the twins. "Go get your mother and sisters." He directed the twins to retrieve the rest of the family. "Let us see the little one."

Sarah showed baby Joseph to his uncle. "Well, we can certainly tell who his father is." Daniel smiled and shook Nathaniel's hand. "Welcome home." His voice grew serious. "We prayed for your safekeeping — the Lord is faithful."

"Yes. Yes he is." Nathaniel shook hands with a firm grip.

James Thomsen, Asa's father, approached the returning travelers.

"How fares my little sister?" he asked, visibly relieved to see them home.

"I am well, James. And Hannah?"

James's face brightened. "Very well. We have a new daughter — Ruth, after your mother. They are both doing well." Emotion infused his eyes. "She eats well and grows strong."

Sarah clutched his arm, remembering baby Samuel who had died.

"I am so glad, James."

Widow Eaton came running as fast as her legs could carry her.

"Sarah! You are safe!" Her mother breathed hard and it was difficult to discern if she was laughing or crying. Perhaps both.

"I am well, Mother. Come meet your grandson."

The widow looked at her newest grandchild and cooed with pleasure. "He is most beautiful, Sarah. And so fat!" She grinned at her daughter. "You have remembered everything I taught you."

"Yes. Thank you, Mother."

"Well, enough visiting in this cold air. Be off for home. And Nathaniel, thank you for watching out for my daughter. And grandson." She cast a grateful smile at her son-in-law.

"I promised you I would. Just as I promised Sarah I would not leave her behind."

Nathaniel stirred the reins to encourage Babe to get the exhausted family home after their very long journey. The family called after them. "Welcome home!"

"Oh look, there is Mary." Her sister trudged through the snow toward the sleigh. "No — it cannot be." Was that a bulging belly under Mary's cape?

"Mary, are we to expect another child in the Lowe family?" Sarah's face broke into a grin. Mary smoothed her hand over her enlarging midsection.

"'Tis true enough." Mary's grin matched Sarah's. "Oh, your little one is precious. The image of his father. Welcome home." She squeezed Sarah's hand, then lowered her voice and whispered. "Remember that night of the corn husking when I knew that Nathaniel had set his eyes on you? I prayed that the newborn we spoke of — the one you might one day have — would be his child. I knew he loved you before you did." Mary smiled and spoke louder. "Nathaniel, take your lovely wife and son home."

As they drove off toward the Eaton farm, Nathaniel bore a quizzical expression. "What was Mary whispering to you about?"

Sarah gave an impish grin. "Oh nothing. Just about love and babies."

He looked at his wife with more than a passing interest.

"Is that so? I was thinking we might discuss those things tonight. Under the quilts. When Joseph is asleep."

Sarah blushed. "Well, Mr. Stearns, I might consider such a proposal from my husband."

He looked at her in such a way as to make her blush even further.

"Promise?" His grin was positively mischievous.

"I promise."

Author's Note

I

t was a joy to begin the sequel to *Road to Deer Run*. I was thrilled to re-enter the lives of the Thomsen and Lowe families, yet fast forward several years to 1790. Sarah is now a young lady who has matured yet still carries the spunky spirit we saw in *Road to Deer Run*. And now I've introduced the character of the veteran, Nathaniel Stearns, who actually made a very brief appearance in the first book. (Can you find him?)

As with *Road to Deer Run*, *Promise of Deer Run* stole my heart as everyone's lives and loves bloomed and as heartache visited them all. The characters of Sarah and Nathaniel became dear to my heart as their personalities and struggles unfolded. Alongside them, Mary and Daniel's story broadened and deepened as their years together progressed, bringing new joys, sorrows, and unexpected challenges. Their faith was at times weakened and then renewed as their journeys in life drew them closer to their spouses as well as their God.

Many of the scenes in this most recent novel were difficult for me to write. The chapter entitled "Samuel" is particularly precious and poignant, as it is based on actual circumstances that followed the delivery of one of my triplet grandchildren. Lucas Samuel, the youngest of the trio, had been having some minor feeding issues but was finally released from the hospital at three weeks of age. He seemed to be doing better, until that night his parents and I will never forget. He could not keep any of his food down. His parents took him to the doctor, who diagnosed a blockage in his digestive tract. A trip to the hospital for a relatively simple surgical procedure fixed the problem and Luke was home and eating within a couple of days. He is now a healthy and adorable six-year-old.

In 1791, the fictitious baby Samuel was not so fortunate. There would not have been any diagnostic tools such as X-rays or anesthesia that would allow a physician to fix the problem today with a fairly common procedure. A baby in those circumstances would likely die from dehydration or starvation. It is a sobering reminder of the blessing of modern-day medicine. And I thank God for the blessing of my precious grandson Luke.

The character of Sarah Stearns in this novel had to face an unexpected situation when she arrived in Boston — a male physician arriving to deliver her baby. By the late 1700s, doctors in England had started playing a greater role in childbirths. They in turn, influenced American doctors, who trained across the ocean and then brought this practice home with them to the United States. Physician-assisted childbirth became popular in the larger cities like Boston, New York, and Philadelphia. These "man-midwives" as they were called, brought with their practice the use of forceps and strong medications. While the forceps could be handy during difficult deliveries — sometimes saving the lives of mother and child — the physicians tended to interfere more in the delivery process rather than allowing the more natural pace condoned by the midwives. The debate over midwives versus physician-assisted deliveries continues to this day. Most feel there is a welcome need for both.

Life in the eighteenth century was difficult in so many ways. And following the victory against England, the joyful mood was short lived, as America went into a deep economic recession. Taxes in Massachusetts skyrocketed to help pay off the war debt and farmers were hit especially hard. Veterans, who fought to free America and had never been paid for their sacrifices, were suddenly trying to survive this assault on their finances. It became a losing battle for many. Some went to debtor's prison. Some — like the drunkard portrayed at the tavern — lost their farms.

It was a desperate time for many that resulted in the 1787 uprising known as Shay's Rebellion. The militia was called out by then-Governor James Bowdoin to quell enraged farmers trying to take over the Springfield arsenal of weapons. In the fray, militia fired and killed four of the rebels and wounded twenty. It was an event that brought a collective gasp to a nation struggling to find its identity. This rebellion became the impetus for the Continental Convention of 1787 to ratify the Constitution that would ensure a strong government. Without resolute laws, it was feared the new nation would disintegrate before it had a chance to take root.

But the years from 1790 on saw the beginnings of new growth and changes in the fledgling country known as the United States of America. Boston and other cities that were scarred by the war began to rebuild and grow at an astounding rate. America was a toddler nation getting its bearings with new legs of self-government. It began to form and mature into a nation known for its liberty and its strength — a government of the people, by the people, and for the people.

The last of the Deer Run saga, *Legacy of Deer Run*, begins in the year 1800. This third book in the series releases in December 2016. I hope you will join me again for the adventures of the Thomsen and Lowe families as they continue to grow in their faith, hope, and of course, love. Until then, may the Lord richly bless you in your journey.

Book Club
Discussion Questions

1. Sarah Thomsen never forgot the kindness extended to her when she was a child (Nathaniel brought bread to her when she was in the stocks). Have you ever received an unexpected generous act that you treasure in your thoughts? How did that affect your relationship with that person?

2. Richard Beal thought nothing of mocking a veteran soldier who had difficulty fitting in with the rest of the community. Do you see any comparison to a lack of understanding of veterans from recent wars?

3. Have you ever known someone who never knew their father? How did they speak about this loss?

4. Compare dating practices in the 1790s with dating today? Were they better? Worse? Advantages and disadvantages?

5. Describe the changes that occurred in Sarah throughout *Promise of Deer Run*. How did her character grow and mature?

6. Discuss some of the practices peculiar to Colonial America such as the way marriages and funerals were performed. Compare to today's rituals.

7. The characters of Daniel and Mary are a strong presence in this second book in the Deer Run Saga. With the growth of their family came many changes and challenges. Discuss how these impacted their relationship.

8. Nathaniel made a bold move in keeping his promise to Sarah. Talk about the ramifications of his decision. What are your personal thoughts about his choice?

9. Changes in birthing babies were in the air in 1790. Yet changes are still discussed today in regards to physician-assisted vs. midwives, male attendants vs. female, home vs. hospital. What are your personal thoughts regarding who should be in charge during childbirth and where the birth should take place?

10. Discuss Nathaniel's thoughts and emotions when he finally comes face-to-face with his father. If you were in his shoes, what might you have done or said?

ELAINE MARIE COOPER

Novelist Elaine Marie Cooper is the author of the Deer Run saga (*Road to Deer Run, Promise of Deer Run* and *Legacy of Deer Run*) as well as *Bethany's Calendar* and *Fields of the Fatherless*. Her passions are her family, her faith in Christ, and the history of the American Revolution, a frequent subject of her historical fiction. She grew up in Massachusetts, the setting for many of her novels.

Elaine is a contributing writer to *Fighting Fear, Winning the War at Home* by Edie Melson, and *I Choose You*, a romance anthology. Her freelance work has appeared in both newspapers and magazines, and she blogs regularly at ColonialQuills.blogspot.com as well as her own blog on her website at ElaineMarieCooper.com.

www.ElaineMarieCooper.com
www.Facebook.com/ElaineMarieCooperAuthor
www.Twitter.com/ElaineMCooper

CROSSRIVER

If you enjoyed this book, will you
consider sharing it with others?

- Please mention the book on Facebook, Twitter, Pinterest, or your blog.

- Recommend this book to your small group, book club, and workplace.

- Head over to Facebook.com/CrossRiverMedia, 'Like' the page and post a comment as to what you enjoyed the most.

- Pick up a copy for someone you know who would be challenged or encouraged by this message.

- Write a review on Amazon.com, BN.com, or Goodreads.com.

- To learn about our latest releases subscribe to our newsletter at www.CrossRiverMedia.com.

MORE GREAT BOOKS FROM CROSSRIVERMEDIA.COM

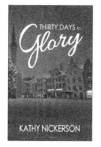

THIRTY DAYS TO GLORY

Kathy Nickerson

Catherine Benson longs to do one great thing before she dies, while Elmer Grigsby hopes to stay drunk until he slips out of the world unnoticed. Against a Christmas backdrop, Catherine searches for purpose while fighting the best intentions of her children. She gains the support of her faithful housekeeper and quirky friends. Elmer isn't supported by anyone, except maybe his cat. When their destinies intersect one Tuesday in December, they both discover it is only *Thirty Days to Glory*.

WILTED DANDELIONS

Catherine Ulrich Brakefield

Rachael Rothburn just wants to be a missionary to the Native Americans out west, but the missionary alliance says she can't go unless she is married. When Dr. Jonathan Wheaton, another missionary hopeful, offers her a marriage of convenience, she quickly agrees. But she soon finds that his jealousy may be an even greater threat than the hostile Indians and raging rivers they face along the way.

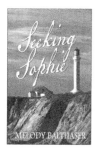

SEEKING SOPHIE

Melody Balthaser

Indentured servant Sophie Stalz stabs her master to protect herself from rape. Escaping through the Underground Railroad, she now finds herself stranded on an island in the hands of a stranger. Surrounded by the sea, Jackson Scott just wants to be left alone with his memories. His fortress crumbles when Sophie shows up on his doorstep. As her master is *Seeking Sophie*, can Sophie and Jackson build a life together free from their past?

POSTMARK FROM THE PAST

Vickie Phelps

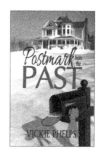

In November 1989, Emily Patterson is enjoying a quiet life in west Texas, but emptiness nips at her heart. Then a red envelope appears in her mailbox with no return address and a postmark from 1968. It's a letter from Mark who declares his love for her, but who is Mark? Is someone playing a cruel joke? As Emily seeks to solve the mystery, can she risk her heart to find a miracle in the *Postmark from the Past*?

Made in United States
Orlando, FL
18 February 2024

43844428R00153